ARMAGEDDON
BY
MORNING

ARMAGEDDON
BY
MORNING

by
Nicky Cruz

New Leaf Press

FIRST EDITION
1992

Library of Congress Catalog Number: 92-81424
ISBN: 0-89221-224-1

Cover art by Pamela Anzalotti, Greer, SC 29650

DEDICATION

This book is dedicated to several pastors in whose churches I have always felt comfortable and at home. I have always felt loved by them and their congregations and have considered these churches to be great places to speak.

To Reverend Jim Cymbala and his beautiful wife, Carol, for their friendship, support, and love over the years, and for their ministry in Brooklyn at the Brooklyn Tabernacle.

To my pastor, Reverend Don Steiger, of Radiant Church and his lovely wife, Loretta, who were there to oversee the spiritual development of my children while I was out on the road.

To Reverend David Wilkerson, my spiritual father, and his wife, Gwen, whose work and passion for the inner city continues daily in the heart of New York City at Times Square Church.

To Reverends Sonny Arguinzoni, Ed Morales, Tony Guzman, their spouses, and all of the "Victory Outreach Gang."

To Reverend Israel Narvaez and his wife, Kathy, a good friend and a living example of the Grace of God.

A special dedication to Cliff Dudley, for his vision and love for me and this project. Cliff was perhaps the most genuine and honest Christian that I have ever met. I was doing a benefit for the homeless in Puerto Rico when Cliff unexpectedly went to be with the Lord. His last words to me on this earth were, "I love you, Nicky. I'll see you soon." Indeed, I will see you soon, Cliff!

SPECIAL THANKS

To my editor, Keith Wilkerson, for his contributions and research which expanded my knowledge in the field of computer technology, and for his assistance in the editing of this project.

To Cliff Dudley for his knowledge and insight into Africa and the Africans, and his love for that continent.

ARMAGEDDON
BY
MORNING

The missionary daughter who had become a smuggler gritted her teeth in fear. Ten thousand feet above Africa's raging Virunga volcanos, in the aluminum belly of her little cargo plane, a terrible malignancy brooded.

Silently, the great evil did not stir.

It did not show itself.

It waited and relished Zuni's growing anxiety.

Up in the cockpit, bathed in the crimson volcanic glow, Zuni gripped her old plane's controls. She glanced at her sputtering right engine and ignored her smudged reflection in the side window. She hadn't worn any make-up in days. Her long, raven hair was wet and plastered to her skull from perspiration.

It had to be 110 degrees in the cabin. Down in the rivers of molten rock below, the temperature was more than 2,000 Fahrenheit.

She had no time to suspect that something evil

seethed in her hold's crates. Her fuel gauge read "empty."

She had gone to sleep expecting her autopilot to bring her within range of home, the African port city of Mombasa, Kenya. Instead, she had bolted awake, startled by the sounds of a volcano erupting literally under her feet.

She was hundreds of miles off course, out of gas, and absolutely baffled as to how she had come here.

Her right engine coughed one last time, then stopped.

" **Dejate de chavienda**," she muttered in Spanish slang at the airplane as if it were a living thing: *You wretched scrap heap.*

She adjusted the controls, whispering again in Spanish although this was not her mother's beloved Puerto Rico. Nor was it Hawaii — that volcanic gem of the Pacific that she could not remember, where her Scottish father had met and married her Hispanic mom.

In a storm of religious passion they had pledged their love, vowed to devote their lives to foreign evangelism — and had stayed in Bible school long enough to graduate . . . and have a daughter, Zuni.

Then, off they had gone to the jungles of the Dark Continent.

Africa.

Thus, Africa was where Zuni now found herself plunging into the raging lava geysers of the Great Rift Valley's Virunga Mountains. She had no idea that she'd been shifted off course by a murderous brute deep in the crates of her hold.

It was a thing that craved pain, that relished suffering, that grew in hellish excitement whenever its human targets blamed Almighty God in their last horrible moments before death.

Zuni did not know that the compassionless thing

in the cargo hold was listening to her racing heartbeat, hooting in silent derision as her adrenaline
surged, as her horror grew, and as her terror multi-
plied.

"**Pedazo de porqueria,**" she muttered to her
plane. *Chunk of junk.* Shakily she gripped the controls.

Quivering, she mentally kicked herself.

It had to be her fault, she thought.

Yes, she had failed somehow to set the autopilot
correctly.

That had to be why she peered into this molten
hell instead of waking to the friendly seaport lights of
Mombasa. Tiny particles of ash and volcanic dust
were beginning to build up on the windshield. It was
like flying through cinnamon.

She tried to retrace her steps.

She had set the controls . . . she shook her head,
unable to think what she'd done wrong. When she
had awakened, she was hundreds of miles off course
in the middle of nowhere and running out of fuel. She
did not suspect it was no coincidence.

In the hold, something evil lusted for her fear.

Now, it gently nudged the plane's stick down —
plunging them toward the blackened slopes of the
fiery mountain.

But it did not take into account an old woman back
in Puerto Rico. A retired missionary on her knees,
quietly praising her Creator.

❖   ❖   ❖

In the great brilliance of the presence of the
Almighty, a great number of magnificent beings
knelt before the great throne of the Creator. Wondrous anthems echoed throughout — with praises
and thanksgivings to the One who made all things.

Gabriel, the messenger of heaven, asked no questions. Michael, the commander of the heavenly fighting forces, stood with head bowed.

The Master of the Universe was in conference.

Before Him was an old friend, a scrawny old warrior on her knees. In her bedroom, she fumbled with an old Bible and a worn prayer journal as she exulted in the presence and holiness of her great God.

She laid her petitions before Him.

She asked Him for the impossible.

"Father," prayed Johanna Graham, "be with my daughter wherever she is. Lord, tonight I am filled with such foreboding. I truly fear for her safety. I feel as if she is involved in something so terrible, so beyond her understanding — Lord, I feel as if she is being used as a pawn in a great and terrible evil. Deliver her, Lord. Bring her home, safely. Turn her heart to You, Father. Touch her. Love her, Father. Guide her. Give her true peace. Let her know that You alone are her only hope, her only salvation . . ."

As the old woman's prayer continued into the night, the Almighty Creator of all things smiled upon her. His hand moved and the old woman was surrounded with great, unseen protectors. As she wept her fervent prayer, a new refreshing fullness gently strengthened her tired spirit.

Johanna stood in great awe, her mouth filled with glorious wonder. Astonished, she turned and sang out a new song of joy, thanksgiving, and faith.

"Oh, Father," she wept in incredible joy. "You alone are God! You are the One to whom I can turn. You never fail. You never falter."

Unseen, a single blink of the eye away, in the darkness of earth's atmosphere, a fallen angel knelt in the presence of his dark and terrible prince. His assignment: to assist in the attack against the old widow — which was already underway.

"Join the battle of oppression and suppression to destroy and mute this interfering prayer warrior. Get her off her knees and shaking her fist at her Creator instead," ordered his dark lord. "Wear her down. Discourage her. Parade defeat and despair before her. Tear apart her faith."

The evil angel was shown a great plan already underway—which this praying, shriveled old woman had already begun to threaten.

The plan was a classic intrigue—a diabolical win-win scenario, a little game that the dark side could not lose. The plan: to use people this old believer dearly loved to place into very evil human hands a malignant machine that would give new and insidious power to truly terrible forces of greed and cruelty.

Whether their delivery succeeded or failed, mere participation in such a mission of terror would destroy Zuni—and perhaps this old believer's faith and confidence in God would be shaken.

The disillusioned Zuni might fall into deep despair and die, broken in mind and spirit over her own willingness to prostitute everything she had ever believed in to make big money. Perhaps her mother, too, would curse the God who would not save Zuni.

If any portion of the plan failed, partial victory would be good enough. After all, just the neutralization of an intercessor would make this exercise worthwhile. Perhaps she would be defeated and seduced into a downward spiral of despair and disillusionment.

For the demonic powers engaged, this was just another daily exercise, a minor battle that might succeed so spectacularly that millions might be hurled into the everlasting pit of fire.

It was a little game in which a few — or perhaps many — would be battered into believing that God-denying lie that, indeed, evil reigns supreme, whereas goodness stumbles and fails.

Their goal: to hurt God, to cause Him pain — to subvert and remove from His loving presence just a few more of these apples of His eye — these humans Lucifer so despises and envies with such evil passion.

As the exercise began, somehow the powers of evil underestimated the scrawny, little old lady on her knees before the throne of God. Johanna Ruiz Graham wept with joy before her Lord. The retired missionary did not rise from her knees.

Her mighty petitions swept heavenward.

Johanna Graham, prayer warrior, humbly beseeched the Lord to awaken her intercessors worldwide.

An army of light.

Across the globe, Christians here and there paused as she danced quietly and humbly before her Lord — just like David had. She sang — just as the Psalmist had done so many times. She would stay on her knees all night — just like the Suzanna Wesleys and so many other burdened mothers throughout history had before her.

Joyous in the presence of her great God, incredibly underestimated by the terrible powers of evil, she was nevertheless just an old woman — weak, tired, human, and vulnerable to the terrible assault awaiting her.

Deep into the night, as fatigue came to Johanna Graham, a new and chilling vision swept her. It was as if she saw Zuni being ensnared by an evil machine, captured by cruel, corrupt people, tortured and killed.

A vision that Zuni was already dead paralyzed, for a moment, the old woman's trembling mind. She hesitated, weeping at the thought of her daughter dying unsaved, unrepentant, forever damned. The convincing picture of eternal doom gripped her heart in a vise.

Johanna fell to the floor on her face. "No, Lord," she whispered, rocking on her knees. "I will not accept this terrible dream. No! Ours is not a spirit of fear, but of faith and joy . . ." she faltered, unable to remember the Scripture verse. "Ours is not a spirit of fear — "

She leaped to her feet.

"I will fear no evil, for Thou are with me. Thy rod and Thy staff, they comfort me . . ." Again, she could not even remember her favorite Bible promises. It was as if a great, dark cloud filled her mind.

She cried out to the Lord.

But the only sound that escaped was a deep, heart-felt groan. Passionately the old woman moaned her terrible, terrible anguish and the cloud swept away.

Great joy filled her heart.

Battered, she rocked again on her knees, pleading her daughter's case — beseeching the Creator to have mercy on this good, mixed-up girl.

Suddenly Johanna was filled with peace and relief.

"Why, Lord?" she whispered. "Where did such fear come from? Was it real? Was it a demonic deception? Is Zuni truly involved in something horrible? Or is this my human imagining?"

She stared into the darkness.

"I see. She's not safe yet, Father," she whispered. "O Lord, protect her with Your mighty hand. Drive back this darkness! Lord, awaken my intercessors. Stir them to battle, Father."

❖   ❖   ❖

The demons squirmed, as in pain, feeling the counterattack, but spitting their defiance.

Zuni's starboard engine coughed a death rattle and went dead. She was enveloped in the roar of the firestorm below. The eruptions sounded like a freight train in a thunderstorm.

Her ex-husband, Noel, would have found dark humor in that. The former newspaperman often joked that people who survived tornados always said their twister sounded like a freight train.

Noel liked to recount that once, when he was a reporter for the Associated Press, he had covered a railway tragedy where a freight train had rammed through a farmhouse.

The farmer had declared it sounded just like a tornado.

Now, this volcano in Africa's Virunga Mountains sounded like both.

Whispering softly to her old plane, trying to coax its engines back to life, Zuni glanced only for a second down into the orange haze. A long string of craters bubbled thousand-foot geysers of super-heated magma. A torrent of golden lava wound across a high crater, then disappeared into the abyss. To the left and right, scarlet rivers of lava poured down blackened slopes. Tiny jewels of flame sparkled on either side of the flows, brush fires igniting as the streams widened.

Zuni's cargo plane was plunging into the midst of it.

She did not give into the panic she was feeling. Instead she resisted the oppressive, invisible hand that seemed to press on the wheel, pushing the plane down into the poisonous mountainside.

She had a wild idea. Once she had been a sailplane pilot, so she began to frantically search for a "thermal" — one of those invisible elevators of sun-heated air that rise off parking lots and pastures, a rising column of hot air that sport gliders ride into the heavenlies.

Surely this volcano is creating such a mighty updraft — if I can only find it, Zuni thought. A mile-high plume of gas and steam seemed to glow below, reflecting light from the bubbling pit. But where was the updraft? "**No me engañes,**" she whispered to her plane. "**No vengas con tonterías.**" *Don't let me down. Come on, quit fooling around.*

There had to be an updraft. Was she already in it? "Feeling" a thermal — and turning a plane around in time to take advantage of it — is almost impossible, if not absurd to attempt, in an unpowered cargo plane falling from the sky. Zuni's heart shuddered under the increasing turbulence buffeting her Martin.

Built in 1947, the old relic just wasn't designed for the rough life it was living — particularly careening into the blistering storm of a volcanic eruption. The Martin 202 had been an airliner.

Zuni knew the very real danger below. Once she had flown a doomed team of university graduate-student researchers to a remote eruption in Zimbabwe. She had tagged along rather than wait for them at the airstrip.

For hours, she had trudged through the forest behind the gear-laden students and their cameras and instruments. She had watched in amazement as they scurried around the edges of their volcano, setting out gadgets that detected changes in the slope of the surfaces, seismic sensors that recorded tremors, and all sorts of other gizmos that sampled the atmosphere, transmitted the temperature, the humidity, wind velocities, and so forth. Every twenty feet or so, the university kids would plop down some sort of contraption, then exclaim in delight at the new photo angle there and begin snapping away with their cameras — like Japanese tourists just off the bus.

Deeper and deeper they descended into the crater, everyone knowing they were getting too close. Their hearts pumping with excitement, they worked their way down toward the rift line — the jagged crack in the earth's crust out of which every few minutes bubbled another new geyser of flame.

Suddenly, that day not so long ago, the air around Zuni had grown much hotter. Stumbling backward on an uncertain footing of crumbling lava, Zuni had turned, sliding down the slope and stared down the very throat of a rocky fountain that had been spraying brimstone only moments before.

She had been terrified, but all around her the university kids were crazily snapping pictures and shouting in excitement as they scrambled closer to death. They would dart toward the main eruption, expose a few more frames of film, then climb back, coughing and laughing. Zuni's clothes seemed ready to burst into flame. Sulfuric fumes thickened the air. Her throat felt like she had been swallowing gravel.

She stepped away from the crater, her eyes stinging. Then, she heard a terrible rumble. As a roar grew within the rift below, Zuni witnessed a sight that few humans ever live to describe. Two new, beautiful fountains thrust torrents of red-hot lava three hundred feet into the air. One quickly died out, but the other grew in magnificence, seeming to pulse and breathe as it splattered seven hundred feet into the sky with blobs that exploded in the air like popcorn.

Liquid rock poured onto the crater floor where screaming university kids were struggling to escape. Their terror still filled Zuni's ears. In absolute horror, she had watched, not believing what she saw — the horrible sight of human bodies aflame. Like Christian martyrs of Nero's madness, young researchers became brief torches, then flickering ash.

Zuni had turned her face away. As she knelt, shaken, gasping for air, three sooty young researchers, their faces gray in terror struggled over the edge of the cliff toward her, no longer shooting pictures as they retreated. But with a fiery rumble, the rift spat a new stream of lava into the air. One of the boys was suddenly afire. He shrieked in agony, then shucked his burning gear, rolled on the ground, and crawled toward Zuni.

Whimpering, he clutched at her ankles. Kneeling, shielding her face from the heat, she found herself weeping and comforting him. She carried him back to the plane and there gently picked tatters of his burned T-shirt out of his blackened skin before he died in her arms. He was just nineteen years old and had wanted to work for *National Geographic* magazine.

Zuni shivered as she remembered.

Never again, she had vowed.

Never again would she tempt a volcano with the flesh of human sacrifice.

Yet now, unintentionally, above this very different eruption, that was exactly what she found herself doing.

This time, she was risking two lives.

From the back of the cabin a young voice called "Mom?" Sleepily, fourteen-year-old Patrick stuck his curly head into the cockpit.

Zuni turned on the windshield wipers and brushed away the ash peppering the glass. Soot was building up on the wings. The plane shuddered, as if slammed by a giant hand. It shook again — battered by the force of new, strong crosswinds.

Patrick reeled, grabbing for a hand strap. "What's going on?" he demanded, his sleepy voice cracking with concern. Then, he stared in disbelief at the

Hades below.

"Hang on," Zuni muttered. "Strap yourself in. We're going down. This thing is falling like a rock."

"Are we out of gas?"

"Buckle up, Trooper."

"What are we going to do? We'll fry down there!" The panic in Patrick's voice rattled Zuni. She did not answer — her face strangely calm, resolute.

She did not know that the evil thing in the belly of her plane was to blame. In its silent madness, it craved death.

It scanned the blackened slopes of the fiery mountain. Yes, this would do just fine. A crash landing would serve quite well. Secure in its crates, it would await the rescuers who would come — slaves of its dark master, servants of the shadowy man who had commanded its creation, who had gathered its components from the ends of the Earth and snatched its insane inventor out of a Chinese prison.

Zuni and this boy would be dead — their agony relished by the thing in the crates.

It loved fear. It thrived on the excitement of human terror.

Startled, Zuni felt a tug on the controls. She'd been hoping for the hint of a warm updraft of rising air that might propel them out of the fiery grave.

Instead, she was puzzled by this nudge downward. It wasn't a wind shear. It was as if something was trying to control her aircraft.

Angrily, Zuni clutched the yoke — the plane's horns, the "wheel." She pushed the craft skyward. The plane responded, reluctantly, but seemed ready to go into a stall. "¡Vamos, lata . . . *levántate, levántate!*" she whispered in Spanish: *Get out of here, you stupid tin can. Get up, get up.*

Even in a rented, lightweight sailplane, Zuni had always depended on a variometer — a clever device that signals to glider pilots when they are inside an invisible thermal. And it was a thermal, no mere crosswind, that would be necessary to get them out of this mess.

Steely-eyed, her hands trembling, Zuni felt like crying. But she was no society belle afforded such dramatics. This moment, her life — and that of her boy — was in her hands. In the next moments, she believed, she would survive by her own cunning and determination or else they would die. Disaster leered at her — taunting her. She sneered back. This evening there was no white knight in shining armor ready to ride to her rescue. It was up to her.

She did not pray.

Instead, from within she stoked a familiar rage that was never far away. It was an anger that had become an old friend — not a fury against her son, nor the airplane, nor the second-hand auto-pilot she'd installed herself, nor even against the volcano. It was an old anger against a world that did not play fair, against parents who had failed her, against a Creator who did not do what she had expected — against a hard life that had robbed her of her dreams and ideals.

"Get your nose up, you piece of junk," she spat softly at the plane. "Don't you stall on me, you old vulture."

But stall the Martin did.

It shuddered — for what Zuni knew well could be its last time and began to yaw dangerously. Below, rivers of molten rock poured from cracks in the earth. She knew the poison gases pouring from the slopes would kill them if the heat did not. "Dear God," she whispered unexpectedly. "Not for me, but for this boy. He doesn't deserve to die like this."

Patrick heard her prayer. He buttoned up his shirt. The boy looked at his mother, then down at the bubbling lava. "Please God," he whispered. "You can help us out! Please!"

Then, it was as if a great hand lifted the plane skyward — up out of the fiery center of the deadly volcano.

As the scarlet stream of hot lava dropped out of sight, Patrick buckled himself into the co-pilot's seat. "All right. A whopper thermal," breathed the boy. "Bango! Can you feel that thing, Mom?"

Zuni nodded tensely — uncomfortably knowing that the old Martin was not designed for this. Corkscrewing upward, the plane rode the miraculous updraft. Zuni sat back.

She could not sense the startled disappointment from the thing in the hold.

Nor did she see the glory.

From the very throne of God, great bursts of light flashed forth. With hands upraised, ancient saints knelt before Him. Lightning flashed as great choirs proclaimed, "Holy, holy, holy, Lord God Almighty, Who was, and is, and is to come." Their voices boomed like thunder.

In the midst of His presence, kneeling in a bedroom in Puerto Rico, an old lady wept her joy. "O Lord," she whispered. "You are worthy to receive the glory and the honor and the power for You have created all things. Everything was created and called into being by Your will!"

She sensed a terrible spiritual storm gathering.

She pleaded for protection for Patrick and Zuni. Incredible sanctuary. Refuge. Asylum against terrible evil.

Excited, Patrick unbuckled his seat belt and stood. "Do you feel it, Mom?" he whispered.

As the little aircraft rose into the heavenlies, Zuni stared at the twinkling stars.

Patrick glanced over and realized she was crying.

Tears rolled down her hardened cheeks. Zuni fought waves of emotion — an unrepentant agnostic forced to her knees, she had renounced her faith and violated most of the Ten Commandments. No, she had never intentionally killed or sincerely worshiped an idol. But she was not a faithful servant.

"Did you feel Him?" whispered Patrick. "Mom? He's here."

Unheard by human ears, the angels sang.

"Patrick . . ." Zuni attempted. But there was no point in explaining that the updraft over the super-hot lava was a very explainable phenomenon — exactly the sort of natural event that Zuni'd been searching for desperately to lift them skyward out of the jaws of death.

Safely the mighty, upward wind carried them heavenward despite her denial of the source of their deliverance.

Patrick stood, his face almost aglow.

Zuni sighed.

From the cargo hold, deranged malice sneered and reached out again — invisibly. Unseen eyes studied the mother and son.

What was Zuni's illegal cargo?

She really didn't want to know. Every time she went near the crates she'd had a terrible feeling — as if something knew she was there.

She just wanted her money for sneaking it out of Johannesburg, South Africa. She had seen the NASA inventory bar codes on some of the components — and the Israeli, Chinese, Japanese, and Russian markings on others.

She had heard Iraqi billionaire Molech Gordini bragging something about the crates holding the only operational "LORRD" computer in existence. Well, Zuni always read *U.S. News and World Report* and knew that a LORRD — short for "Lasing Optical

Reffluent-Repanding Drive"—was expected to do for computers what rockets had done for space exploration.

What was a LORRD? The world's greatest micromega computer.

A mighty device with supposedly infinite abilities. A computer with a mind of its own.

A doomsday machine, some said.

But it was much more than that.

❖　　❖　　❖

Aboard a jet speeding toward Mombasa, a rumpled Russian inventor with the hint of a mustache on her lip shoved cola-bottle glasses up on her greasy nose.

Valentina Vasilieva glanced out the airliner's window and stuffed a cream pastry into her puffy face. She peered disdainfully at an American computer magazine, then glanced out the window again.

She wore tiny earphones, which thumped the bass of a heavy metal rock group. "The last time I was on an airplane was last week when I was being sneaked out of China," she proclaimed suddenly to a New York businesswoman napping in the seat next to her. Valentina shook the magazine. "What foolishness, all this renewed fascination with virtual memory. It's absolutely useless — obsolete."

Startled, the New Yorker glanced up. She smiled, unsure of what she had just heard. Valentina babbled on. "It says that the portable computer will be the only telephone most people will need." She smirked. "On our portable computers, we will be able to see who is calling before we answer. Three-dimensional holographic images will bring us TV shows and movies with clarity. Interactive shows." Valentina's voice rose — much too loud for conversation.

The tired New York woman winced in disinterest.

She tried to ignore the heads turning in their direction. Valentina did not act as if she noticed.

She did sense the businesswoman's obvious, growing dislike of her. But regardless, "Personal portable computers will put telephones, fax machines, and interactive TVs into every car," Valentina yammered. "High-resolution satellite navigation will pinpoint any vehicle's location giving the driver a digitized view of any road ahead." She sniffled, but a small stream of nasal mucus glistened on the fine whiskers of her upper lip.

The businesswoman turned away. Revulsion showed all over her face. Valentina had bad breath, too. "You've heard of refluency, of course?"

The New York woman started to say something, but Valentina cut her off. "I invented refluency. That's what will make all of this practical. We're talking about a storage solution that totally eliminates any need for media. We're talking about infinite reliability. Infinite capacity. Limitless. Limitless. Limitless."

"Very interesting," muttered the businesswoman, turning in her seat and fluffing her pillow. "Excuse me, but I am very tired."

Valentina nodded. Peering over the pillow at her Valentina demanded, "Want to know the secret? Biochips. Live computer chips developed from human cancer cells. Cancer cells. That's right. Cancer cells. Living biochips give you a billion times more memory. Plus cryogenics. Cryogenics. Sub-zero environments give you much more than mere speed. Crack the absolute zero barrier and you get adimensionals. You know what that means? Proof of anti-physics. Entry into parallel universes. A door into the unknown — beyond the mystic veil. Unlimited access to all the knowledge in the world — and absolutely beyond. Whatever you download is there, available."

The businesswoman sat up with a sigh. She dug under her seat, opened her briefcase, and took out a handkerchief. She held it to her nose, then dabbed her eyes, glaring sideways at Valentina.

"Repanding interface is what will make it really work," babbled the puffy-faced Russian. "Repandency! Yes! Repandency solves the speed limitations of every computer that has ever existed before!"

Her words were pure nonsense to the business-woman.

"I was the first one to see repandency's application," Valentina ranted on. "Me and Naoto Horii at Kyoto Polytechnical Institute in Japan. See, he knew that I was the first true genius to put repandency to work. I was the first one to see how repandency would allow constant downlink — updating without pause — from every transmitting device bouncing its signal off of a satellite anywhere."

Not understanding a word of Valentina's obnoxious technical gibberish — or caring about any of it — the businesswoman craned her neck, looking for a flight attendant. Valentina lit a cigarette and blew smoke into the air, then laughed and babbled more seeming nonsense.

It would be hard to explain the emptiness, loneliness, and hunger that filled the ranting Valentina. Abandoned at a Moscow hospital shortly after birth, she had spent her first five years in a sterile, state-run orphanage, denied affection or attention.

As a kindergartner, she had been placed with a childless ex-submarine officer and his young psychologist wife. But the retired commander had demanded military perfection of little Valentina and did not hesitate to pull off his belt to lash the strong-willed little rebel for the smallest infraction.

At school, Valentina became unmanageable, a violent, spitting, defiant little scab of a girl, always

the reject of the playground, accused of having coo-
ties, the perennial object of scorn — the fat, ugly girl
that the hooting boys accused each other of liking.
She had responded to their insults by scratching
their ugly faces with her well-sharpened fingernails.

By high school, she had been in three mental
institutions and four more foster homes. Scarred
from sexual abuse she had suffered from older boys at
the last hospital, she had become an introverted
wanderer in fantasy worlds.

Magical worlds became real.

It was there that she first encountered imaginary
friends who actually talked with her, liked her, and
told her amazing secrets about her tormentors.

Her spirit friends had shown her how to burn
down the girls' dorm at the Bakliev Reformatory
Camp in the Urals. And, true to their promises, she
was not caught — nor even suspected.

Silently, she had laughed as the three bodies had
been brought out — the lifeless forms of girls she had
not known, but did not like. They were athletes.
Proud of their full, shapely bodies.

Arrogant.

Unworthy.

Now, Valentina had seen her country bow and
pander before the haughty Arabs, the vengeful Japanese, and the short-term, opportunistic Americans.
She had growled with fury as the Eurodollar became
the world standard.

Valentina had made a vow.

She would avenge the humiliation.

She would return glory to Mother Russia.

She had never been a Communist. No, her loyalty
was to the mighty mother bear of the North — the
Imperial Russia of Catherine the Great.

Russia. Magog.

"Look at this," Valentina exclaimed at the businesswoman, waving the magazine in her face.

The New Yorker clutched her belongings and awkwardly squirmed into the aisle. Without a word, she sat down in another seat.

Valentina snorted.

The businesswoman did not look back around. Valentina muttered under her breath.

She whispered her disgust.

Wandering out beyond the human limits of time and space, Valentina had quizzed the master spirit guides — who always divulged such wondrous secrets of a far greater universe.

To Valentina, the mystical worlds of science fiction had long been an intense, personal reality. Her spirit friends took her to magical places unseen, unenvisioned by mere mortals. They had birthed in Valentina a personal vision of a new world order. It would begin with a new monetary arrangement — a new financial system forced upon every living human being, a new fiscal order dropped into place overnight in a technological coup that would catch even the superpowers by surprise.

All nations of the world would start over from zero. Everybody!

Mother Russia would begin life anew, too, on an equal footing. And a daughter of Russia would control the system.

Valentina had chuckled at the simplicity of the scheme. Everything had been made ready. The day's financial structures were already interfaced into communications systems accessible from any pay phone. The need to rob armored cars lugging around bags of cash was long past.

Now the financial world was electronic. Real money only existed in the computer memories of banks and financial institutions. Now, overnight, all human-kind would bow to a benign dictatorship out of the North.

No monetary exchange would take place without Valentina's knowledge.

The eccentric Russian genius chuckled at the utter simplicity of it all. Her spirit masters had shown her how to tap into the computers. Repanding refluency made it a reality with limitless memory and instantaneous worldwide communication.

The New York businesswoman didn't care.

That was okay with Valentina.

The next time the New Yorker tried to cash a check or use a credit card, she would discover that everything had changed.

Deviously, Valentina grinned to herself.

She would have to ask Valentina Vasilieva for permission to spend any money.

Crazily now, Valentina laughed under her breath as she flipped through the computer magazine, her eyes devouring every word. "Obsolete," she muttered aloud. In a sudden fury, she hurled the magazine at a flight attendant in the aisle. "Take that trash away!" she squealed in a frantic rage. "Take it away, away, away!"

The attendant did.

Later, the airliner's captain strolled back through the cabin to check out the disturbed political refugee. The flight attendant had mentioned, "She may have a medical problem, Sir."

Valentina was staring intently at the seat back in front of her. In her mouth she clutched a pillow. Her eyes were vacant. She was soaring. She was orbiting a marvelous planet straight out of the rich imagination of Jules Verne. Out in the astral wilderness, a grotesque being explained the concept of worldwide madness.

This was far more powerful than Hitler's big lie. This was the miraculous, global acceptance of a great delusion. Global hallucination.

"Truth becomes whatever you declare to be true," explained the spirit guide, "particularly to a generation taught that truth is relative and whatever they want it to be."

Valentina jumped up and down in glee. How delightful. How godlike it would make her — but, "What does it have to do with my computer?" she demanded.

"Everything, my little sister," calmed her grotesque mentor. "Everything."

Back on the airplane the pilot was yelling hello at the Russian defector. "Hello?"

Blankly, Valentina turned and blinked. "What?" she roared.

"Are you okay?" asked the captain.

"Certainly," spat Valentina. "I am the inventor of refluency. You, on the other hand, are a mere mortal and probably never heard of it. You probably think that the universe is curved. Well, my friend, Einstein was a half-baked fool."

Gently feeling the stick, instinctively sensing where to guide the plane within the rising column of hot air, Zuni fumbled for a cigarette.

She muttered under her breath, remembering she had quit smoking at Patrick's constant urging. Wearily, Zuni did not swear — since the boy was sitting beside her.

She had turned her back on everything else in her strict moral upbringing, but swearing really had not become one of her habits.

Lately she had found herself shedding all sorts of other vices as the responsibilities of middle age overtook her. Of course, she knew how to curse — dramatically and violently in a number of languages.

She believed she swore for impact, not from reflex. In this man's Africa, she knew she had to act meaner, tougher, and harder than any male, gringo bush-pilot. She had to maintain a fireball image. That's why a World War II-vintage Luger automatic pistol was strapped to her leg.

She'd never fired it in anger. She had certainly showed it off for effect. Once she had even put a very calculated slug through a gun dealer who'd taken too much interest in her femininity. She'd carefully just winged him and the big Austrian had gotten the message. Without protest, he had allowed her to lift from his wallet her complete payment for the load of shoulder-fired missiles she had just sneaked into her easy-going home port of Mombasa.

Again, she fumbled for a cigarette, then winced, irritated all over again. Deep inside, she was glad she'd brought none. But she yearned for the tough-ness and steely coldness that good, strong nicotine gave her.

What she really wanted was a cigar.

In the darkness of the night, old Johanna Graham again knelt in her threadbare nightgown. Before her on the bed she had laid photos of Zuni and Patrick.

"O Lord," Patrick's grandmother whispered in intensity. "I continue to feel a great burden that I cannot understand. Again, Lord, You have awakened me from my sleep with this burning conviction that something truly evil is afoot.

"Lord, I don't know what's going on but I bring before You my daughter. O Father, Zuni has never recovered from her father's murder at the hands of the native guerrillas so many years ago. Lord, please touch Zuni tonight. Give her complete safety and protection and a yearning for You.

"Give her peace, Lord.

"Draw her to You. Hold her in Your mighty arms and protect her. Open her eyes to Your goodness, to the reality of Your protection. Let her see You as You truly are!

"And Patrick. O Father, I do not know how to pray tonight. I am baffled as I struggle for words. Lord, I am so burdened for that boy. Is it for his spiritual development? Is it for his personal safety? I don't know. Was that terrible vision from You? He is such a sweet boy. But he is at such a fragile and impressionable time in his life. Send him — Lord, send him someone who will explain Your truth to him in simple and exciting terms. Let Patrick know You, Father.

"Lord, I sense such a deep, deep evil reaching out to Zuni and Patrick. I do not understand it, Father. I see a terrible, black hand overshadowing them. Lord, I ask for Your mighty protection. Father, whatever it takes, break through, O Lord, and protect them with Your mighty angels.

"Lord, I feel as if a great battle is beginning.

"Father, again awaken my intercessors. Lord, stir those who pray for me and my ministry here. Fill them with a great urgency tonight. Direct them in the way that they should pray."

Up, up, up, glided Zuni's heavy airplane.

Undoubtedly customs rangers are tracking us on radar, she thought. Again she could have kicked herself. She really should have taken care of that little misunderstanding back at Lake Kiva airport.

She hadn't meant to run out on her big fuel bill but she was broke.

You can't pay anybody if you don't have a cent.

The strict little British martinet who ran the tiny Lake Kiva airstrip by the regulation book had filed felony charges against her. She'd steered clear of his air space ever since. She figured if she mailed him a check someday, he'd be satisfied.

But now, here she was, in his lap — with a contraband mega-computer packed in three little crates — conspicuously tied down in the middle of the empty hold.

It looked so tiny. It hardly weighed a thing.

Patrick had laughed when Zuni had asked him if it was alive.

"Mom," he had hooted. "It's a machine. Give me a break."

"I don't know," she had muttered. "I think it breathes."

"Breathes?" exclaimed the boy incredulously. He roared with laughter.

"I think it's evil."

Patrick winced. "Mom," he had whined, "a machine can't be evil."

"It can be possessed by evil."

Patrick had groaned. He had rolled his eyes mysteriously and began tooting the theme song of the old "Twilight Zone" TV series.

"Holy, holy, holy is Your name, O Lord..." Johanna's prayer intensified as she began to sway. It took on almost a sing-song as she pleaded her daughter's case at the throne of the Most High.

Then, she began to groan again. Even she did not understand the meaning of her moanings.

But God did.

And He smiled upon her.

In Melbourne, Australia, an Aborigine hotel maid

named Helen gently closed the linen room door behind her. She locked it. She then began to do what looked like a little dance. "Oh, Lord," she whispered in the language of her ancestors, "I do not know why I feel such an urging to walk about before Your throne and bring before You Johanna Graham. But I lift her up, Lord. Father God, in the precious name of Your Son, the Lord Jesus Christ, I present before You Johanna Graham. Hear her prayers, Father.

"I ask you, Father, to send great legions of angels to her. Give her might and power, Lord. I do not know why I am asking this. But I ask for a great army of angels to be dispatched to her aid. Surround her! Protect her. And protect those for whom she fights, O Lord . . ."

In Gdansk, Poland, an eleven-year-old boy named Ladislav sat up in bed. Over his dresser was a faded picture of the Black Madonna of the old shrine near his grandfather's house.

"Our Father," prayed the little boy, "who art in heaven . . ." He paused. "Thank You for bringing my papa home from the army. Now, please, help that missionary lady I saw on television. God, I don't even remember her name, but I believe that she is very, very important. Lord, help her. Hear her prayer."

The youngster paused, perplexed. "Okay," he murmured, "I am going to do what Father John told me to do. As I just prayed, I saw a terrible machine in a crashed airplane. Father John says that when I see things like this, I am to go to You, O Lord, and ask how I should pray."

The boy paused.

He whispered. "Let that terrible machine be hidden from the great evildoers who want it so. Let there be a great and terrible fog over their wicked eyes. Let them stumble right over the thing and not see it. Make them blind, O Lord. Deliver instead that machine into the hands of those who ..." the boy paused. "I don't know who is supposed to get it. Maybe it is supposed to be destroyed. I don't think so, but Lord, let that machine be used for only good. Let no evil come from that thing."

In New Hampton, Iowa, a farmer paused at his home computer. He grimaced, then pulled down his prayer journal that he kept on the computer's hard drive.

"O mighty God, Maker of all things," he tapped out. "I was trying to figure out my estimated taxes for this quarter when I was consumed with an urgency for Johanna Graham. Reach out, O Lord, and protect her from whatever evil is advancing against her. I ask this in Jesus' name. Amen."

Then he closed the file and returned to his quarterly report.

Across the globe, similar incidences occurred.

In East Los Angeles, a former crack addict with gaudy tattoos all over his forearms and neck stood in the twenty-four-hour grocery where he worked. The loud street flowed with slowly moving, beautifully customized cars. Angry teens yelled, laughed, drank, and shouted insults from vehicle to vehicle.

Motorcycles roared down the broken sidewalk, littered with crack cocaine vials and broken liquor bottles. Leaning against graffiti-covered walls, young men with quick eyes and dark clothes were selling almost any kind of street drug available. Scantily clad girls flaunted their merchandise under a corner street light.

This was the rush hour on Whittier Boulevard.

The tattooed store clerk glanced sideways at customers browsing for munchies. Just for a moment, he closed his eyes. "Praise You, Jesus," he whispered, opening his eyes.

A stoned customer advanced, a soft drink cup

trembling in his hand, coins offered between tightly gripped fingers. Silently, the tattooed clerk rang up the purchase and asked for special, divine protection for "that boy."

What boy? As Miguel closed the cash register, he wondered to himself, *Just what boy suddenly needed such urgent prayer.* Again, under his breath, Miguel whispered intercession for a blond, gringo kid lost somewhere near a . . . volcano?

A volcano? As he waited on the next customer, Miguel grinned to himself. "Thank You, Jesus," he prayed silently. "Hey, I don't have the slightest idea what that sudden urge to pray was all about, Lord. But I could see a blond gringo kid near a volcano. He reminds me of my little brother, José Chimon. Lord, protect José, too. José, he's in the gangs, I know it. This *anglo* kid near that volcano, his danger is just as real. Thank You, Jesus."

Johanna Graham's intercessors were, indeed, awakened.

Unseen, the evil forces in the heavenlies attempting to cloud her mind and darken her vision were thrown back once again.

Zuni did not turn on her radio. She didn't want to know if she was being ordered to land. The government of Zaire had blasted smugglers out of the sky before — but never ones that had not been warned.

Fighting the control stick, she tapped on the lifeless fuel gauge as the old Martin continued its spiral toward 27,000 feet. Worried whether the old plane could withstand a descent from any greater altitude, she decided to guide it out of the thermal.

"Pues, tan pronto como estés listo," Zuni muttered to her plane: *Well, whenever you're ready.*

The ancient bird began its final landing. Strong upward winds might be plentiful over the mountains, she knew — but they would blow in every direction. So that was why she needed enough altitude to get out of the mountains and see if she could wrestle the creaking plane safely into a grassy clearing somewhere in the jungle.

Saving this cargo was worth a lot of money to her. Delivering the crates would get her out of trouble with a certain loan shark waiting in Mombasa.

As Zuni gently and tensely guided the Martin earthward, she gripped the stick and marveled at her own alertness. It was if she had been given a second wind.

She sighed, watching the air speed indicator.

Everybody had been so tense at the airfield outside Johannesburg.

Molech Gordini himself — one of the world's most shadowy power brokers — had been at the field in his gold Rolls Royce, personally walking the entire strip, nervously searching for potholes, anxiously examining her flight plan — asking too many questions of Patrick.

Of course, the mysterious Italian-born Iraqi did not lower himself to speak directly to Zuni.

She had pretended not to recognize him.

Knowing full well he claimed to be a non-drinking Muslim, in Spanish she had offered him the rest of her beer. In English, he had protested his indignant refusal.

She had smiled innocently.

She had heard the old lecher had twenty-seven concubines.

Carefully now, Zuni coaxed the old, unpowered Martin through the starry, starry night — her anger fueling her resolve to find a makeshift landing field.

In the milky moonlight, she came out of the clouds

and zoomed silently over a grassy plain filled with night-grazing Thomson's gazelles. She marvelled: She did not know this plateau. Was this the beautiful, famous Serengeti Plain? No, they could not have come that far. Besides, the altitude was wrong. The herd stampeded out of her way as the cargo plane made its single possible approach.

Zuni reminded herself that if middle-aged Space Shuttle pilots could put their stubby-winged craft down safely on one pass, then she could, too.

As the ground rushed up, as Patrick's knuckles turned white on the dashboard handle, as his adolescent face turned toward her in incredible respect, she touched down on the wild, uncharted pasture. Madly the plane rushed through the high grass, bouncing Zuni and Patrick and their high-tech cargo against the walls and off the ceiling. Suddenly, the ancient Martin slammed to a metal-screeching stop as one wheel was sheared away by a hidden termite mound. The old airliner swung wildly around, then quivered, collapsing against its starboard wing.

Shaken, Zuni stared at Patrick. Then, although they had not hugged in months — she was holding him and stroking his curly hair. His breath was shaky, trembling. She realized he was trying to comfort her.

"It's okay, Mom," he whispered. "We're safe. You are one great pilot."

He was then gone, back into the hold — checking on their precious cargo. "It's okay, Mom," he yelled victoriously. "The crates aren't even broken. The straps are shredded, but the boxes are okay."

Like any boy, he was enamored with the idea of possessing the world's most incredible machine. Like the hero of a science-fiction movie, he believed he had been entrusted with the key to universal peace, he had told her. The future rested in their cargo hold.

Zuni had smiled patiently.

It was just a bunch of electronic junk to her.

"No, no, Mom," exclaimed the boy. "This is a LORRD computer. You know, it's got the world's first Lasing Optical Reffluent-Repanding Drive.

"It's the next decade of computers, Mom! This is the very best that the Russians, the Americans, and the Japanese have! A LORRD computer takes advantage of the ultimate in American microminiaturization. That's why it's so tiny.

"It's fast, fast, fast, Mom, because of the new Israeli and Japanese cryoconductors — you know, using super, super cold stuff right down there around absolute zero.

"And Mom, this is radical — it is powered by something Molech told me the Russians have been frantically developing called the Karolian Component. It harnesses the same natural force that makes the universe spin and the earth rotate.

"See this crate, Mom? Six guys died getting it out of Moscow. The KGB was desperate to keep it out of Molech's hands. See that crate? At least a dozen people had to be wasted in Japan to get it. That nervous little Chinese technician working for Molech told me the computer is not restricted by our ideas or theories about time or space. Mom, that's anti-physics.

"Mom, this is a return to true medieval magic. Like Merlin. Like genies in the legends. You've heard of the New Age? This is New Age. But far, far more. It is a . . ." he fumbled with his hands, "more than religion."

"Uh-huh," Zuni had grunted in disinterest.

"Imagine that you are an ant," the high-strung Chinese technician had told Patrick. "You are little insect ant — never see sky. Spend all life in wonderful tunnel world taking care of eggs. One day, a wicked thing with terrible shovel end your world and put you and fifty others in plastic thing. Day and night, great giant stare at you, sprinkle delicious food into your new, confusing, pointless home. In terror, you run about, trying to find eggs, searching for queen, trying to understand, forming theories about what the wicked giant want. But you only die of stress, unable to know what is expected of you."

The technician had blinked, smiling broadly at the boy. "You never understand that giant want nothing. He only five-year-old boy and got an ant farm for birthday. Such concept too far, far beyond your reality. Not system. Spiritual. Not math. Not physics. Nothingness is not inexistence for there is no nothingness."

"Right," Patrick had exclaimed excitedly. "The sound of one hand clapping."

"No, no," sputtered the technician. "That is Zen. This is more."

Zuni winced. It was all nonsense to her, but she was glad Patrick took such an interest.

Now in the darkened cockpit she said, "Well, let's figure out where we are," as she turned everything off.

Opening the hatch, she peered outside behind Patrick. Her faithful old bird would never fly again. The fuel tanks were empty — so there was no danger of explosion — but the starboard wing was at a sickly angle. The fuselage sat cock-eyed, barely 18 inches off the ground. Zuni feared the worst. The ancient Martin's fragile back was probably broken for good this time.

"Mom," exclaimed Patrick. In the bright moonlight a great gang of impalas exploded into high jumps not fifty yards from the crash site. Spellbound, the fourteen-year-old stared at the springing animals.

"Beautiful, aren't they?" exclaimed Zuni, dropping to the ground with a painful lurch. Oh, no, she realized as she sat awkwardly in the dirt.

She had broken her ankle. She sighed.

This was ridiculous.

Released out of the very jaws of hell, carried heavenward by a miraculous thermal from nowhere, delivered to an unmapped highland plains perfect for an emergency landing, she now had broken her ankle getting out of her plane.

"Patrick," she called.

But the boy was captivated. On a nearby rock outcropping, a pride of lions lounged, pretending boredom with the human scene in the sea of high grasses.

"Patrick," Zuni called.

"Mom!" called the fourteen-year-old, pointing. A herd of giraffes grazed on the treetops of a distant grove. On another pile of boulders surrounded by purple wild flowers, thirty balls of fur — purring rock hydroxes, warm, fuzzy little animals of the elephant family — huddled together. A tiny pair of dik-dik antelopes no larger than a poodle stared at the boy watching them.

Zuni didn't move. The pain in her ankle told her she was not going to walk to Mombasa. Holding her breath, she watched her son.

Captivated, he exulted in the glory of life.

It was a rare and beautiful moment. He was almost a man — yet not enough to be ashamed to revel in the joyous creation spread before him or the wondrous gift of life he'd just been given.

Silently the boy stood tall, breathing it all in.

"Mom," he exclaimed. "Where are we? I didn't think anywhere like this still existed. Look — there's a real herd of wild elephants."

Zuni peered.

Wild elephants. Still free in Africa? Was it possible?

The Africa she had loved as a kid was increasingly an over-populated, over-grazed, defoliated, asphalted-over shadow of its former glory, torn by endless revolution and counter-revolution, terrorized by despots, ravaged by terrible diseases.

"Trooper, I've broken my ankle," she said evenly. "You're going to have to help me."

The boy knelt beside her.

"Does it hurt?"

"Badly." She groaned, leaning against his strong, adolescent back. "Oh, Trooper, it is bad. Uhhhhh." She fumbled at her bootlaces.

"No, Mom," Patrick exclaimed. "Leave it laced up. I'm not kidding. If your foot starts swelling, we'll never get your boot back on."

"Well, that'll be too bad," she sputtered darkly. She yanked the boot away. Sharp knives of pain shot up her leg.

Patrick winced. When his mother was really upset around him, she swore in Japanese — or actually the Hawaiian slang of her cousins, uncles, and aunts. Her parents were from Puerto Rico and Scotland, descended from the cane-field workers and whalers who had settled in Hawaii in the 1830s.

"I'll go get the first aid kit," he announced.

In minutes, he was back, studying a yellow manual and unwinding an elastic bandage. "If any bones protrude, control the bleeding and cover the wound with a large clean dressing or cloth. Do not clean the wound," he read aloud.

"No bones are protruding," growled Zuni.

"If no bones are protruding," continued the boy, "immobilize with a padded splint. Use boards, magazines, and so forth for rigidity and cloth or a pillow for padding."

Zuni closed her eyes. She felt light-headed. Sleepy. She winced and glanced up at Patrick.

". . . but if you are unable to improvise a splint," he was reading, "place padding between the legs and tie them together, using the good leg as the splint for the broken one. Hey, Mom, that sounds really smart. Oops. Listen to this: Very important. Seek medical aid. Do not try to reset dislocations yourself. Treat the same as fractures. Watch the patient carefully for signs of shock."

Zuni nodded groggily. She just wanted a nap.

"Hey," mused Patrick, "that's for broken legs. Look at this. Ankles. Hey, I was wrong. It says to remove or cut away the shoe or boot if possible and to immobilize with a padded splint. Tie the foot snugly, but not too tightly. Use a blanket or pillow and watch for signs of shock. Are you feeling groggy?"

Zuni grunted sleepily.

"I'll get you a pillow," announced the boy.

His mother nodded.

When she awoke, she was alone. She trembled, cold, under the full moon. The strange noises of the African outdoors unnerved her as she awakened, half in, half out of a recurring nightmare from her child-hood.

She had been dreaming that she was a little girl again, crammed into the back of a run-down truck with thirty other women and children during a murderous local uprising. The missionaries were on their way to be executed, but you would have thought the drunken guerrillas were on their way to a carnival. The truck kept stopping and picking up Africans hitching a ride to villages along the way — piling the executioners' truck with boxes and bales, goats, chickens, and stalks of bananas.

Even during the French Revolution's Reign of Terror, Queen Marie Antoinette — shoved into the back of a mule cart en route to the guillotine — was afforded more dignity.

Zuni had been only seven. She had sat up against the back of the cab and surveyed the twelve adult whites in their sun helmets, their neatly pressed khaki shirts and shorts, and their openwork sandals, clutching their Bibles and their neatly packed suitcases.

Fear prohibited any conversation . . .

Now, the adult Zuni laid still, listening — trying to remember where she was.

She was stretched out flat on the grass, covered with Patrick's sleeping bag. Under her head was his rolled-up flight jacket. Her injured ankle was 18 inches up in the air, placed in the crashed Martin's open hatchway. Her boot was gone and her foot was encased in her own rolled-up sleeping bag, secured by Patrick's belt.

Feeling ridiculous, she looked around.

She was amazed that Patrick had gathered acacia thornbushes and had piled them in a makeshift hedge under the broken plane and around her. She sighed her satisfaction with the way the boy was turning out. He was meticulous whereas she was impulsive.

He thought of the little things — such as gathering thornbushes. A good thing, too — as Zuni's nose caught a rather awful smell. She craned her neck to see what it was.

She was horrified to stare eye-to-eye with a dozen half-grown lions with bloody jaws. Clutching at the pistol on her hip, pulling up on her elbow, she realized they were not really looking at her. Instead, they were devouring the carcass of some sort of buffalo —

probably a wildebeest. The young lions were intent on their meal and ate silently, except for strange gurgles as they swallowed gory chunks of meat.

Zuni fought an urge to gag — or throw something at the lions to drive them away from their disgusting binge. Instead, she lay still. Zuni spotted a single jackal peeking over the tall grass, staying safely out of reach of the lions. The tiny, wild canine, too, awaited its turn.

Wincing from the nasty stench of the big bull whose bloody guts lay spilled on the ground, Zuni watched the lions and wondered why they had not noticed her.

Then, she remembered something from her missionary childhood in Africa — before her mother had been widowed. Zuni was downwind. That meant she was relatively safe since lions have notoriously bad eyesight.

She carefully glanced down at her Luger.

It was loaded. Would it stop a determined pride of lions?

She hoped she would not need to find out.

In the distance, she heard the unmistakable laugh of a hyena. A terrible memory from her childhood awakened. Hyenas. The sneaky scavenger-hunters of the Great Rift. Again she heard the haunting bark, nearer.

She knew that was worth worrying about.

Those ugly hunchbacks could be a problem if they decided to try to get through Patrick's hedge. Where was the boy?

Behind the Martin's fuselage, Zuni heard ghostly grunts that she knew all too well. The hyenas had caught her scent. What few non-Africans know is that hyenas are often far more aggressive than lions. In the Ngorongoro wildlife preserve, lions seldom made their own kills — instead letting hyenas do the work, then driving them away from it.

Zuni's heart leaped as a hyena loped across in front of the hedge. Zuni did not move. The slopeheaded canine did not sense her presence at first.

Then it turned and stared right at her.

In sudden panic, Zuni unsuccessfully tried to struggle to her feet.

And she was gripped with another terror. In the tail of the plane was an automatic transponder beacon that was broadcasting her location — sending out a steady appeal for help. "Oh, no," whispered Zuni. The inexplicable fear that consumed her was numbing. As she stared eye-to-eye with the mangy hyena, she knew she had to get to that beacon and disable it.

This time she didn't want to be rescued — it was something she and Patrick simply could not chance. Too many evil people were too intently interested in their contraband cargo. Instinctively, Zuni knew she did not want to encounter any of the sorts who would be coming to look for her.

Molech was a single-minded man.

If he sensed any sort of double-cross, he opened fire first, then apologized later.

She and Patrick had to get the computer to Mombasa — somehow — on their own. Painfully, she again attempted to stand. The lions looked up, startled, as she stood to her feet — her sleeping-bagged ankle held out like a weird pendulum. She clutched at the metallic skin of the Martin, her head light.

The hyena cocked its head. Seeming to smile, mocking her, it coughed to its cohorts. Four more slipped up out of the shadows and eyed her hungrily.

"Oh, no," she whispered to herself.

There was a dog-like whine, then the evil laugh for which hyenas are famous. Two more panted at the edge of the thorns, inspecting the hedge for a hole. One began digging, then paused, looking inquisitively at the others.

She grabbed at her pistol. "Come on, you," she snarled. "I'll feed you to your brothers."

The hyena cocked its ears and grunted, as if accepting the challenge. Painfully, Zuni dragged herself back into the dark airplane. Panting heavily, her foot throbbing tortuously, she bolted the door closed.

She leaned against it in relief.

And she collapsed, dreaming again a terrible memory of Africa and revolution. She did not notice that the mega-computer in the crates had developed a hum. The control panels glowed in the darkness.

It was operational — although it was still in pieces.

It was getting ready.

Its time was coming.

Fitfully, she would sleep until morning — as the automatic beacon proclaimed her location to every satellite passing overhead.

Patrick knelt in the shallows of the river, clutching a Swiss army knife. Thirty enormous hippos seemed to be rioting over something he could not figure out. Then he saw the nasty wounds gleaming pink and raw against their dull, gray hide. Squawking tickbirds were perched on their boulder-like shoulders, their wings flapping, their beaks open in protest.

Then the hippos settled down. Patrick watched them, puzzled. He had no idea what was bothering them. Crocodiles? Whatever it was, he was not about to take a swim.

Nor was he going to try wading.

Perplexed, he gazed at the river.

Then, he had an incredible feeling that he was

being watched. Tensely, he spun.

And there, not five feet away squatted the blackest man he had ever seen in his life, clutching an enormous spear, wearing nothing but St. Louis Cardinals athletic shorts, and grinning as if he knew the answer to a clever riddle. Patrick tried not to stare, but this guy was genuinely black — not brown. He was almost purple and had incredibly kind eyes.

He squatted, grinning, watching the boy.

"Who are you?" demanded Patrick.

The native squinted at him.

"I am Patrick," said the boy. He thumped his chest. "Me Patrick. Me Patrick. Patrick Graham MacDougal. Mighty warrior. Kill many men. King of the jungle. Not afraid."

The black man nodded. He squinted at the hippos and did not speak.

"You havum name?" asked Patrick. "Um-ga-wa?"

"Um-ga-wa?" laughed the native. "Who do you think you are, Tarzan?"

"What?" exclaimed Patrick. "You speak English! How long have you been watching me?"

"Oh, long enough to know that you are not the king of the jungle," laughed the man. " Are you thinking about going swimming with those guys?"

Patrick looked at the hippos and shuddered. "I was trying to figure out how to get to the other side. Do those things eat humans?"

The black man shrugged. "Upon occasion, but only if they think you are something else. Men do not taste all that good. Why do you want to get to the other side? How did you get up here? Tourist safari?"

"Our plane crashed," answered Patrick. "My mom's injured. I have to get help."

"Ummmm," said the native.

Uncomfortably, Patrick looked away. "Do you always run around like that?"

"Huh?" asked the man, glancing down at his gym shorts. And he turned to go.

"Hey," exclaimed Patrick. "Hey, come back."

The man turned.

"Hey," protested Patrick. "Hey, take me with you."

"I cannot do that."

"Why not?"

The black man squinted at him. "I just can't."

"Well, can you take me to a doctor? My mom's got a broken ankle and I left her out there in the grass."

Alarmed, the man stood, peering at the horizon. "Where?"

Patrick stood, trying to get his bearings. Suddenly, everything looked the same. "I don't know," he said.

"Ummmm," said the black man. He studied the ground. "Well, we will just follow your trail. Come on." And he was running through the grass.

Patrick jumped up and galloped after him. "Wait!" he called.

The man stopped. "Oh, I am sorry," he exclaimed. "You cannot run like an African. I will walk. But please come quickly."

"I can run," defended Patrick. "Go ahead. I'll keep up with you."

The man squinted at him. "Ummmm," he said, then set off in a slower, easier jog.

Patrick charged after him. "Do you have a name?"

"Of course I do." The man answered with a bemused dignity.

"Yeah?" panted the boy.

"It is Matthew."

Patrick was expecting something more like Bugga-Bugga-Jojo or Mohammed Ali. "Matthew?" the boy panted. "That's really your name?"

"It is," answered the man. "Matthew Britanga, son of Titus Britanga. I grew up with brothers named

Mark, Luke, and John."

"Wow!" exclaimed Patrick. "I bet you know my grandmother."

Matthew squinted quizzically. "Why would I?"

"She's Johanna Graham," said Patrick. "She's a missionary."

"A missionary? I do not know her. You are a Christian?"

Patrick grinned. "Do I look like a pagan?"

The black man did not smile. "Do you know Jesus, Patrick?"

"Sure," chuckled the boy. "Well, I've seen the movie, but I never met the dude. You know, He died several thousand years ago." The fourteen-year-old smiled at his own joke.

The man running beside him did not laugh. "He is not dead, Patrick."

"Yeah, right. I guess He lives around here and is working as a beekeeper?" Again the boy snickered.

The man did not. "He lives within my heart," Matthew said, his voice majestic and proud — yet very humble.

"Oh, yeah," said Patrick. "Okay. I got ya. So, you're religious. That's cool. I got no problem with that. You have your right to your own beliefs."

"Yes," said Matthew.

The two ran for perhaps ten minutes without another word. Then, softly, "You are more pagan than anyone I have ever met, Patrick," said Matthew.

"What?"

"Yes."

Again they ran in silence, Matthew watching the ground intently, occasionally making abrupt turns.

Patrick's side began to hurt. He was a fair athlete, but this was considerably more rigorous than he was accustomed.

"Can we stop?" the boy exclaimed.

"Yes," Matthew halted. He studied the horizon. "Your mother may be in trouble."

"What?"

"I see your crash. There is a vulture."

The boy exhaled in sudden concern. Without a word, both were running again.

"Why did you call me a pagan?" gasped Patrick. "My grandmother is a missionary."

"Are you a Christian?"

"Of course. I mean, I guess. I'm kind of into Zen and neat New Age stuff, you know, but I'm really not anything. Look, my grandmother has been a missionary for fifty years. That makes me a Christian, doesn't it? I was born into it."

Matthew shook his head vehemently. "God does not have grandchildren," he said.

"What?"

"God is your Father. He will not settle for being your grandfather. Your grandmother's faith doesn't do a thing for you."

"Are you a preacher?"

The black man smiled. "All who believe are members of a royal priesthood. It is our call to go unto all the world and preach the gospel unto all who have not heard the good news."

Matthew nodded, with only the hint of a smile on his face. "Where are you from?"

"Nairobi," said Patrick, huffily. "I go to the British Royal Academy."

"Mmmmm," nodded Matthew. "British boarding school."

Matthew nodded saying, "You are not one of us."

As Zuni cringed in her broken Martin, a pack of determined hyenas suddenly yelped and ran for safety.

Like Balaam's burro, they saw a great warrior angel of the Lord standing over the airplane — an invisible sentinel with a burning sword and eyes of fire that Zuni did not even sense.

"Glory, honor, power, and strength to the Lord..." Johanna's voice was growing hoarse. "Greater is He that is in us than he that is in the world."

Worldwide, intercessors were also praising His name and asking for miraculous protection from what each sensed as enormous evil — more vicious and murderous than anything they had ever encountered.

Insane vengeance.

Venomous hatred against all humans.

In Australia, Helen knelt in her linen room door and wept before the Lord.

In Poland, Ladislav whispered again: "Let that terrible machine be hidden, O Lord. Make a great fog over the wicked eyes of the evil men who are looking for it. Let them stumble right over it. Make them blind, O Lord. Let no evil come from that thing. Now, protect that boy." Ladislav paused. "Yes, Lord. Whoever he is, Lord, protect him." The Polish lad trembled. He began to repeat the Lord's Prayer. "Our Father Who art in heaven..."

On the grassy plains, beside Patrick, ran a great troop of heavenly warriors. Matthew clutched his spear and studied the boy as they ran toward the crumpled plane. Who was this boy? Why had the Lord so urgently sent Matthew to the hippo hole?

Matthew winced, perplexed. At home, his wife tended the cooking fire, nursed their four-month-old son, and offered up a prayer for her wonderful, faithful husband. She prayed that he would bring home delicious venison. Beside her, their too-serious son, Daniel, read aloud to her from the Psalms.

In the tail of a crashed Martin, the batteries of

Zuni's transponder beacon weakened and went dead. The distress signal faded, then stopped.

In the spirit-infested heavenlies over earth, demonic screams reverberated in angry frustration. Great fallen angels pleaded for reinforcements from their dark supervisors. Dark hatreds swelled among the troops. Chaos reigned.

In the belly of the broken plane, the tiny megacomputer stirred. It fought back against the heavenly meddlers and sent up its own beacon — mimicking the emergency transponder.

But overhead, a great solar flare disrupted communications worldwide. At least eight satellites went dead briefly as their orbits took them over central Africa. At Lake Kiva airport, a radio operator dozed in his office — his receiver turned down. In the office next to him, the customs radar operator read a paperback novel. His log sheet was blank.

Aboard his yacht in Mombasa harbor, an Iraqi arms dealer named Molech Gordini fumed and sputtered as the long-distance operator apologized profusely that she could not get through to Johannesburg, nor Nairobi, nor Lake Kiva.

Kneeling beside her bed, Johanna Graham wept before the Lord. "O Father, You are so good to me. I do not understand why, but I thank You. Now, bring Zuni and Patrick home safely. Give them peace that passes understanding. And joy. And deliverance. Holy, holy, holy is Your name, O Lord. Thank You, Jesus."

"Your ankle is broken," diagnosed Matthew in the moonlight. "Thank You, Jesus." He held her foot gently.

A startled Zuni surveyed the black giant kneeling

over her like some sort of witch doctor.

The man began to tremble. "What is that?" he demanded, glancing back toward the computer crates in the hold.

"Equipment," mumbled Zuni.

Matthew shook his head.

He edged slightly away from the boxes. "I sense a truly terrible evil," he declared. "In the name of Jesus Christ, I come against this evil. I say that it cannot touch us. Satan, you have no power here. I proclaim that we are covered by the blood of Jesus. Go!"

As he proclaimed the strange words, the lights on the control panel flickered and went out.

Matthew gently held Zuni's throbbing foot. The man paused, his eyes closed. "Thank You, Jesus," he whispered. Then, he began to massage her foot. "I hope that I do not amaze you too greatly. When my grandfather gave up his great and terrible sorcery, he burned many such evil things that had . . ." Matthew squinted over his shoulder at the crates, ". . . such evil as that over there. Are you aware that many people have been killed because of those boxes?"

"Yeah," exclaimed Patrick. "How did you . . ."

"Many more are intended to die because of them," said Matthew softly. "There is malicious and vengeful evil surrounding every part of that machine's creation."

Patrick wrinkled his nose, amused. "It's just a computer."

"Yes," nodded Matthew.

"Do you think computers are evil?" laughed Patrick.

"Anything can be used for evil," responded Matthew. "What kind of computer is that thing?"

"You understand computers?" exclaimed Patrick.

"Somewhat," said the tall native. "I also understand the migration of elephants and how to dry millet grain. Would you like me to tell you about the rebirth of sculpture during the Italian renaissance?"

"Never mind," chuckled Patrick.

Matthew bowed his head. Then, solemnly, he turned and took Patrick's hands, placing them on Zuni's swollen ankle. "Pray with me, Patrick Graham MacDougal," he said.

"You bet," exclaimed the boy.

With his eyes closed, the black man folded his enormous hands over Patrick's hands, covering Zuni's ankle. "In the name of Jesus," the man pronounced, "you are healed."

Zuni sighed. Great, a jungle faith healer.

Then, Zuni saw Patrick's eyes. In absolute amazement, the boy stared at her ankle. "Mom," he breathed. The swelling was going down so quickly that Zuni's stretched skin was wrinkling.

"Oh, Mom," whispered Patrick.

"Now do you believe, Patrick?" asked Matthew.

"I believe," exclaimed the boy. "Mom, did you see that?"

Zuni sat back, her eyes closed. She felt very, very tired.

She sensed her mother's distant but nearby concern. "Mother," she said aloud. "Quit praying quite so hard."

"What?" asked Matthew.

"Just a joke," deadpanned Zuni.

"Yes," mused Matthew.

"Can you do that for the plane, too?" asked Patrick. "Come on, let's try it."

Matthew looked up at him, searching for mocking in the boy's eyes. But the child's faith was pure. "I do not hear the Lord telling us to pray for this airplane," said the man.

"Oh," said Patrick. "Okay." He shrugged, obviously disappointed.

"But," said Matthew, "I feel at peace about something else. I am permitted now to take the two of you to my home in our secret, hidden valley."

"Your what?" exclaimed Zuni, climbing gingerly to her feet. Carefully, she tested her ankle. She grimaced in irritation that she did not truly understand.

Basically, she wished that God would leave her alone.

She stumbled back to the tail of the plane.

There, she saw that the beacon was already disabled.

She turned.

"You live in a hidden valley?" Patrick was asking.

"We call it Britanga," said Matthew.

Zuni's eyes filled with sudden, unexpected tears. "**Eh, che,**" she whispered to the aircraft. "**¿Qué tal, mi nene?**" *How you doing, kid?* She ran her hand along the ceiling of the broken Martin. It had been a good friend. It was a well-built old bird.

She knew it would never see Mombasa again.

❖   ❖   ❖

"Lord, protect my little brother."

The heart-felt prayer did not rise out of the African forest. Instead, it came from inside the walk-in refrigerator at an all-night convenience grocery deep in the heart of East Los Angeles, California.

"Protect little José Chimon," prayed Miguel Rodriguez as he restocked the two percent low-fat milk racks and watched the front cash register. In front of the counter lounged an armed security guard, a former gang member and longtime friend. By the candy counter, three grade schoolers studied the bubble gum. It was 3:15 in the morning.

"O Lord," prayed Miguel as he loaded the last half-gallon onto the shelf, "José is being really stupid. He's gangbanging with all his stupid buddies. He's running numbers and drugs. He's gonna get killed unless You protect him from himself, Lord."

The convenience grocery hugged a corner on busy Whittier Boulevard, its small windows covered by security bars, its cash register watched by surveillance cameras. The owner had decided to try staying open 24 hours without the expense of enclosing the cashier in bullet-proof glass. Instead, he kept an armed guard on duty from 10 p.m. until 6 a.m.

Except for Al Ochoa, the guard, who began playing pinball at the front door, and the little kids worrying over the candy counter, the store was empty — despite a busy street filled with four lanes of slowly moving, highly polished cars. Teens and young adults yelled, laughed, joked, and shouted from one vehicle to the other.

Across the street was a brilliantly colored Mexican-style mural of Aztec warriors refusing crack cocaine from street peddlers. It loomed three stories tall on the side of an old apartment building. Down in the garbage cans on the ground, two cholos — youth gang members — were unexcitedly defiling the artwork with spray-can graffiti.

Inside the walk-in refrigerator, Miguel checked the eggs and whole milk, then the soft drinks and beer. A former addict, he now didn't even drink wine. As he loaded the beer shelves, he offered a strange prayer: "Lord, restocking the beer is part of my job and I thank You for giving me this job. Now, Lord, I pray that You will turn this beer into vomit in the cans. Make it nasty, awful tasting stuff with so little alcohol that drinking it is a waste of time. Lord, ruin this beer, I pray."

Miguel's arms and neck were covered with ugly tattoos of mythical, demonic-looking creatures and scantily-clad chicano beauties — the marks of a *vato loco*, a hard-core street warrior. He had gone onto the streets at age eight, rising through the ranks of a gang called the Little Lions or *Leonitos,* then the Young Lions or *Leoncillos.* He had learned how to survive on the street with all the other little guys in the gang. It wasn't considered a rebellious thing. All the boys' parents were friends of Miguel's parents — most of whom were former members of the feared street gang, the Lions or *Leones.*

The mighty Leones had a street picnic every summer. The mothers, fathers, sons, daughters, the kids, and their friends all got together to reminisce about old gang fights, old triumphs, old battles. Miguel's had been a world turned upside down: small-time extortion, jail for stealing candy from stores, watching the older boys kill rivals to prove their honor, to take revenge — sometimes just to demonstrate their bravery.

Many of the fourteen year olds sold drugs to support their drug-addicted parents. Drugs were a major part of the economy. Early, Miguel had learned the drug trade: The boss puts up the money, the carrier makes the buy, the runner brings the stuff into the spot, the bookie keeps track of the money. Other young runners brought it to the pitchers and the clockers selling it on the street — often ten year olds who could not be charged as adults if picked up by the police.

Often on the sidewalk, a three or four year old — wearing the colors of the Leones, sometimes clocking — could be seen delivering drugs from a pitcher watching with a gun in the shadows. The colors the child wore were important. Few outsiders paid any attention, but from the viewpoint of the gang members, a toddler in colors was a little home boy who in the next few years would be called on to stake his life to defend the honor and reputation of his neighborhood.

Indeed, the newspaper only days before had mourned the drive-by shooting of a six-year-old boy, cut down by automatic rifle fire from a speeding car. "An accident," the police had said.

It had been no accident. The kindergartner was wearing the wrong gang colors. The archrival Fantasticos had hit the boy in revenge for a street fight killing of one of their young members. Murder was a rite of passage, too. You could not join the full-fledged Leones until you had killed a man.

Why murder? Nobody seemed to know when it had started. But the common experience of having killed an enemy in cold blood — premeditated, planned, first-degree murder — was like a social glue, uniting each of the gang members into a brotherhood of trust and love and an unquestioning willingness to die for each other.

Miguel straightened up the back room and walked out into the store. As he did frequently, he was quietly praying for his little brother, a fifteen year old deep into the exciting world of the Leones.

José Chimon had joked just the day before that he didn't expect to live to be twenty. He didn't care, he was having fun, flashing the gold jewelry and expensive running shoes and satin jackets of a drug seller. For that matter, what was there after age twenty for a home boy except jail, drug addiction, or the agony of working for a living? Few drug dealers were older than twenty-five.

His was a world of violent death, AIDS, crime, and despair. More than one in three adults got some form of public assistance. This was el barrio, the 'hood, the neighborhood. In the aisle across from the pinball machine, the convenience grocery sold aspirin, antacids, lip balm, and nail polish remover next to crates filled with yucca, pitaya, yams, batata, plátanos, and mangoes. On the walls were the bright flags of Mexico,

Guatemala, Puerto Rico, and Cuba.

In the alley behind the store, the pavement was littered with crack cocaine vials and broken bottles. Leaning against the dirty walls were people with quick eyes and dark clothes.

"Hey, Man, windowpane, windowpane," a man shouted at the traffic. He was selling LSD. Other people were hawking angel dust, brown cocaine, white cocaine, crack cocaine, methadone, heroin, and some of the new synthetic drugs flooding the marketplace.

This was the rush hour on Whittier Boulevard. The drug peddlers in the alley and sitting on the curb just a block down kept regular hours. Their employers jealously guarded their turf. Loitering around in the dim light were gang members whose only job was to protect the sellers. Under their trench coats were expensive Israeli automatics and Argentine pistols.

There were more than twenty brands of crack on the street that month. The day before, a punk kid from San Diego had tried to break into the East Los Angeles scene by underselling the competition. Now, he and all six of his street peddlers were dead, their bodies laid out in the city morgue.

As Miguel strode to the cash register, his ears perked up at what sounded like firecrackers. He didn't even glance outside. It was gunfire.

"Lord," whispered Miguel, "I don't know what it's going to take to get José out of the gangs. But do it, Father. Do it. Don't let go of that boy. He's my blood, Father, I can't just let him die. Bring him back to us, Father."

A motorcycle roared past on the sidewalk.

Miguel checked the cash register. It never held more than $20. At the pinball machine, Al cursed loudly and put in more quarters. "Man, I almost beat my best score," he called over his shoulder to Miguel.

The little bell over the door tinkled. An enormous kid in the colors of the Dukes walked through, his eyes glassy, his movements quick. Miguel could smell marijuana. The bell rang again and again. More Dukes pressed into the store. Laughing and calling to each other, they began emptying the beer cooler.

At the pinball machine, Al calmly pulled out his revolver. But before he could, a knife was at his throat. Laughing, mocking in his face, the big Duke leader took Al's gun. "I know you," yelled the Duke. "You killed my brother Ramon in the big rumble at St. Cecilia." His hunting knife pressed against Al's neck, his eyes quivering, the Duke slammed his knee into Al's groin and cut his throat.

Before Miguel could grab the shotgun under the cash register, the Duke leader slammed the security guard's gasping body over the counter into Miguel and pinned the two against the cigarettes. Laughing like devils, the Dukes knocked over shelves as they exited with armloads of beer.

"No, Man," whispered Miguel as he stared down the barrel of an enormous revolver.

"You are a dead man," laughed the big Duke leader.

He fired twice.

The sound of gunfire caught Valentina's attention. She looked up and winced in irritation. The in-flight movie was some violent American film with musclemen and karate heroes. Irked, Valentina yanked the movie earphones out of her armrest.

She was anxious to arrive in Mombasa.

There, she intended to see her vision become reality.

She would assemble her computer components —

hustled out of Russia by South African soldiers of fortune recruited by Molech. Together, she and Gordini would finally bring the world to its decadent knees.

Valentina and Molech had been strangely drawn together a year before at a reception at Moscow's Italian Embassy.

Valentina had heard of Molech.

Gordini knew all about Valentina.

At the party, their eyes and evil minds met in a way that shocked those in attendance. One would have thought that two twins separated at birth had suddenly rediscovered one another. It was as if massive spiritual forces in the air shoved them together.

Oblivious to the others at the reception, the socially graceless young Russian computer genius and the billionaire Muslim power broker reveled in all that they had in common.

An intense hatred for Americans and Saudis and Israelis. A sneering disdain for the new, impotent Russian reformers.

And absolute scorn for the money-grubbing Japanese — so anxious to sell their souls to the highest bidder.

What a pair they made.

As the crowded room grew quiet, the loud Valentina babbled seeming nonsense to the dark, evilly smiling Molech — a mustachioed, abrupt man given to expensive Italian suits and gold jewelry.

Molech Gordini was as difficult as Valentina was fat. He was a complex, self-possessed man, convinced of a world-leadership destiny ordained by God. Yet, Gordini was a tortured man — lonely — terribly threatened by the talented people he recruited.

Watching Molech fidget during conversation, a casual observer sensed his deep self-consciousness. However, Molech's insecurity was far more — an intense sensitivity to the slightest disrespect.

He was constantly watchful for the smallest insult — which did not have to be verbal. Turning his back to Gordini during a party had doomed one top New York corporate executive who was unaware that the boss was telling a joke on the other side of the crowded room.

Molech was obsessed with conquering everyone around him. He enjoyed the chase much more than the kill — the process far more than the result. One might expect a man of such immense power to be incredibly tolerant of the personality quirks of the geniuses necessary to his goals.

However, he was incessantly critical on even the most personal levels. He enjoyed controlling people's lives, frustrating creative genius, stifling initiative, and fighting with his own executives and generals, forcing them to battle with him to do their jobs.

He would fire them out of boredom when they quit fighting back. Their performance didn't matter. What was important was whether or not Molech enjoyed the contest.

He was constantly surrounding himself with the very top international talent, chewing up the strong-willed and keeping only the submissive, most nonthreatening bureaucrats who kept out of his line of fire. He encircled himself with ambitious, brilliant flashes in the pan — and bootlicking warlords past their prime.

His most effective executives dreaded his visits. They enthusiastically encouraged diversifications that drained their cash flow, but took him elsewhere.

In his absence, great things were accomplished.

Unfortunately, he always returned.

His lieutenants trembled at the thought of his involvement in their projects. The result was invariably illogical reorganization, unnecessary disorder, rash initiatives from aspiring zealots in the ranks, and the destruction of the project.

Molech would arrive, find order, create chaos, destroy morale, rebuild his own bizarre and ineffective system, then leave with effectiveness at a standstill. However, Molech always felt good about what had happened.

That was all that mattered.

Somehow, in the process he made billions upon billions of dollars. So, he reigned worldwide, frustrating and destroying the most brilliant, rewarding the vicious and greedy.

Indeed, he took pleasure in intimidating the brightest and best into compromising all that was important to them. He loved seducing them into moral bankruptcy, emotional paralysis, and sinister dependencies. He enjoyed forecasting the onset of a targeted employee's nervous collapse, physical decline, and suicide.

The destruction of the weak proved to him that he was the only genius worthy to lead the world.

Molech's organization rotated around his raging ego and ran on the raw ambition of those who "bowed down" to him. His vicious, profit-spewing, multinational companies were just an extension of his greedy, nasty, destructive obsessions.

His evil empire would die when he did.

And no one would weep.

That was why all who were watching were amazed at Molech's fascination with the bizarre Russian computer genius Valentina Sergevicha Vasilieva.

At the Italian ambassador's reception, Molech had listened with deep interest and total seriousness to plump, pink Valentina's mad vision of a worldwide monetary revolution — and her wild dream of an overnight takeover of the reins of international financial power.

As the room grew quiet, Molech had laughed and

joked with the spitting, cackling, Russian psychic genius — while signalling to his aides to take careful notes.

They did.

The next morning, Valentina had been invited to an elaborate breakfast aboard his private jet parked at Moscow airport. There, Molech astonished his closest lieutenants by sharing with Valentina his current pet project — his vision for eliminating his biggest frustration, the constant threat of American military intervention in his projects.

He would defeat the world's last superpower with a super drug.

Solemnly understanding the secrecy of what she was being told, Valentina laughed, her eyes dancing with delight.

Of course it would work.

The idea was hardly original.

Britain had used the strategy to bring China to its knees in the 1800s. Opium had swept through China, enslaving everyone that it touched, including the royal family. In the last half of the twentieth century, the Colombians and the Cubans had attempted the same thing in America's inner cities with marijuana, heroin, and cocaine. Billions of dollars had been made. The already crumbling cities had been turned into bloody war zones. In the place of the 1800s Tong gangs of China, there rose up the vicious Bloods and Crips — nationwide, rival street armies peddling power, violence, instant wealth, and terrible addiction. But their terror had been limited to the poorer metropolitan areas.

Now Molech wanted complete destruction.

He shared with the young, mad Russian his vision of an America robbed of its soul, its creativity, its ambition, and its future — with its young clutched in a fist of hate, rebellion, and sensual gratification. The key would be a super drug created not in the jungles of South America, but in any lab — a synthetic wonder that any chemist could concoct over a Bunsen burner.

A drug two thousand times more powerful than crack.

A drug that would give its disturbed addicts instant peace and joy and passivity — and deep feelings of wisdom and creativity and security.

It would not have to be smuggled into the country. It would just appear overnight, enslaving and enticing a generation.

"Now," whispered Molech, "here's the brilliant part of the plan. We'll put it out on the streets, but we'll also package it as a healthy sugar substitute. It will be completely organic and wholesome. For the first year, it will be sold in supermarkets and convenience groceries and gas stations and candy stores."

Valentina squinted in evil glee. "Sure, but how long is it going to take to develop a drug like that?"

"I've already got it," leered Molech. "It is almost identical to sugar."

"Sugar? Table sugar?"

Molech nodded. "In the lab, you take three grains of ordinary refined sugar. With one, you alter a single molecule, creating a super opiate very much like heroin.

"With another, you alter another molecule, creating a mild hallucinogen rather like LSD, but with no immediate effect. It builds up in the blood stream.

"Then with the third, you alter another molecule, removing the sugar's calories, but intensifying its sweetness. Mix the three together and you have SuperRich."

"I've heard about SuperRich!" exclaimed Valentina. "The ads are already in all the magazines and on TV. The Super Sweetener of Tomorrow!"

"Of course, of course," said Molech, his face twisted in evil delight. "The great new artificial sweetener created from sugar itself!" He laughed. "We're spending billions in marketing. We controlled the Food and Drug Administration testing and approval process — which was not that difficult. Next summer, the major cola companies and the biggest candy makers and the most popular diet product manufacturers will release their new, long-awaited SuperRich diet products — with complete cooperation from the mighty sugar industry this time!"

"Wow," gasped Valentina, stunned. "You're going to make trillions."

"More. Much more," nodded Molech. "And then, of course, a terrible discovery will be made that SuperRich is so terribly addictive. Our company will issue shocked and heart-felt apologies, then go into bankruptcy. Meanwhile, every druggie and skin magazine in America will be publishing the easy laboratory process for creating America's favorite candy drug. It will be Prohibition and Woodstock and Haight-Ashbury all over again. The government will attempt to stamp it out, but on every street corner will be the new bootleggers and pushers, satisfying a selfish, addicted nation's violent hunger for its powerful new pacifier."

"Wow," whispered Valentina.

"And the superpower will be rocked to sleep," hissed Molech, "like a baby sucking on its lollipop. In the Third World, we'll just give it away. In Japan and Germany, we'll bring the factories and the brain banks to a sleepy halt. Everybody will be too happy to care."

"Molech is incredible," had whispered Valentina to her spirit guides that afternoon. "He's like something out of a Saturday morning cartoon or a Superman movie."

As Valentina trod an alien landscape, her demonic friends smiled, their eyes evil slits. "That's why his plan will work," they hissed in unison.

"What?"

"Nobody is afraid of its happening. They imagine that if it did, Superboy or Wonder Woman or Batman would speed to the scene of the crime and destroy the rascally villains. The only problem, of course, is that there is no Superboy or Wonder Woman or Batman. The groggy human world will call out for a saviour and there will be no one. That means, of course, that we must produce one for them."

"A Batman?"

"No, no," hissed a great spirit guide. "A prince."

"A prince?"

"A prince. In shining armor. Riding to the rescue on his white horse, his eyes filled with courage, his voice strong and assuring. A superchrist."

"Me?"

"Certainly not! To wield true power, you need a prince who will be your figurehead, your lightning rod. In this age of television, he just has to have an honest face, an earnest set to his jaw, the self-deception that he really is in charge, excellent speechwriters, and the ability to remember his lines."

Valentina squinted in thought.

"With the human world terrified, reeling on its knees, pleading for help, you will give them a great prince with all the answers, wielding the might of the real power. If your prince turns on us or wanes in popularity, we will sacrifice him and come up with another. But the bottom line is that you will grow hideously rich and unbeatably powerful while the entire world is watching — and blaming your prince."

The next time she saw him, Valentina bounced the idea off Gordini.

"That's hardly original, my dear," said the Italian-born Iraqi. "A countryman of mine originated the concept in the Middle Ages. You've just ripped-off the ideas of Machiavelli."

"Wow," whispered Valentina.

"Some people say that's what Ronald Reagan was — a prince," mused Molech, "just an actor who knew how to play the greatest role of his career." Molech shrugged. "Ronnie was not that easy to control. But he rose to power because of those who saw that potential. After all, somebody else was really running the world while he was taking naps and giving speeches and visiting Nancy's astrologers."

Valentina grinned in delight. "What about Gorbachev?"

"Same idea," said Molech. "But he wasn't controllable, either. He kept surprising everybody. I hate surprises."

"What about Margaret Thatcher?"

Molech pretended to be in pain and rolled his eyes. "Every once in a while a loose cannon appears on deck. She was the biggest problem with Reagan. He kept listening to her and thinking he really was in charge. And at his right hand, he had a quiet, ever-advising vice president — George Bush. Let me tell you, Bush was a Sadat."

"A Sadat?"

"Quiet, like Egypt's President Anwar El-Sadat — a pencil-pushing bureaucrat who laid low for years and rose to power only because rival power makers saw him as no threat. Sadat was an agreeable errand boy for Gamel Abdel Nasser, who took the Suez Canal back from the British and French and who first stood up to Israel.

"When Nasser died, the power brokers pulled out their long knives. Then, somebody suggested that Sadat run the government temporarily. He agreed. Nobody expected him to last a year. Instead, he grabbed the hearts and minds of the Egyptian people, wrestled control away from the political self-servers, and turned Egypt into the greatest and most powerful Arab non-oil power on Earth. Today, Egypt is at peace with everybody, even arch-enemy Israel, because of Sadat."

"Wow," gawked Valentina.

"But it will not be a lasting peace." Molech's eyes danced, evilly. "I will see to that."

Valentina grew steadily in awe of her new friend. Molech opened incredible doors for the young woman.

A month after they met, Molech bailed her out of yet another mental hospital.

One morning, Valentina had just gone blank and stayed that way — staring into nothingness, her muscles rigid, her mouth slack. She did it so regularly that her co-workers were not enormously concerned. They thought she was epileptic. Sometimes when her eyes rolled back and she disappeared into her fantasy lands, she soiled her pants. Usually, she drooled.

Of course, she was completely conscious, frolicking in a personal Never-Never Land shared with beautiful and wonderful beings who hammered into her preposterous lies about the "true" nature of man — such as that humans can all evolve into little gods.

It was one such being who first showed Valentina the seductive power available from submitting to spirit lords.

Another time, the subject of Jesus Christ came up and the spirit master had clucked his tongue in disdain at the stupidity of a misguided cult that would believe that theirs was only way to eternal life. "Godhood is free to anyone who seeks it," he leered. Once, Valentina's spirit master had explained how humans had abused and defamed the poor, misunderstood former regent of Heaven, that ex-archangel named Lucifer.

"Such lies have been told about my master," whispered the spirit guide. "Just look at his name — Lucifer, Latin for 'light-bearer.' Even the prophet Isaiah called him by his true name, 'Son of the morning.' He is the Bright Morning Star. We call him Seraph Nachash — the great, fiery dragon."

Such a wondrous time Valentina had among the forces of the spirit world. They were so much more fun than selfish, staring, mocking humans. And so it was that Valentina was staying longer and longer in the great beyond — and losing her grip on the physical world.

Molech had visited her at Moscow's Yakolev Mental Clinic. Valentina had not spoken in weeks. She had wasted down to mere obesity. Gently, Molech whispered into her ear, coaxing her back.

Only reluctantly did Valentina return.

"We have so much work to do here," Molech had reminded. "Now, I have that equipment you have wanted so."

Indeed, stolen from Japan's premier cryogenics institute at Kyoto Polytechnical Institute, Molech had obtained the gizmo that would make one of Valentina's strangest concepts actually work. Molech did not tell the young Russian that Japanese cryogenics pioneer Naoto Horii had been killed during the burglary.

But Molech arranged for Valentina to be given an adjunct professorship at the Naval Technology Institute in Volgograd. There, young Vasilieva began to demonstrate the reality of refluency. As defined by Valentina, it was the incredible elimination of magnetic, optical, digital, or any other media to store information. Instead, using Naoto Horii's breakthroughs in anti-physics, stored information was "folded back into emptiness," according to Valentina.

"Adimensional" was her preferred term. "You open the window into any of the infinite parallel universes coexisting simultaneously with ours and just borrow a piece of space they don't need."

The young Vasilieva became immediately controversial in the international scientific community. A team from Massachusetts Institute of Technology voiced its suspicions that the murdered Naoto Horii's entire lab had been stolen by the Russian KGB. Another study group from Paris packed up in disgust after pronouncing her theories to be "childish gibberish."

But a crew from Los Alamos returned saying that her mysterious machines worked — or at least appeared to.

The German scandal magazine *Stern* did a wild exposé that declared there was some sort of curse on LORRD technology — on the scale of the King Tut Tomb curse. Everybody involved either was murdered, died in strange accidents, or else went mad.

The magazine claimed Valentina was heavily into the occult. That wasn't true, she had snorted in derision. In fact, she was far too sophisticated to affiliate herself with spiritualists or devil worshipers. She merely hated having too much contact with fellow humans. Instead, she preferred close friendships in the parallel "non-dimensions" she loved to roam with her spirit guides.

Stern quoted a noted Russian Orthodox Church exorcist declaring Valentina "mad, truly mad — a deranged genius in the Russian tradition of Ivan, Stalin, and Rasputin — quite possibly in touch with beings from other worlds that I cannot label as being anything but demonic emissaries masquerading to her as masters of truth."

Vasilieva had laughed as she read the article. Was she demon possessed? She laughed in glee. Of course!

But she was in control — or so she had shouted aloud to her apartment's walls and ceiling.

Her interdimensional friends did her bidding.

They came and went at her beck and call.

They had already told her that all her equipment was being gathered from Moscow and was on a plane headed for Mombasa.

They were her slaves.

Her messengers.

She was the master.

Was Valentina truly possessed by medieval devils? Evil spirits? Goblins? Most people would have winced at the idea. Devils and ghosts to them were the stuff of primitive folklore and bad movies.

However, Valentina's erratic behavior was enough to make anybody give the idea serious thought.

Two weeks before, she had impulsively defected to China.

Even Molech had trouble getting her out of that mess. In a malignant fit against her Russian government keepers, Valentina had announced her defection at an international technology conference in Beijing where she had been scheduled to speak on repandency.

She realized almost immediately that she had reacted impetuously and shortsightedly. She had realized it too late as usual. She had not considered beforehand the consequences of her actions.

It had set her vision back an entire month.

She was that close to success.

Visiting her at the Chinese foreign ministry, Ambassador Alexander Moiseyev had laughed aloud at Valentina's shrill demand that the Russian government immediately send her complete lab and all her equipment.

"Allow me to understand this," the diplomat had chuckled. "You, our perpetual international embarrassment, our renegade wunderkind, want Mother Russia to send you all your beloved equipment so you can immediately go to work for our enemies?"

Weeping, Valentina had pledged that she would never do anything to hurt her beloved homeland. Whispering in his ear, she blurted her plan to take over the world's economy.

The ambassador had patted her on the back and wished her the best of luck. "You have thrown in with the most persistent and effective persuaders in the world, my friend. They are not likely to be impressed if you hold your breath and turn purple this time. Perhaps you should just commit suicide at your first opportunity. It may be easier on you."

Terrified, Valentina immediately informed her Chinese hosts that she would do anything that they wanted. She gave them complete details of her intentions on the international monetary system.

It was as if the Chinese could not see why it would work.

Valentina became louder and more abusive as her keepers attempted to get her to explain the concepts behind refluency.

One interrogator suggested strongly that she be sent to a re-education camp to work in a rice paddy for a couple of years.

Valentina retreated into her spirit world and refused to utter another word. The Chinese were ready to strait-jacket her off to a Tibetan insane asylum.

Only through Molech Gordini's personal intervention — actually his generous bribery of the highest officials in China's corrupt secret police — was Valentina smuggled out of Beijing in a wicker basket packed into an Nicaraguan cargo plane and delivered to Molech's sprawling ranch outside of Cali, Colombia, South America.

But now, in the Kenyan port city of Mombasa where he based his African gun-running operations, Molech was assembling her complete lab.

Finally, she had everything she would need and revenge was going to be sweet.

A new world order was about to be birthed.

It would rise from the ancient cradle of civilization, from the very source of the mighty Nile — out of the fertile valleys of Mother Africa.

In Africa's Great Rift Valley, Simon Webster sat at his laptop computer in a nylon tent on the shores of smelly Lake Nyamulalengai. With short stabs he poked the keyboard and peered at the manuscript before him.

In the distance, the Virunga eruption still raged. A photographer from *Life* magazine had flown in that morning. He had marvelled at the dead lake, which three months before had begun bubbling the nasty stench of rotten eggs — sulphur dioxide. Birds straying over the middle of the lake frequently dropped out of the sky. The gas was deadly.

Even the weeds along the shore line were dead. Instead, the lake was rimmed by a brown-yellow crust — a foul bathtub ring of putrid death. No fish survived — just insects, swarming, biting, laying eggs in human skin, spreading diseases that most doctors encountered only in textbooks. This was no industrial disaster, but the sort of natural catastrophe that has occurred for centuries around Africa's Great Rift.

In the distant crater, spectacular fountains of fire reached 3,000 feet into the African sky — beginning to attract tourists, network cameramen, and even barefoot sightseers from nearby villages.

The stench seemed to bother them.

They did not stay long at Simon's camp.

It did not bother him particularly. It had crept up gradually, irritating at first, but not enough to make him ill. Now, it just lingered, making Simon occasionally sick at his stomach, sometimes even strangely light-headed. But he had grown used to it — although he worried about a new puffiness in his fingers, his increasing fatigue and, now, unrelenting nightmares.

He believed sacrifice was his gallant destiny if he was to do God's work. Simon was a Bible translator, bringing the written Word to illiterate savages identified by analysts in New York and Amsterdam as needing the Scriptures in their own language.

Simon hated his job. It paid almost nothing. He lacked rapport with the natives — whom he viewed as stupid, ethnically uncultured, racially inferior, unambitious, without potential for improving their lot, and lacking mental processes necessary to coexist with civilized people. Enduring what he considered to be the inevitable suffering of the righteous, Simon accepted his heroic fate — stuck on a smelly lake shore, trying to put an obscure, unimportant native tongue into writing — a dialect that no more than fifteen thousand tribespeople still spoke. By the time he had their Bible translated, they probably would all speak pidgin English. He was wasting his time.

However, it was his calling.

Realistically, it was all that he knew how to do. So, a religious literature translator he remained — enduring the institutionalized enthusiasm of his distant superiors, putting up with the stupidity of the natives.

He wished he had a drink. He nudged open a chest beside his chair. He yanked out a hip flask, unscrewed the lid, and downed a slug of the alcoholic contents. He cringed. Native moonshine had quite a kick — and tasted like licorice. He shivered as the evergreen brew chilled his throat, then spread a warm glow through his chest.

He noticed for the first time a plume of dust out on the road. Another van full of tourists headed for the volcanos? He sighed and put away his hip flask.

Soon a battered little car roared into view. In it was a lone figure.

Simon peered.

Was it a woman? The profile seemed much too slight to be a man. Whoever it was wore a helmet — straight out of the Tarzan movies.

Simon pecked at his keyboard, then stood.

The rusty car sped down the lake road — straight toward his compound. It skidded to a stop. A skinny boy — straight out of college, it appeared — climbed out. Excitedly, he looked around. "There are hyenas around here!" he exclaimed in greeting. "Pew, it really stinks here!"

Simon strolled out toward the car. The kid was frantically digging in the back seat. "I watched one chasing a wildebeest just as I was coming in," he declared, holding a red kerchief to his nose. "Yuck, what is that smell? I thought they were just scavengers. But it was a hyena. I've read all the old Pogo comic strips and that was a hyena all right. I watched it chase a cow for two miles. It was awesome."

Simon didn't know what to think of this unannounced visitor — who was pulling a couple of brand-new compact computers out of the back. "Every once in a while . . ." The kid coughed, his eyes beginning to water. He clutched his bandanna to his nose. ". . . the hyena would jump up and nip the wildebeest in the hindquarters or tug at his tail or legs. Then, out of nowhere, five more hyenas turned up and joined the chase. They disappeared behind a pile of boulders and I didn't get to see how it all ended." Coughing, the boy puttered with a box, then pulled out something electronic.

"Do you have a name?" grunted Simon.

The young man blushed, then grinned, and extended his right hand, holding the bandanna to his nose with his left. "Huckleberry Finn. What is that stench?"

"Huckleberry Finn?" exclaimed Simon. He shook hands and tried to suppress his amusement. "Huckleberry?"

"Just like in Mark Twain's Tom Sawyer and Huckleberry Finn," the kid coughed, fanning his face more than a little self-consciously. "Ol' Huck, Tom Sawyer's best friend. Only I didn't bring Tom, Becky, or Aunt Polly, just your new portable computer. They've really improved the access time. What model is your satellite dish?"

Simon grunted something incomprehensible.

"I didn't catch that," gasped the cheerful Huckleberry, digging in another box in the back. The kid grabbed out an industrial oxygen mask and slipped the elastic strap around his head. He turned the knob of an oxygen bottle, then tucked it into his belt, "Where am I going to live?"

"What?"

"Where am I going to set up? Where do I sleep?"

"Look, boy, I don't know how you got here. Do you have any idea of the danger you are in? Americans — especially children — simply do not travel in Africa alone."

"God protects me," exclaimed Finn — who had to be at least twenty-five. "I'm hardly a child. You're not still living in your tent, are you? Where's your house?"

"The natives here live in thatched huts, but most of them have moved away from the lake. They haven't been much help. I don't mind the tent. I've grown rather attached to it."

"Well, praise the Lord," Huck bubbled holding up his oxygen mask. "I'll put my tent up over there. Oh, I know — I can stay in the church!"

Simon winced — as if in pain. "We don't have one, yet," he growled. "I've concentrated on work."

"Huh?" breathed Huck through the oxygen mask.

"I don't have a church."

Huck lifted the mask. "You're surely teaching the native leaders how to read, aren't you? How have you learned anything about their language?"

"Most of them speak English," snarled Simon.

"English?" exclaimed Huck. He lowered the mask, took a deep breath, then lifted it again. "Then, why are you still here? Did you tell your district supervisor? He told me you've been out of contact ever since you arrived."

"Who the devil are you?" demanded Simon.

"I'm your new team leader. You were told I was coming. I sent you a greeting this morning on the computer bulletin board. Didn't you see it when you logged on to the system?"

Simon sighed. "No," he grunted. "I rarely network with headquarters. I just run off of my own equipment."

"Well, hallelujah anyway," exclaimed Finn. "I think we're going to have a miraculous time here. I believe I heard the Lord speaking to me as I was driving here that it is time for a great revival up here — a mighty stirring of the Holy Spirit. I feel really excited about it."

Simon muttered something snide under his breath.

"What?" asked Huck.

"Is that your real name?" snorted Simon.

"My real name is Horatio Ogilvy Finn. I much prefer the nickname Huckleberry."

Simon winced, considering the possible nicknames.

"Where is your satellite dish?" asked Huck.

"In that crate over there. Did you bring any American food? How about some potato chips?"

"You've never set up your dish?" exclaimed Huck. "How long have you been here?"

"Look," said Simon, "I'm on the payroll of the local superintendent of education. He's a Hindu, two generations out of India. We get along just fine. I don't do anything to rock his boat and he does nothing to rock mine. I'm no missionary. I'm a linguist. I'm here to do a job and I make no waves."

Huck stared at him in disbelief. "You're not in contact with the office?"

"Who needs 'em? A bunch of meddling, do-good, know-it-alls sitting in their air-conditioned cubicles in Amsterdam and New York — blessing us poor grunts with their little daily Bible verses and their daily prayer requests. If it was up to them, I'd have to wander all over the U.S. every three years pleading with little old ladies to send me money. No thank you. I get the dish out whenever I need it. Otherwise, back it goes into the box."

"You're kidding!"

"Look, you little cream puff, why don't you just go home? I don't need you bossing me around. I'm doing just fine."

Huck blinked at him in disbelief. He yanked off the oxygen mask. "You've got to be kidding," he bellowed. "Look at this mess! Your tent is going to fall apart from rot. You don't have any contact with the natives and you're not even attempting any sort of evangelism. What is it that you are doing that you would call 'just fine'?"

Simon stared at the kid in disgust. "I don't have to answer that sort of insult. I have seniority here. Who are you, anyway? I know your kind, showing up with all the answers, ready to reform the whole program before you've even unpacked your hippie backpack.

"At least you could settle in before you criticize. Why don't you get out of here before I kick your little tail? Take my word for it, you'd better not ruffle any feathers. The government is Muslim. The superintendent hates Christians. And the natives either worship all sorts of ancient hocus-pocus mumbo-jumbo or else they're into Christian mysticism. But they are happy. Leave them alone."

"But what about the ones going to hell without Jesus Christ?"

Simon swore and stared at the sky. "They've sent me a Bible-thumping fundamentalist."

In disbelieving silence, Huck stared at him. "Why are you here?" he demanded.

Simon laughed cynically under his breath. He muttered something the young man could not hear.

"What?" Huck demanded.

Simon made a lewd suggestion that was not meant to be taken literally — merely to insult. The naive Finn peered at him in incomprehension. "What? You are disgusting!"

Simon laughed in disgust. He stalked back to his tent.

"Where do you want me to put your new computer?" called Huckleberry.

Simon told him exactly where to put it. Huck blushed. Nobody had talked to him like that since junior high school. Stunned, he went back to his car. He sat down behind the wheel and shook his head, disbelieving what he had just heard.

He dug in the back and found no more oxygen bottles. He would have to drive back to Lake Kiva.

But he really didn't have any money for bottled oxygen.

He sighed and pulled off his mask. The oppression of the lake's stench gripped his senses like a tight fist. "Lord," Huck gasped in sudden panic. "Get me out of here. I hate this. I don't want to stay with that man. This is a terrible place."

He leaned against the steering wheel, his cheeks damp with tears. "I want to spread the joy and wonder of Your gospel — not fight with a defeated jerk who has surrendered. Father, I can't even breathe here. Please, get me out of this mess. You've given me a vision of magnificent revival sweeping the plains and valleys and rain forests. Signs and wonders and miracles. Praise You, Lord. Now, get me out of this hellhole."

Huck paused, surprised at his own language. He had never cursed in a prayer before. "Forgive me, Father," he prayed. "I'm sorry. See, this place is already affecting me. I gotta get out of here."

He waited.

Then he realized that there was a gentle stirring in the air.

A gentle wind.

A great, strong, quiet breeze, blowing the sulphurous fumes back over the lake. Huck took a deep breath.

It was good.

Fresh.

Clean.

"Lord," he prayed. "Thank You. Now, please get me out of here."

He reached for the ignition key. "I'm going back to town, Lord." He twisted the key.

The car grumbled, then was silent.

"No," whispered Huck. He turned the key again.

The car shivered once more, then did not make another sound.

"Oh, Father," he whispered. "Don't do this to me. I can't stand it. I can't take it!"

He stared over the lake. The sun was coming out of a great, billowing cloud. A magnificent, golden ray illuminated the sparkling waters. Then, as the cloud closed again, a beautiful rainbow suddenly shimmered into view. It was the most vivid Huck had ever seen. A gentle rain began to spatter down on the dusty windshield, then was gone.

"No, Lord," protested young Finn. But he knew he had been given an answer.

Reluctantly, he got out of his car, unloaded his gear, and trudged over to Simon's tent.

Webster was staring out over the lake. "Maybe you'll get to meet our local cultists," he drawled.

"What?" responded Huck, blushing again, but hating himself for it.

"See that plateau out there? Somewhere out in the middle of it is a tribe of refugees from Uganda. They claim to be Christian, but the men hunt wild animals like savages and the women toil all day like slaves. Their leader, a giant of a man who calls himself Matthew, drops by here from time to time. He trades their products for gym shorts and baseball caps. He speaks perfect English, but won't tell me where they are camped."

Huckleberry stared out at the horizon. He saw no plateau. He shivered. This was not what he had been told to expect.

"Where are you from, Wheaton College?" asked Simon.

"How did you know?" exclaimed Huck.

Simon snorted derisively. "I knew. Probably did your doctoral work at Fuller Theological Seminary?"

"Yeah," exclaimed Huck.

"Well, you will love Matthew. He will drop in some morning when you are least expecting him — and will want to discuss the fruit of the Spirit. In my family's denomination back in the United States, Matthew is the sort of cult leader who the minute he surfaced would be stripped of the ecclesiastical authority he has taken upon himself."

Huck frowned. The idea of a half-naked cult leader was not exactly appealing. He walked back to the car.

Minutes later, he lifted Simon's tent flap. "Well, here's your new computer."

Simon grunted and did not look up from his work. He typed in a few lines on his old keyboard.

Huck sighed and put the new computer down.

Then he went away and put up his own tent. Simon didn't particularly care where he went. Simon had seen too many of his kind before — self-styled young visionaries straight out of seminary, claiming to "hear" God.

Like this gym-short trading Matthew.

Simon chuckled. This little bran muffin with a name from children's literature would hit it off great with Matthew and his tribe of Bible thumpers. Matthew did not know a single word of ancient Greek. He could not read even a letter of Hebrew.

Yet he considered himself qualified to debate predestination with Simon.

It was a sad joke.

The blind leading the blind.

The naive savages that Matthew led with songs of pie in the sky in the sweet by and by needed a shot of reality. They needed to learn how to save themselves.

Simon snickered. He listened for Huck's footsteps and cautiously fingered the moonshine flask.

Simon peered at the Bible text before him.

He would like a shot at Matthew's people.

If he could only trick the simple hunter into taking him to the hidden valley.

Matthew's valley was seemingly invisible from a distance.

He pointed toward it in the morning twilight. Beside him, an exhausted Patrick studied the horizon, but saw only a dusty landscape of rocks, grass, acacia, and baobab trees.

Patrick, Zuni, and Matthew picked up their burdens and trudged onward. The trio must have presented quite a spectacle. In the early morning humidity Zuni had shed her flight jacket and had tied up her hair with a brightly colored scarf. With his pocket knife, Patrick had reduced his jeans to jagged shorts.

Each carried luggage from the plane. Matthew had refused to bring the LORRD crates.

Matthew stopped. Patrick gasped in surprise. The earth dropped away from under their feet. Patrick found himself teetering atop a 350-foot cliff where the plateau came to an abrupt halt.

Below in the sunrise's dusty pastels was a thin, green valley hugging a rich, blue stream.

Carefully, Patrick and Zuni clutched their suitcases as they followed Matthew down a narrow path. Patrick's pulse quickened as he glanced over the edge. There was no gentle angle to the cliff wall — it went straight down. Carefully, he hugged the sandstone wall, his heart pounding, his feet feeling carefully for the ledge of the path.

They turned a corner and Matthew pointed out the distant outlines of the town called Britanga — sand-colored clusters of huts with rounded, thickly thatched roofs. In the middle of each family circle was a square, adobe-mud tower — a strange, beautiful, unique creation of mud and straw.

"What are those?" whispered Patrick.

"What are what?" responded Zuni.

"Those short towers," asked Patrick, "what are those square buildings?"

"Granaries," answered Matthew. "We are farmers."

At the bottom of the sheer cliffs, Matthew led them along the river, pointing out plots of millet, rice, cotton, eggplant, onions, peppers, and melons. Proudly, he led them through a rich grove of orange trees.

As they neared the village, Patrick studied the 25-foot square-topped towers. "How come the granaries don't have grass roofs like the houses?" he asked.

Matthew pondered the question. "I do not know," he responded.

A rooster sounded its morning alarm.

A bunch of little kids ran out, laughing, greeting Matthew, delighted at the sight of strangers. Shy ones hid behind houses and peeked out, giggling. Bolder ones hung on Zuni and Patrick, touching their skin, chattering all sorts of comments that evoked laughter. Some of the boys scurried to pull out of Zuni and Patrick's socks the irritating stickers that clung to the fabric.

Leading the way through the village's narrow lanes, Matthew hailed onlookers, who were obviously taken aback at the sight of white strangers. Chickens flapped under foot. Men asked explanation of Matthew. Ducks and geese squawked and honked. Old women frowned disapprovingly. Scrawny dogs yipped. Younger women smiled politely, chattering obvious concern to one another. In little cages hanging from the sides of the houses, fluffy balls of fur — apparently guinea pigs — whistled noisily. Patrick tried not to stare.

Most of the little kids of the town ran around completely naked. But their absolute innocence clothed them well. They were as oblivious as any toddler who had shed its diaper.

Older kids wore whatever they wished, apparently. Girls and women wore loose, ankle-length bolts of bright cloth. Their hair was braided ornately with beads, coins, and gold chains. Patrick saw three boys his age wearing long pants. Few of the boys wore shirts, but many wore athletic shorts and brightly-colored baseball caps.

One kid, perhaps twelve years old, ran up to him in leather sandals and a faded pair of soccer shorts emblazoned with the Manchester United team logo. "Ça va?" exclaimed the friendly kid. "Ça va?"

Patrick glanced at Matthew inquisitively.

"That's French," said Matthew. "It means 'What's up, dude?' "

Patrick grinned. "Bien." he answered.

The twelve year old grinned, obviously puzzled at the response, then tugged at Patrick's crate, offering to help him carry it. Gratefully, Patrick shared his burden.

Immediately, women were all around Zuni, helping her with her luggage. Matthew disappeared into a hut.

❖   ❖   ❖

Inside, unseen by Patrick or Zuni, a quiet exchange took place between Matthew and a statuesque woman who was treating a small child's sore throat with swabs and an expertly quick injection before the toddler could protest.

"Well, Matthew, my husband," she greeted him — formally and in the native tongue of the Britanga tribe, "you have brought home another stray puppy for me to nurse back to health?"

The ailing child's mother ushered the toddler outside, discreetly leaving the two alone in the spartanly furnished clinic.

Without a word, Matthew slipped his hands around his wife's waist, his chin nuzzling her temple, his broad hands moving up her strong back. She responded to his gentle kiss, teasing his neck with her fingertips. He sighed as she melted against him. He held her tight.

This was where he belonged.

Now he was home.

She rested in his arms, secure, at peace, knowing he was faithful and true — but she was a little anxious to continue her day.

"Two puppies," he whispered.

"Two?" she chided softly. "The kids ran in here hours ago and said you found a lost white boy at the hippo hole."

"Yes," sighed Matthew, "and the little puppy at the hippo hole has a mother."

"What?"

"You have ears, woman," smiled Matthew gently. He grabbed a ceremonial shirt-tunic off a pile of folded laundry — but in his haste picked up two by mistake.

"You brought a white woman to this safe valley that God gave to our people for their protection and security?" exclaimed his wife.

"Now, Lydia," he responded. "Listen, I sought the Lord and was given great peace."

"Without even consulting the elders?"

"They will agree when they hear the whole story."

Lydia's eyes flashed. "I have ears," she whispered, her voice almost a mocking sing-song. "Tell me."

Matthew sighed, summoning patience. "I believe that the Lord is going to do a mighty thing that will strengthen the faith of millions and millions of people — and that this boy and his mother will be the catalyst to get tens, then hundreds, then thousands, then millions of believers on their knees, seeking God, interceding on behalf of one another and throwing back the forces of darkness."

Lydia Britanga — who was the valley's only trained

nurse — stared at her visionary husband with consternation. "You think that the Lord showed you this?"

Matthew touched her chest right at her heart. "Here," he said, "He showed me here."

His wife nodded. "Well, bring them in."

Matthew shook his head. "They don't need to see the clinic. They already believe that we are very primitive. I'm going to get Daniel and the other boys to take the white boy fishing. You take the woman to my mother's."

"Why there?"

"She has lots of room, she's lonely — and she speaks English. Plus, I believe that she can break through the deep sadness of this woman."

Lydia nodded.

Her husband looked troubled still.

"What is it?" she asked.

"They are smugglers. The boy is just barely an adolescent and is very open to the gospel. The woman is very cynical. She was once a believer, but has turned away."

"Apostate?"

"Perhaps. She was smuggling a machine that is like nothing I have ever seen. It was not cursed, but seemed to have a brooding, evil side to it. I sensed that it has caused the deaths of many already."

"Is it a weapon of some kind? A doomsday device?"

"Perhaps it is meant to be something like that, but it was really not so different from those computers the Bible translator uses on the other side of the lake."

"It's a computer?"

"I think so. But it is very active — doing what I do not know. I believe that great and terrible forces desire to use it for enormous wrongdoing."

"Maybe the Bible translator will help you."

Matthew shook his head abruptly. "No," he said with a smile.

❖   ❖   ❖

Matthew emerged from the hut wearing sandals and a long, white shirt. He threw Patrick the extra shirt he'd grabbed — knee length and homespun, but bleached white.

Patrick caught it, but did not put it on. He grinned at his new friend his age and held up the shirt. The kid grinned, then laughed, pantomiming putting it on. Patrick snickered and refused, shaking his head — pointing to the boy. Nodding enthusiastically, the kid pulled it on, buttoning it expertly, and then danced around as everybody cheered.

Matthew smiled. "Welcome to my home," he said grandly. "This is Britanga — our hidden valley." Then he made a long speech to the gathering crowd. A group of older men, obviously the village elders, pushed to the front and listened as Matthew described the entire adventure.

More boys Patrick's age gathered around him. The twelve year old, whose name apparently was Andrew, strutted around in the long shirt Matthew had given Patrick, making eyes at the giggling girls, who stayed in their own group or with their mothers.

Patrick studied them. Their hair patterns were each slightly different, but there was a definite pattern that each followed. He wondered where they got the bright sea shells.

"You are English," said a kid who looked maybe sixteen or seventeen.

Patrick stood, relieved to hear somebody speaking his language. "No, Kenyan. Actually, American," he said. "My mom's more Kenyan than American, but she's got passports from almost any country you want. My dad is an American. He works for the state department — in the consulate in Cairo."

The kid listening to him was enormous, a full foot taller than Patrick, but not yet filled out in the shoulders. "You sound British."

"I go to the British Royal Academy in Nairobi," said Patrick proudly.

"Yes," said the boy. "My father went to school back in Uganda. He was going to go to college. I am Daniel Britanga."

Awkwardly Patrick smiled, then thrust out his hand. "I am Patrick Graham MacDougal," he said.

The black youngster wore red shorts, leather sandals, and a St. Louis Cardinals' baseball cap. He looked concerned. "The mayor said you are a Christian."

Startled, Patrick tried to smile. "Well," he tried to joke, "I'm not much of a Christian. Who is the mayor?"

Daniel pointed at Matthew. "My dad. Matthew Britanga." Then, concern in his eyes, Daniel looked at Patrick squarely. "Don't stare at the girls."

"What?" sputtered Patrick.

"It is not proper for you. You are not of the people."

"I was just looking at their hair."

Daniel shrugged and didn't answer. Up front, Matthew was expounding on his worries about the contents of the LORRD crates. An animated debate followed.

Daniel squinted, puzzled by the question. "Is there terrible evil in your wrecked airplane?"

"Huh? I don't think so. It's just some computer stuff that my mom and I sneaked out of South Africa. It belongs to this really vicious Iraqi-Italian drug and gun dealer who is supposed to be meeting us in Mombasa. I mean this guy is bad. He owns whole countries. They're paying us a ton of money. He promised to pay my way through Oxford — you know, in England, if I come work for him."

"You are smugglers?"

"Yeah!" grinned Patrick. Then, realizing that it was the wrong answer, he added, "Not really. We are just couriers. We don't hurt anybody. We just take stuff from one place to another."

"You break the law?"

"Hey, if it's a stupid law, you ignore it."

Daniel grimaced his concern. Then, he looked up and listened to Matthew, who was arguing now with one of the elders. "Do you like fishing?"

"What?" asked Patrick. "You bet, but I didn't bring my tackle. Are there trout in your river?"

Daniel held up his hand, listening to Matthew. The debate was growing in intensity. Matthew was nodding, then made what was obviously an official pronouncement.

"What did he say?" asked Patrick.

"The crates cannot come here, but you may stay, even though your mother is now an unbeliever."

"That's stupid."

"It is not," said Daniel solemnly. "You need to learn some respect."

"Right," snorted Patrick in distaste. "Are you the only kid in town who speaks English?"

"Yes," said Daniel. "Do you speak Swahili or Afrikaans? Portuguese?"

Patrick shook his head. "My mother knows Spanish and a little Arabic."

Daniel nodded. "My grandmother speaks French, Afrikaans, three kinds of Arabic, and English. She went to the American University in Cairo, Egypt. That's where she met my grandfather. She was not born Britangan. She was a Nigerian. She wanted my father to go to college, but when the war drove them out of their home, he had to look after her and all our people. Someday, he says, I will go to college."

Patrick sighed.

He was stuck in a stone-age village in the middle of Africa able to talk only to his renegade mother, a giant black mayor in gym shorts, and a stern sixteen year old who didn't want him to have anything to do with the local girls.

"Let's go fishing," ordered Daniel.

Patrick rolled his eyes. "Naw, I'll stay here with my mom and Matthew."

"You must call him Mr. Britanga, mayor of Britanga."

"Look, Jerk, he told me to call him Matthew. Who are you, anyway?"

"His son, Daniel Britanga. I told you that already."

Patrick groaned. He strolled over to his mother, who was trying to talk with the women surrounding her. She had given her colored scarf to a large woman, who fastened it around her neck.

"Mom," muttered Patrick, "let's get out of here."

"Patrick," she responded, softly, through clenched teeth, "are you aware that we have no idea where we are? I think we are stuck here for a while."

"Mom, I gotta get away from these geeks. They are getting on my nerves. I'm going back to the plane."

"You will do no such thing and don't call them names."

"Mom, Matthew's son is a religious drill sergeant. He told me not to talk to any of the girls. He says you are an apostate."

"Well?" Zuni laughed. "I wouldn't have you be anything else."

"What? I'm a Christian."

"Baloney. You don't know Christian from Kristofferson."

"What does that mean?"

"Patrick, these people are strict, traditional, fundamentalists. They are into faith healing and probably weird, weird stuff like snake handling."

"So?"

"So, you were brought up to question authority, to be skeptical of rules, and to defy restraints on your personal rights. You are going to have some real adjustments if you are going to fit in here. It will be good for you. You're going to be truly cross-cultural."

"Mom!" protested the boy.

"Do some evangelizing of your own," suggested Zuni. "Teach the little kids to smoke cigarettes. I bet none of them can swear in Spanish."

"Mom," protested Patrick. "I don't smoke. That's you. And I don't cuss."

Zuni smiled innocently.

Patrick's buddy, Andrew, sidled up beside him and sat down on the ground. "Ça va?" he asked, grinning.

"No worries, Mate," answered Patrick.

"Nowurrese, Make," parroted the African.

Matthew walked over and knelt down beside the two. Two other men stood beside him. "Is there anything else you need from your plane?"

"I need my log book," said Zuni. "I use it as a personal journal, you know. Are you bringing the computer here?" Matthew shook his head.

"What are you going to do?" demanded Zuni. "That equipment is worth a great deal of money to me."

"We will put the crates in an old burial cave up in the cliffs. It is dry and safe," answered Matthew. "The bones of the ancient ones who lived here before we came have been preserved safely for centuries."

"I'm coming," exclaimed Zuni. "Those crates are my personal responsibility. You simply do not understand what will happen to me if they are lost. Molech Gordini is not a good person to double cross."

"No,'" said Matthew. "You need to stay here and rest."

"Then take Patrick with you."

Matthew turned and conferred with the village elders. Then, "No," he said, "it cannot be allowed. I am sorry."

Zuni crossed her arms and sighed. "I don't like this."

"I am truly sorry. Your evil machines will be safe."

Zuni clenched her eyes shut and nodded abruptly. Patrick started to protest, but Matthew glanced at him sharply and he was silent.

Beside him, "Where is your father?" asked Daniel.

Patrick looked up, surprised. "What?"

"Where is your father?" repeated Daniel.

"Gone," muttered Patrick. "I told you he lives in Cairo. He's a state department analyst at the U.S. Embassy."

Daniel looked puzzled. "He could not come on this trip?"

"We don't ever see him," said Patrick uncomfortably. "He doesn't live with us."

"Why not?"

"Because he has his own life."

Daniel looked puzzled. "Let's go fishing," he suggested.

"Less gow fichy," parroted Andrew.

"Yeah," grunted Patrick. "Let's go fichy." He stood and marched off with a suddenly enthusiastic mob of boys. One of the kids took off a Dallas Cowboys cap and put it on Patrick's head. Other boys pounded him on the back and talked a mile a minute.

Soon, they were all running, Patrick in their midst, whooping about something that Zuni could not understand.

In the hold of the wrecked Martin, lights on the control panels flickered back into life. The LORRD computer hummed, downlinking, compiling, watching, listening.

The evil within sensed approaching humans.

Who?

Their voices were native.

The thing watched them, blood lust growing in its dark core. Who were they? What did they want? A hideous, silent whine resounded unheard, an unsettling taunt — the same inaudible hum that had attracted the hyenas and the lions to Zuni when she was unconscious and crippled.

Only this time, the intensity grew — tweaking the nerves of the approaching Britangan hunter-farmers. They did not sense it or suspect its source. But they felt its subtle, irritating annoyance, its needling aggravation — like fingernails on a blackboard.

Within minutes, an argument broke out — a stupid disagreement based on old, unresolved angers and hidden, unspoken resentments.

"Stop it," whispered Matthew.

The men fell into silence.

But Matthew was not speaking to them. He was commanding the crates. "I command you to keep your demonic manipulations away from my people," Matthew said softly.

There was a scream. Matthew turned and saw one of the younger men rolling in the dirt, his hands clutched to his ears. Matthew turned back. "I command you," he said.

Another one of the young men shrieked, dropping to his knees.

"Stop it," declared Matthew with unflinching authority, pointing a long finger directly at the crates. His voice was unafraid. "You cannot touch us. In the name of the Lord Jesus Christ, I order you to stop this foolishness."

Suddenly, the men on the ground relaxed. The

irritation was gone.

In a terrible panic, the dark evil surveyed Matthew.

He would have to die.

❧   ❧   ❧

In the very throne room of the Most High, a beautiful yet horrible presence stood proud and unbowed.

"What have you been doing?" asked the Lord.

"Going to and fro in the earth and walking up and down in it," answered Lucifer. "And I have seen one whom you protect with a great hedge of thorns, this Matthew Britanga."

"Yes," answered the Lord.

"His people only follow You because of his strong leadership. Without him, they would fall back into paganism."

"I think not," responded the Creator.

"Let me take him," whined Satan. "Then we will see just how much they truly believe."

"No."

"He is disobedient," sneered Satan.

"How so?"

"Look at him dealing with that computer. He has not prayed specifically for the evil that infests it to be thrown out."

"How is that disobedient?"

"He has failed to seek You. He did not ask You what to do. He operates in his own strength. Let me take him. Then You will see whether the people will follow You."

"No," said the Almighty.

"He must die," whined Satan. "It's the only way."

❧   ❧   ❧

"You will save my brother's life now or you will die,

you filthy gringo scum," fifteen-year-old José Chimon was shrieking in the East Los Angeles emergency room.

Miguel awoke in the crowded trauma center of Boyle Heights Medical Center. Around him were the yelling, demanding, gun-waving kids of the Lions. A doctor was pinned against the wall. A nurse was screaming.

"You will save my brother's life now!" José was howling at the doctor, profanities filling his screams. "I don't care nothing about who is next or who has had to wait for hours. You will save my brother's life right now or your wife will be a widow. What is your choice?"

Miguel could not see out of his left eye. The pain in his head was intense — unbearable. Before drifting away again, he wondered to himself why they had come all the way to Boyle Heights, a relatively nice part of East L.A. Perhaps the ambulance driver had radioed ahead and all the public hospitals were full.

How had little José arrived so quickly? Where was Al Ochoa? Such questions did not seem important although he wondered about the answers. Instead, riding above his terrible pain, he closed his eyes.

And he remembered his dad.

His real father, not the last three or four guys who had lived with his mother while Miguel was still at home.

His real father had always bragged that he was the record holder for the fastest time in a powerboat between Miami and New York.

He had told little Miguel about it many times — bouncing the boy on his knee in their dirty apartment. "Someday, we will be rich again, Manito," he would say, calling the boy by his pet name. "Did I ever tell you about the time when I had seven powerboats in my own name? I was just like a partner to the famous Eduardo Tolliver, a very rich, rich man from Chile.

"Ah, yes, Manito," Miguel's father would say to his son, holding up his palms so little Miguel could practice his boxer punch. "He and I, we owned our own airline — we did. We had five little jets based out of Opa-locka Airport, just outside of Miami, and, my little man, they were beautiful."

As little Miguel laughed and punched his father's hands, the man bragged on and on about the elaborate security system that he oversaw and the thirty people he supervised — and how their closed-circuit TV system was the very best that existed.

None of it made much sense to the little boy — who listened intently anyway, basking in the attention of his beloved father. "I was best friends with the pilots," the man once told little Miguel. "One time, Octaviano Morales, our very best fly boy, he had to run two loads of guns down to our ranch in Costa Rica and bring back a thousand kilos of the purest cocaine. It was like the driven snow, my son."

"What's cocaine?" laughed the little boy. "**Drogas?**" *Drugs?*

"Yes," his father nodded very seriously. "Bad chemicals that only fools put into their bodies. You must promise me that you will never, never take drugs."

The pre-schooler laughed in his high, little-boy voice and vowed never to take drugs.

"Swear," said his father, a strange desperation in his eyes.

The little boy stared at his face, mocking in the way only a loving, admiring five year old laughs at a bigger-than-life role model — brashly snickering in the face of the man that he worshiped. "I swear," laughed the boy.

"Hold up your hand and swear like a man," insisted his father.

Little Miguel was confused. He held up his hand and whispered a naughty word he had heard the bigger boys say.

"What?" roared his father — startled that such a little boy would know such a blunt profanity. "Why did you say that?"

Little Miguel began to cry, embarrassed. His father held him closely, nuzzling his forehead with unshaven cheeks and chin. "Hey, **Manito mio**," whispered the big man. "**No llores.**" *Don't cry.*

"You told me to swear," gasped the little boy.

"No," whispered his father, hugging him, and grabbing the boy's clenched fists. "I told you to swear that you would not take drugs."

Miguel looked confused.

"**Hagame una promesa**," urged his father: *Make me a promise.*

"I promise," whispered the little boy.

Then one day, his father disappeared. A long line of step-fathers and "uncles" came and went, some only for a few nights, others for months. Where was his dad? Miguel remembered something that his father once had told a friend. "Tolliver and me, we have to remember all sorts of fake names to fool the authorities. I have to keep track of twenty different passports. Whatever I have in my pocket is who I am that day. And that person is legit — yeah, just like a real person with his own credit rating and insurance. If the customs officials stop me and check me out, no problem. It is just paperwork. I have to be able to move freely."

So, was he underground and on the run?

Or was he dead — thrown in some unmarked grave in Central America? Miguel did not know. But the little boy longed for the big man who had made him make that promise. The disappearence of his father caused Miguel to have many strange dreams and nightmares. He couldn't understand how a father who said that he loved him would leave him alone. As he grew older he became angry that his father had dared to leave him all alone. Remembering those precious moments when his father talked to him about taking drugs suddenly became a mockery. *Why should I do anything that no good %@#&^$%# told me to do? I take back any promise I ever made to him,* Miguel thought. And from that day on things changed.

Try as he would, Miguel took no drugs, even when his Leonitos buddies were getting wasted on glue in the third grade or sneaking around to try marijuana in the fifth grade. Miguel loved to party — but he stuck to alcohol.

By age fifteen, the good-looking ladies' man was warlord of the Leones. He had earned the position just before he was a suspect in a drive-by shooting — of which he was completely innocent.

In jail, he was befriended by a social worker named Ramon Calvert. The retired Marine gunner and former gang member got Miguel out on probation and even took him on a trip with his girlfriend — a week-long camping trip in Yosemite National Park.

It had been the most exciting week in Miguel's life. He'd hiked to the top of beautiful, tree-covered mountains and swam in the crystal, freezing water of Yosemite Falls. He'd met a girl from Texas who thought he was cute and liked the gaudy, macho tattoos he had all over his arms. Her name was Patricia. She took him to an evening campfire where a preacher from San Jose told funny stories and told everybody they ought to come to Jesus.

Miguel had no idea what that meant, but he figured it had something to do with confessions and rosaries and candles.

He went up front with Patricia, and a bunch of

people who were not nuns or priests prayed with him and laid hands on him and carried on about his being born again and talking about stuff that didn't make a lot of sense to him. He went along with it because it seemed to make Patricia really happy.

And he really wanted to know a lot more about her.

Miguel returned to the Calvert campsite grinning that night. Patricia had gone on a long walk with him after the campfire and had let him kiss her.

"I think I got religion," he told Ramon's girlfriend.

"You did?" she exclaimed in concern.

"I think so," grinned Miguel. He shrugged. "Is it true that church girls don't want to have sex?"

Ramon had confirmed that church girls like Patricia usually were quite difficult on that subject. Miguel had sighed as he stared into the Calvert campfire. What a waste. She was beautiful.

The next day all she wanted to talk about was Jesus Christ. She had a paper with four spiritual laws that she insisted he repeat after her. Disgusted, he had walked off by himself. She was crazy. He was a good Catholic. He had been to confession with his mother several times before she ran off to Texas with her new boyfriend. Miguel had been to Christmas high mass every year as far back as he could remember. His uncle had been an altar boy.

But if she wanted him to repeat the four spiritual laws, that was cool. She really knew how to kiss.

But that was all she would let him do.

Miguel forgot about Patricia and her religious stuff when he got home and one of the home boys was there waiting for him. "Miguel, I have some bad news for you, Man. Your step-father was just killed in a bar fight," the home boy nervously related to him.

Miguel, wanting to show no sign of weakness, merely said, "No big deal, Man. Get lost so I can do some thinking." Miguel went inside, sat on the couch and cried like a baby. He hadn't cried in years. His entire being was overcome with grief and insane anger. *It won't be long until someone gets me too,* he thought.

Suddenly his tears and grief turned to blazing anger. Screaming at the top of his voice Miguel yelled, "I'll kill that *&@#*^! Papa, I swear by the blessed Virgin, by Jesus, and Joseph, I will kill your murderer!"

Depressed and lonely, Miguel had gotten drunk and looked for his old buddies in the Leones.

Now the gang was his only family.

That night, they had gotten a copy of the newspaper that told who had killed Miguel and José's stepdad. Around 5 a.m., one of the twelve year olds from the gang banged on the dude's front door.

A drunken giant lunged into the doorway. He demanded to know what the kid wanted.

Out of the shadows, Miguel stepped with a shotgun. He blew the man away.

The next years were a violent blur. Miguel was jailed quite a number of times and there started to smoke crack. Despite his best intentions, despite the promise he'd made so many years ago to his real father, he became a crack head, sleeping in a trash-littered lot in the middle of the barrio.

José stayed wherever he could. At one point the nuns took him.

Meanwhile, Miguel sank deeper into drugs. No longer did he enjoy fighting or the other things that had made his East L.A. adolescence less the hell that TV made it out to be. No longer did he play baseball in the sandlot, or do his hilarious rap with the wannabes practicing on the corner with their mail-order Mr. Microphones.

No longer did he leer at the thirteen-year-old girls dressing up and pretending it was time for their fifteenth birthday coming-out parties.

Instead, he drifted through the darkness of his own personal purgatory, drunkenly hustling a little money here, holding up a liquor store there, rolling drunks, pickpocketing people in line at the tuberculosis clinic, mugging tourists, ripping off cars for the chop shop on the corner, spending months in jail and in de-tox.

Whether he knew it or not, Miguel was under a death sentence. Crack had become his mother, his father, his gang, his family, and his executioner. It took everything he had, every penny he put his hands on, his appetite, his ambition, his hope.

Then one day, Miguel ran into a street crusade — or rather, one almost ran over him.

Groggy and crazy from a synthetic heroin-type fix that he knew had been spiked with rat poison, Miguel had been sleeping on a sidewalk after drinking dry cleaning solvent. A bunch of kids with a megaphone came marching down the broken concrete. They were passing out papers to everybody and some dude was yelling something about the blood of Jesus over the horn.

Miguel had hidden his face in his hands. A girl knelt over him. She was no more than twelve. "Mister," she said. "Are you redeemed by the blood of the Lamb?"

"Wha —?" protested Miguel.

"Do you know Jesus Christ?"

"Yeah," Miguel muttered. "I got religion."

"Have you accepted Jesus as your personal Saviour?"

"Right, sure. I got it in Yosemite."

"What?"

"I got it. Leave me alone."

"Are you a believer?"

Miguel cursed her loudly and ordered her to leave

him alone. Instead, he was surrounded by a bunch of zealous boys he didn't know. They started preaching stuff at him that he didn't even hear. He wanted to be left alone. He wanted to sleep.

Then, there had been a scuffle. Miguel remembered looking up and realizing that his little brother, José Chimon, and the Leones were challenging the strangers, facing them off with knives and broken bottles.

But the outsiders had lifted their hands in surrender. "We ain't in no gang, man," said one of the leaders, obviously shaken. "We are royal ambassadors of Jesus Christ."

"I've heard of the Ambassadors," snarled one of the Leones. "They a bad bunch of black dudes from Watts. You from Watts?"

"No, Dude," José had laughed. "These boys, they're preacher boys. They got God all over them, y' know, Man? They want us to have religion and make love to our enemies, you know, Man? They gonna want us to pass the hat." The Leones howled.

The young street witnessing team did not. "We just saw our dear brother here on the sidewalk and we wanted to help him," said the twelve-year-old girl who had first approached Miguel.

"Oh, yeah?" barked José. "Well, I'll tell you what. That dude ain't your brother. He's my brother. He's a crack monster. He's trying to kill himself and make me cry."

On the sidewalk, Miguel had begun to whimper.

"Would you like your brother to live?" asked one of the preachers.

"You know it," said José, his eyes deadly serious. "I would like that, Man. You think you can clean up Mikey?"

"His name is Mikey?"

"Yeah, he's Mikey. He'll try anything. He eats acid,

speed, synthetic crazy stuff, angel dust, you name it. He likes coke, rock coke, though. That's what's got him now, man. He's inside the crack vial and don't want out."

The kids picked Miguel up and, despite his protests to José, hauled him off to a car, then drove him away. He found himself sobering up in an abandoned apartment building that had once been a crack house. Adults were cleaning it up. The second floor was cleared out and filled with beds.

Hurting badly for a fix, Miguel listened to their religious babble. He agreed to whatever they asked of him, all the time watching for a chance to escape.

But his mind cleared.

After two weeks, he was clean and sober. But he wanted out. Their religious talk was getting through to him and he didn't like it. Yes, he wanted to live in peace. He wanted to be free. He wanted to quit fighting with God. But he didn't like wanting any of those things.

Instead, he wanted to get loaded. It was only when he was flying on drugs that all his gnawing wants and hurts went away. He wanted to get high.

High as he could fly.

As if reading Miguel's mind, "You want a high like you never experienced before?" asked a tall, skinny black preacher.

Miguel stared at him, then spat a racial insult.

"Hey, Man," whispered the black preacher in his ear, "you can call me anything you like, but it still is true."

"What's true?"

"That Jesus Christ is the greatest high in the world."

Miguel cursed him.

"Hey, listen, really man," insisted the man.

"How am I gonna get high on God, Black Boy?"

Staring silently at him, the preacher had not answered for several long seconds. Then, smiling, "Man, I would have killed you not very long ago for the way you talk." He smiled broadly.

Miguel sneered and cursed the man's race again.

Closing his eyes, "Father," prayed the black man, shaking with intensity and emotion, "show Your love to Mikey here. Let him know that You are the only way for him. Show him that Your love in me is the only reason that I do not kill him." He paused. His eyes glanced over Miguel. He smiled and continued.

"Lord, You know I could break his puny neck with my bare hands. Lord, You know I could break his head open or splatter his spleen all over the wall. But You have given me a brotherly love for Mikey — even though I want to grab his filthy tongue and cut it right out of his mouth. Tonight, give Mikey a special understanding of Your love and Your power that keeps me from carving out his liver. Lord, give Mikey that supernatural high that is beyond anything that any drug can give. Lord, I pray that Miguel will know You in a supernatural way tonight. Let him soar in the heavenlies and know Your perfect high."

Miguel peered at him, surprised.

"Will you ask Jesus to reveal himself to you tonight?" the preacher asked.

Miguel laughed and swore aloud.

The man stared at him, then moved on to someone else.

That night, Miguel escaped.

He got to a window and opened it. He peered out. He knew that somebody was guarding all the doors. This was his only chance.

He clutched onto a rain drainpipe and stepped out into space. Crazily, he slid down the pipe and plopped into the dust, his hands bloody. He swore, his ankle twisted and hurt with a terrible shooting pain.

He cursed the black preacher.

He cursed the people who ran the abandoned apartment building.

He started to curse God — then paused. With the blasphemous words on his lips, he halted, stopped by some deep fear that he did not understand.

He dared not curse God.

God was his friend.

He winced. Where had he gotten that idea?

He knew it was true. God was his friend. God wanted him to have his heart's desire.

"God," he whispered, "get me away from these crazy people. That big dude would enjoy killing me."

Limping, he walked down the sidewalk, his hands stinging from the cuts on his fingers and palms. It felt good to have talked to God. He clutched his eyes shut.

"I believe in You, Man," he prayed silently.

At the corner, a crack dealer was shivering, his hands in his pockets. Miguel grinned and said to himself. "Thank You, Jesus."

"Hey, Man, I got three star," the pusher greeted.

"I got no money, Man," said Miguel. "I'll have to pay you some other time."

"Sure," agreed the dealer, handing him a vial.

Miguel pulled back his hand in shock.

He stared at the guy in absolute disbelief. Nobody ever gave junkies credit.

It was never done. No way.

This guy had to be a cop. Or worse.

Miguel stared at him.

Grinning, the pusher held out the vial.

"You are the devil," exclaimed Miguel. "You are Satan!"

"Man, I'm giving you a free high," whispered the pusher. "Don't blow it. You're from that rehab house, ain't you? You are hurting, Man. You ain't had no dope for a week. You gotta have it, Man. Well, I'm giving it to you, Man, for free. Here, here it is. You ain't going to turn away no free gift, Man. Take it. Then, you come back with some money and I'll sell you lots more."

"No!" howled Miguel. "You're Satan. You want me dead. You want me hooked. Man, I'm clean." And suddenly, he was running down the sidewalk, crying crazily. Halfway down the block, he slammed into a parking meter. Spinning around, weeping, clutching his bleeding head, he fell to the concrete.

"God!" he howled. "I am so screwed up, Man. I don't know nothin'."

He cried and cried.

And he asked God to forgive him.

And God did.

Just as the sun was coming up, he banged on the door of the abandoned apartment building.

"I like God," he announced to the wrinkled old woman who opened the door. "And He likes me." Behind her, the tall, skinny, black preacher loomed. He peered at Miguel in disbelief.

"Hey, Mikey," he said.

"Hey," said Miguel. "Don't call me that no more, Man. That's an Anglo name. I'm Miguel."

"You got it," exclaimed the preacher.

Two weeks later, Miguel was baptized in the ocean and went to live in the home of one of the volunteers. It turned out that they went to a very non-traditional church right in the middle of East Los Angeles — a church that believed that little was accomplished in hit-and-run evangelism, such as Miguel had experienced in Yosemite.

They believed that it was necessary to love new converts enough to bring them into their own homes and make them a part of their families.

Miguel was wary at first. He became angry when one of the first requirements was that he spend at least three hours every day looking for a job.

But he did get a job — at a taco stand. He did well.

He started doing volunteer work at the abandoned apartment building. The church had gotten the deed to the property from the city and members were putting in their spare time trying to keep it from falling down.

The one who was the most impressed with Miguel's rehabilitation was little José Chimon. But he would have nothing to do with church.

"Hey, Man," he told Miguel. "I ain'no Evangelistica. I am Aztec. I am learning the ancient religion of our people. It is what we are. It is what is true for me."

Miguel was amazed by the very idea. Everything he had heard in school about Aztecs involved sacrificing humans atop Yucatan pyramids and hurling virgins into sacred pits.

"Naw, Man, it's nothing like that," snickered José. "That's all gringo lies. Anglos, they always lie about the Chicano way, you know. They want to keep us down in the barrio. That's what your stinkin' Christianity is about — keeping us quiet and stupid and poor."

Miguel winced. "Man, Jesus Christ wasn't no white man," he told José. "He was a Jew, Man, like them guys Hitler murdered, you know? He lived in Palestine, like Yassar Arafat. His people hated whites, Man. White Romans came in and conquered them and made them pay taxes. You don't know much about Jesus Christ, Man."

Miguel had been a Christian only a few weeks when he volunteered to be an intercessor for an upcoming crusade.

"Man," he had told José, "I am filled up with the Holy Spirit! No kidding! He is all inside of me, telling me how much God loves me. I have God inside of me now, Man. And He shows me things — like how I need to pray for people who have troubles."

"You're nuts," José exclaimed, grinning.

"No," disagreed Miguel. "Before, I was nuts. Now I know the truth. And it is setting me free — more and more every day. And, hey, Man, you're number one on my list."

With Matthew and the men of the village hurrying off to take care of the LORRD crates and with Patrick and the boys of the village sprinting off to the swimming hole, Zuni had found herself suddenly alone in a gawking crowd of women and little children.

A little girl at her elbow babbled something to her and laughed. When Zuni did not reply, the child pushed her toward an open hut. In a hysterical titter at her own bravery, she then turned and ran down the street, laughing and yelling in her native tongue.

In the doorway, a large woman in a bright tunic, her hair covered and wrapped in a scarlet turban, smiled. Her gestures were unmistakable as she loudly urged Zuni to enter.

Unsure, the American woman crossed the threshold. A rickety door shut behind her and Zuni felt a great sense of relief and security. She was inside; the loudly talking, gawking villagers were outside.

Inside the hut, another, older woman, thinner and smaller, stood and nervously twisted her hands, wrinkling her forehead, smiling, and babbling incomprehensible gibberish at Zuni.

She squatted over an open fire and carefully made a cup of tea, which she finally held up to Zuni.

The larger woman showed with gestures that Zuni should sit on the ground. Awkwardly stumbling, Zuni did. She sampled her tea. It was strange and sweet — a cross between Earl Grey and hedge clippings.

The two native women sat down across from her and sipped their tea. Both tried to smile politely, but the worry lines on the eldest's forehead gave her away.

Zuni knew her presence presented a problem they were trying to solve. Outside, children began shouting at each other and pushing against the door. Embarrassed, Zuni realized for the first time that she was sweating profusely in the heat. The older woman continued to talk to her urgently, her forehead deeply furrowed, her hands continuing to twist in concern.

But Zuni could not understand a thing. She watched the old woman's face, feeling like a moron. The old woman asked her a question and waited for an answer. Zuni tried to look intelligent, but instead felt certain that a mask like an idiot covered her exhausted, sweaty features.

She really needed a bath.

A nap would have been nice, too.

Suddenly, both native women stood. Awkwardly, Zuni did, too. One on either side, they escorted her through the door, where the gawking, pointing crowd of women and small children seemed to have doubled in size. The older woman guided Zuni down a side street and whispered something Zuni did not understand.

When the American woman just stood in the street stupidly, the younger woman took Zuni's hand and pulled her across the open courtyard quickly, then down into a narrow, cramped side street.

At her elbow, the older woman tried to tell Zuni something, then smiled patiently when Zuni, for the hundredth time, indicated that she did not understand at all. In the lead, the younger woman gripped her hand and almost dragged her down the narrowing passageway.

The alley became so narrow that Zuni could touch

the rough stones and mud walls on each side — but the noise of the crowd lessened. The mob of women and children trooping along behind shrank — dwindling to a sparse parade. The walkway turned and sloped downward into another courtyard where two separate cooking fires were burning. Women bent over the low flames and turned to look at Zuni, then excitedly greeted Zuni's two escorts. Zuni smiled mutely.

The younger woman stepped ahead and pushed open a woven mat that served as the front door of a large hut. Zuni strode into a large, neat room. Bed mats lined three walls. A long, beautifully woven mat hung from the fourth. Above the mat was a faded painting of Jesus Christ, a national flag that Zuni did not recognize, and several photographs in glass frames.

Each was pointed out to Zuni and explanations were given — which, of course, she could not comprehend. In one, Zuni's guide stood beside a much younger Matthew. She, too, was much younger and wore a long, white wedding dress. Her hair was bound up in a scarf and festooned with coins and golden chains. Matthew towered over her with a new haircut and a suit that did not fit well.

Zuni realized that it was their wedding picture.

This was Matthew's wife and Daniel's mother.

They went back out into the courtyard. The women cooking over the open fires did not look up this time, but tended their pots. The steam rose up into the morning air to the top of a high wall where a bird was perched in a tuft of grass growing between the mud bricks.

Zuni stood awkwardly for a moment while Matthew's wife said something to the women at the fires. Then, Zuni was guided into another room.

It was enormous.

She realized that it was a cave, carved long ago from the wall of the tall cliffs that hid the village. Zuni wondered what it would take to get a soft drink — maybe a diet cola.

The women gestured repeatedly to her. She began to realize that the mat next to the window was being given to her. She looked up and smiled her appreciation. The older woman left, then returned with a pitcher of water and a clean, folded rag. Both women babbled, but Zuni was now much too tired to try to understand anything.

She smiled her thanks and sat down on the mat, hoping they would leave her alone.

They watched in silence.

She sighed and dipped the rag into the pitcher. The older woman exclaimed, then took the rag from her. Carefully, she showed Zuni how to pour a little water onto the rag. Then, gently, she sponged the American woman's forehead.

Zuni smiled reluctantly. She closed her eyes and leaned against the cool mud wall. Where was Patrick? Matthew's wife took her hand. Zuni looked up with a start. She tried to smile.

"Lydia," said the woman. "Lydia." Her name was Lydia. She was Matthew's wife.

Zuni nodded and closed her eyes.

The women conferred among themselves, then quietly left her alone.

Carrying a crate from the airplane, Matthew stepped gingerly. Ancient human bones pressed around his ankles in the dusty dimness. Fifty feet up in one of the cliff's hundred burial caverns, he peered around, his eyes adjusting to the darkness.

Carefully he put down his crate amid dusty shreds

of cloth. With his foot, he nudged aside the remains of old ribs and femurs. Who were these dead? How had they come to rest in this cemetery in the cliffs? Where had they disappeared to hundreds of years before Matthew brought his Britanga people to this lush valley?

No one knew.

The evil within the LORRD computer certainly did not care. It was summoning help. Not only was it broadcasting an emergency beacon for any passing aircraft or satellite to detect, but it was calling old cohorts: dark, nasty assistance from the same occult shadows in which Valentina Vasilieva loved to play.

Come and see, whispered the malignancy. *A whole valley of naive, simple savages. Come and join this seduction. Death, destruction, chaos, terror! This will be fun . . .*

"See his disobedience!" whined Satan as he stood before God.

The Creator, indeed, was saddened.

Why had Matthew not sought guidance?

"Let me take him," whispered Satan. "I want to kill him."

"You may not," thundered the Lord.

With Patrick in tow, whooping Britanga boys pushed dugout canoes into the blue river.

"They are crazy," muttered Daniel, kicking off his shoes and throwing off his baseball cap. Cautiously, Daniel stepped into the water, peering into the depths, a long spear held carefully over his head.

From one of the canoes, Andrew called to him,

pantomiming throwing a spear into the water. The other boys chattered encouragement. A twelve year old splashed out of one of the boats and gave Patrick his spear. Suddenly, there was a flurry of activity downstream and several spears were thrust into the water. Amid shouts of victory, the young fishermen held high their spears — flapping with fish.

Soon, they had a fire going. Two boys rushed into the circle carrying armloads of rubbery-shelled eggs. Self-consciously, Patrick unlaced his boots, sat down in the sand, and pulled them off. Carefully, he removed his filthy socks and stuffed them in the boots. He doffed his cap, then glanced around. He pulled off his shirt.

Nobody was watching him.

Instead, a water fight was underway. A few of the kids were roasting the fish on spits, but most were splashing wildly and apparently trying to drown Daniel.

Rolling his eyes and taking a deep breath, the fourteen-year-old American started to yank off his ragged shorts and go skinny dipping like everybody else. Then he hesitated.

Instead he decided to keep them on. Yelling, he splashed up to his waist into the water. Andrew whooped and took his side, splashing up a tidal wave, then escaping the onslaught that followed.

Patrick was delighted to find that nobody cared if he wanted to wear shorts or not. He found that few actually could swim. Easily he freestyled away from his pursuers, then laughing, dived underwater and tackled Daniel, pulling him under the surface.

When he surfaced, there was absolute pandemonium. None of the Britanga boys could swim underwater. But they were great imitators. Immediately, each tried whatever Patrick did — most of them successfully.

Before the morning was over, he had exhausted his entire repertoire — showing off the Australian crawl, the backstroke, the butterfly, the classic breaststroke, and a goofy underwater dolphin kick that his dad had taught him on Patrick's last trip to Cairo.

Determinedly, Daniel worked hard at each style. Quickly, he mastered the crawl, even breathing under his arm. But only Andrew managed an acceptable butterfly.

There was then an enthusiastic yell on the far riverbank. The gang of adolescents splashed across, and before Patrick realized what was happening, they were clamoring up a narrow path up the side of the cliffs.

Up on the plateau, the boys hid in the grass as a small herd of zebras stampeded past, their hooves thundering loudly across the plain. In a meadow of scarlet wildflowers, the boys sneaked up on seventy grazing elephants. Suddenly, the great beasts sensed their presence and, trunks upraised, moved off, trumpeting loudly with a dozen infant elephants barely visible in the great forest of baggy legs.

A vast flock of iridescent birds whirred out of the bush as the boys attempted to stalk a herd of wildebeests. "Look," whispered Daniel, pointing. Patrick peered at a thick sausage tree and saw the leopard — perfectly camouflaged in the leafy shadows — lounging in a fork of the branches. Quietly the boys watched. The big cat yawned, stretched, extended a thick paw, and slipped away into the tall grass, raising a sudden cloud of white butterflies.

Patrick stood as the boys began to laugh loudly. Several converged on the tree, scrambling up into its branches. Daniel called a warning. Sure enough, a red, spitting cobra was knotted up in the branches. The boys threw rocks at it until it slithered away. Then they took the tree — mighty victors. As the sun climbed high in the sky the American and his new African friends played a rough-and-tumble king-of-the-mountain, throwing each other out of the tree and down onto the soft, grassy dirt. When a thunderstorm moved in fast from the east, the boys took refuge under their tree — with three uncomfortable marabou storks, which huddled in a clump, watching the boys suspiciously.

The rain passed and produced a spectacular double rainbow in the deep blue sky. "I will ask God to restore your father to you," said Daniel. "To stir within him the great love he has for you. To bring him here to you and your mother so you can be a real family."

"What?"

Daniel smiled and did not answer. He just nodded to himself approvingly.

A hung-over Noel MacDougal dug out his wallet as the big boat's engines roared. "That's my son Patrick," he mumbled to the scuba instructor. The Sinai shoreline of Taba, Egypt, fell away as the launch sped into the Red Sea's Gulf of Aqaba. "He's my boy. Great kid. Wish I could spend more time with him."

"How old is he?" asked the Egyptian, his voice too loud for Noel's aching head.

Patrick's father winced and tucked the photo back in his wallet. "Twelve. No, he's older than that. He's fourteen. He's fourteen or fifteen."

The instructor squinted in surprise at the American embassy employee. No Egyptian father would be unaware of the age of his only son — particularly one advancing into manhood.

"Is he in boarding school?"

"Yeah," said Noel, his eyes faraway. "No. Well, he

lives with his mother in Kenya. We're separated. She's a bush pilot. He goes to the British academy in Nairobi."

The Egyptian nodded. Americans never failed to amaze him with their irresponsibility. "Why are you not still married?"

Noel didn't answer. It was none of this Egyptian's business that Noel and Zuni had grown steadily apart. When Noel had grown lonely and had an affair with a secretary, Zuni had taken the opportunity to leave.

But their marriage had been on the rocks for years.

Repeatedly, Noel tried to get back with her, but she wasn't interested. *How I had loved that woman,* he thought over and over again.

So, he had immersed himself in his career, the embassy party life, and his half-hearted hobbies, such as scuba diving.

That morning, his group was diving off the Sinai in a little-known spot known as Phoenician Wreck. Diving off of the Egyptian coast was mostly confined to the Red Sea — since the Mediterranean off the Nile delta is clouded with silt.

The instructor divided his students up into groups of three. Noel's partners were two researchers from the Cairo embassy commercial desk — a husband and wife team named Dave and Melody.

Except for Noel, everyone toted a spear gun because of the heavy shark infestation.

The three jumped off the side of the boat and slowly made their way to the bottom. It was the deepest Noel had ever dived, about 110 feet. This was no ancient wreck, just a brightly colored reef that looked somewhat like the hull of a boat.

Just as Noel had been told, the ocean floor was spectacular. It was alive with marine life and lush with vegetation.

Like a plumed warrior, a jet-black razor fish glided past his mask. Noel instinctively reached out his hand. Instantly, the fish tilted sideways and fluttered to the ocean floor like a piece of discarded paper. Astonished, Noel watched.

Only after Noel held still for more than a minute did it come back to life, graceful and beautiful again. Unfolding beneath it, a sea anemone that looked like a dozen miniature roses bloomed from the sea floor and swayed in the gentle currents. Was the anemone watching him? Noel could not tell.

Melody tapped him on the shoulder and pointed off to his right. A large, dark object hovered over them. A nine-foot requiem shark was looking for lunch. It nosed down, investigating them. Only a few feet away, the man-eater broke its approach and started to circle.

Eight reef whitetip sharks — five to six feet long — joined it. They followed each other in a tight, closed circle, never taking their eyes off the divers. Noel felt unexpected terror. He had swum with sharks before. Why were these any different?

Dave and Melody held their spear guns ready and slowly moved Noel between them. The great killers represented unquestionable danger, but Noel couldn't help but admire their beauty. Their streamlined, perfect bodies moved effortlessly through the water. It was hypnotic to watch them. They were, indeed, nature's perfect eating machines.

The Egyptian instructor's words came back to Noel: "Don't be intimidated if you see sharks. They're very curious animals and they are scavenger-hunters. If you look too interesting, they may try to take a taste. But usually they are just as wary of you as you are scared of them. Very few sharks will attack humans. So, act natural. Don't splash or struggle or try to swim away quickly. Sharks feed on injured fish, so don't do anything to tell them you are in trouble. Remain calm and they will go away."

Sure enough, after a couple of minutes, the sharks wandered off in search of other prey.

Noel returned to his exploration. He moved across the floor, then glanced around for his diving partners. Instead, he noticed three circling sharks. Nervously, he glanced around. Dave and Melody were nowhere to be seen.

Noel sank to the floor and lay there motionless. Keeping one eye on the circling sharks, he watched a beautiful, scarlet sea urchin move slowly across the sand. A good six inches across, it bristled with prickly spines like an undersea porcupine.

Noel glanced up. Two more sharks had joined the circle.

Noel did not move. He glanced around, but still did not see Dave or Melody.

The sharks above maintained a uniform circle around him. They seemed to broaden their circle — as if examining other prospects as well.

But a jackfish seemed in love with Noel's mask.

Time and again, the big fish butted his mask, apparently convinced it was a rival. Noel slowly hovered off the bottom and moved his arms toward the jack. With one hand, he batted it off.

Then, from out nowhere, another diver was in front of Noel. Whoever it was waved a greeting, took aim, and fired a spear pointblank into the jack.

It struggled violently on the end of the spear as the young diver reeled in the line. Dark clouds of blood filled the water.

"No!" thought Noel, glancing in alarm up at the sharks. The young diver grabbed the spear and held it up proudly as the impaled jack struggled crazily about on the other end. Indeed, the sharks broke their circle and began to swim toward the blood.

"This is it!" thought Noel, envisioning a feeding frenzy—dozens of sharks out of control, sinking their teeth into everything in sight.

The nine-foot shark chomped down on the thrashing jack, surprising the young diver, who dropped his spear gun and fled toward the reef as the big shark veered sharply toward Noel. It swung around, its rough hide scratching his shoulder, its tail slapping him in the face. Careening backward, Noel held up his hands and tried not to move a muscle. Chills ran up his spine.

The shark turned sharply again and swam back toward him, veering after a piece of the jack. It spread its massive jaws and swallowed the debris, then began to survey the area with its great, round, unblinking eyes.

Its attention was diverted suddenly by Dave and Melody swimming in from the reef. Waving their arms and swimming directly at the shark, the two held their spear guns in front of them, aiming directly at its head.

"No!" Noel wanted to yell — but could not in the water. It was hard to believe anyone could be so stupid. The blood from the jackfish was already exciting other sharks all around. Now, if Dave and Melody attacked the requiem, a frenzy would certainly result.

"Help me," Noel prayed. This was not his usual tactic, as he was no prayer warrior.

Nevertheless with the jack's blood clouding the water and gung-ho divers with spearguns charging, ignorant of the mob of hungry whitetips poised to strike, Noel prayed.

"God," he exclaimed silently, "God, please, get me out of this alive."

As a whitetail appeared in his mask and nudged

him inquisitively, a quiet calm settled over Noel. He felt strangely confident and relaxed. Real danger remained all around, but Noel knew everything was going to be all right. The whitetail returned to the circle.

He floated effortlessly in the water, passively observing the storm around him. It was as if he were in a dream. He simply knew everything was going to turn out okay.

Dave got to within a foot of the requiem, aimed his spear gun and pulled the trigger. But nothing happened. Dave yanked the trigger again and again. Each time, there was nothing but an empty, clicking sound. The shark veered off and moved back toward the perimeter. It rejoined the other sharks and continued to swim in a circle around the divers.

Noel knew the misfiring speargun was no coincidence. Shaken, he glanced at his air gauge. The entire drama had taken only five minutes, although it had seemed like an eternity, and to say the least, it had shaken him.

He surfaced and climbed aboard the boat. His instructor yammered something at him that he did not hear. He noticed that all the other dive teams were already aboard, looking alarmed. Noel waved and went below.

He had been spared for a reason, and he felt an urgency to go visit Zuni and Patrick.

This time, it would be different, as he had a son who desperately needed a loving father.

A son who . . . Noel paused, unsure.

A son who was in trouble. Whose life was in extreme jeopardy. A boy who needed his father. "Patrick," whispered Noel. He glanced around self-consciously, then ducked his head. "Patrick, I'm coming. I'm coming to love you, my son. Zuni, please be there for me. I really need you. I love you, too."

❖   ❖   ❖

As if gripped in a new madness, Valentina shrieked urgency at the Mombasa cab driver and waved money in his face.

The morning sun was beginning to bake Mombasa's decaying dock district. As the sin-filled city basked in the tropic warmth, the heavy air shimmered, distorting the distant silhouette of Mount Kenya.

This morning, a laid-back feeling seemed to permeate the grimy waterfront. Rusting cargo ships of Panamanian and Liberian registry floated lazily at their moorings in the oily harbor. Near a tumbled-down lighthouse, a beautiful white yacht was anchored 500 yards offshore. It flaunted the Iraqi flag.

Molech Gordini had not yet roused. He seldom awakened before noon. He snored loudly between two oriental sisters clad in gaudy, flimsy Arabian Nights-type harem costumes. They yawned, but did not dare leave his enormous bed. Molech's tantrums were legendary.

Along the wharf, longshoremen ambled along the docks, hugging what little shade existed. Out of scores of taverns and brothels, loud music wafted out across the water. To outsiders, the music sounded repetitious — as if the bands and juke boxes were playing variations of the same monotonous song. Provocatively dressed girls moved languidly around sailors who had not yet begun drinking in earnest.

In a cab, an animated Valentina Vasilieva pulled up to the dock.

She climbed out and huffily threw a wad of money into the driver's window — seemingly unaware of the extreme danger into which she was placing herself — a white, European woman alone on the docks.

"Ma'am," yelled the cabbie, "this is no place for a lady."

Valentina kicked the side of his cab. Startled, he

looked at her, then at the dent in the door. "Don't worry about me," spat Valentina.

Muttering his irritation, the cabbie sped away.

Valentina muttered under her breath — only dimly aware of the attention on her. She shielded her eyes and spotted Molech's yacht. As dock workers began to stroll onto the sidewalk, she fumbled in her briefcase and pulled out a cellular phone. With her fat fingers, she banged out a familiar number — then demanded loudly to speak to Gordini.

In irritation, she listened to apologies that Molech was not yet taking calls, then demanded to know if her computer had arrived.

Her face grew purple. A crowd of dock workers gathered. "Lost?" she screamed. "How could the plane be lost! You fool! You cannot possibly know what this means!"

As she howled her protests, a speed boat moved away from the big boat. Weeping aloud, Valentina threw down the portable phone and furiously danced a tantrum over it, stomping it into junk in a display that evoked a bemused murmur from her audience.

"Find it!" she wailed as the launch pulled up to the dock. "Find it! I will not wait another moment! Take me to my computer!"

With assault rifles slung over their shoulders, the yacht's sailors parted the sea of gawkers. Laborers, stevedores, teamsters, and dock workers stepped aside as the portly Valentina continued her mad dance over the debris of the portable telephone.

She was beside herself by the time the sailors got her to the yacht. Gently, female attendants guided her to her plush room. But she did not seem to see or hear. She was elsewhere, floating in the cosmos, weeping her protests to the astral guides. "Where is it?" she cried pitifully.

She was floating over a sheer, sandstone cliff. Up

350 feet over a narrow river it twisted above a fertile ribbon of bottomland — a tiny Nile-like stream giving life to the desert — the secret valley, tucked away in the depths of the secluded plateau. Below stretched a cultivated Eden hidden from white traders, unspoiled by modern ways, unvisited by tourists.

In her vision, Valentina saw hundreds of caves honeycombing the great cliffs. Entering one 150 feet over the river valley, she glided among a mass of ancient human bones. Dusty bits of cloth bearing faded patterns lay snagged in the pile of ribs, skulls, and vertebrae.

The young Russian did not care about this ancient graveyard of a people long vanished. Impatiently, she stood at the doorway and watched Britanga women at their daily chores. Several carried water jars on their heads and chattered with others washing clothes in the river, barefoot on a narrow, rocky beach shaded by thorny acacia trees. Along the river, tall, lean men worked alone, chopping at broad fields of millet and corn. Valentina turned, hearing women pounding grain in the village, singing in pure joy.

In her vision, young Vasilieva soared over the secret village — nestled in a dusty landscape of massive boulders, tall grass, and great trees. Her eye was caught with the beautiful, square granaries, the short adobe towers filled with the tribe's wealth.

"Where is my computer?" she howled impatiently. Abruptly, she was thrown through a thicket of acacia thorns onto an overgrown hillside. She was shown hand-laid stones marking a little-used trail, a chockstone stairway masoned between massive boulders. Deep within the cracks of the cliffs, she came upon ancient ladders with steps worn shiny by decades of bare feet.

Fifty feet up, hugging the sheer cliffs, her feet searched for a narrow ledge. Inside, thousands of bones lay snug in their ancient, cotton shrouds as they had for centuries, preserved by the dry, hot climate. She exclaimed aloud as she saw the crates of her LORRD.

Then she awakened from her vision.

Consumed with a frantic urgency, tearing open the door of her stateroom, she lurched into a passage-way and grabbed the first crewman she encountered — demanding to be taken to Molech.

The billionaire was still in bed, but was yelling into a telephone.

Howling, Valentina demanded to be given a heli-copter — that she knew where to find the computer.

Molech winced at her, but did not grow angry. He covered the mouthpiece with his hand. "Valentina!" he greeted. "Sit! Have some tea! I am mobilizing a search. I own the commanders of these pitiful little governments."

A uniformed man appeared behind Molech. "Sir," he said in a deep voice, "as we speak, the armies and air forces of five little countries are scurrying over their nasty wildernesses, frantic to please you, prob-ing for our missing airplane. They will find it and kill that unworthy wench we so foolishly trusted. She has disappeared from radar deep within the Great Rift Valley. It will be a simple matter to find and kill her — even though she apparently silenced her rescue beacon."

Molech looked at Valentina and smiled. He shrugged. "Come, relax."

Valentina's eyes were dilated. "I know where our LORRD is!" she declared. Urgently, she blurted out her vision. "My spirit friends do not lead me astray! Fly me to this Great Rift and I will know that valley when I see it from the air."

Molech signalled silently to his aides.

They quickly scurried about. They knew that he

took this mad Russian woman completely seriously.

Within minutes, Gordini's personal helicopter was airborne over Mombasa.

Vasilieva yammered on about a hidden village and caves filled with bones. Molech's pilot listened with skepticism, glancing worriedly at his boss. Gordini unfolded a map. Intently, Valentina pored over it — then studied a spine of mountains on the long border separating the African countries of Zaire, Uganda, Rwanda, Tanzania, and Burundi.

Her face not an inch from the map, Valentina closed her eyes and began to moan. Her nose passed over Lake Kiva, then paused. "There!" she shrieked, her finger jabbing the map. "It is here on an uncharted plain! Let's go! I cannot wait another second!"

Molech nodded. Reluctantly the chopper pilot changed his course, quietly voicing concern about crossing at least four international borders without posting a flight plan. He tapped the fuel gauge, but fell silent as Molech gave him a deadly stare.

Molech took the microphone.

As the pilot listened gravely, he heard the billionaire spit venomous threats at government officials in Kenya, Tanzania, Uganda, and Zaire, ordering that the missing pilot and her son be killed the minute they were found.

"They are unwieldy," Molech smiled to Valentina. The Russian laughed her agreement.

Zuni must have dozed for quite some time. When she awoke, the shadows were short and the air was much more humid. She stood, then faltered, surprised that she was so weak.

"Why have you brought such danger to our hidden valley?" asked an old woman in the doorway.

Zuni looked up in surprise, amazed to hear English. "What?" she whispered.

The woman stepped into the room, shut the door quietly, and smiled at Zuni. She produced from the folds of her skirt a great, round loaf of brown bread.

"Would you like some mint tea?"

Lightheaded, Zuni nodded.

The old woman left, returning with a steaming pottery pitcher. Carefully, she flaked a pile of dried mint leaves into a cup, then handed it to Zuni. Almost ceremonially, she poured hot water into the mug. Zuni sat in silence, watching the steam rise into her face. Slowly, the water turned yellow-green.

"Drink," said the old woman, lifting her own cup to her lips.

Zuni looked up at her. "Why am I here?" she asked, her lips trembling. "Why was I brought here?"

The old woman scrutinized her without answering. She slowly began to pull apart the loaf of bread. She held a wad out to Zuni.

"I don't understand." Zuni's eyes filled with tears of frustration and anger.

"Come now, my dear," said the old woman briskly, putting her hand on Zuni's and placing the bread in her palm. "There is no need to cry. You just have to be thankful."

Zuni wiped away her tears but still looked troubled.

"Come," said the old woman, "let's go up on the roof."

Out in the bright sun, birds twittered and sipped from a cistern. Zuni panted behind the old woman — who had almost run up the four flights of steps to the top of the family granary.

The woman stood on a roomy balcony complete with sitting mats. Below, the swirl of the village went on uninterrupted by the day's excitement. Out by the river, women were singing and beating their laundry against the rocks. In the fields, men and boys were hoeing and weeding. At the edge of town, a man and two boys carrying spears were running — apparently headed out to hunt.

The town raised quite a hubbub — babies crying, kids playing, guinea pigs whistling, roosters crowing, hens cackling, donkeys braying, men and women haggling, women sweeping the courtyards, scolding children, and calling to husbands. What caught Zuni's ear, though, was the constant clapping. In little groups here and there, teenage boys and girls, small children, older children, clapped off and on, loudly, in different rhythms. It was human percussion — incessant. It never seemed to stop.

Zuni caught the scent of freshly baking bread. She looked around.

The old woman was studying her. "Do you believe in the end of the world?" she asked.

Zuni considered the question, but did not know how to answer it. "What do you mean?" she asked.

"Do you believe that one day God will end things and bring His children home?"

Zuni turned, her long hair caught in the light breeze. She took in the rich scents and sounds of the village. "I suppose," she answered. "I've really never given it that much thought."

"I believe that the end is upon us," said the old woman. "God in His wisdom will never tell any of us when He will bring it all to a close. That is not His way. However, He has provided signs so that we will recognize the beginning of the end."

Zuni listened, but did not comment.

"For centuries, a great battle has been fought unseen to our human eyes," continued the old woman. "It has not been a real war, but more a continuing rebellion which has never been out of God's control. He could have terminated the conflict at any stage, but whenever He actually wills it, the struggle will cease.

"The history of the end of the world has been written down in advance. The final events will follow a certain course, just as the flood waters come to this valley every spring. How far away is the glorious time of His return? I do not know. It is our place to watch and wait — to trust and obey." She paused.

Zuni stood beside the cistern, watching the city below.

"I believe you are here because this is a place of safety," said the old woman.

Zuni turned, her eyes betraying her shock.

"You are greatly loved," said the old woman. "Great prayer worldwide has been offered on your behalf and on the behalf of your son."

"How would you know that?" whispered Zuni.

"Some things are imparted by the Holy Spirit of God," said the old woman.

"Hmmm," muttered Zuni.

The old woman smiled. She leaned forward and touched Zuni's shoulder.

Zuni found herself crying, hugging the old black woman as if she were her own mother. "I'm sorry," Zuni whimpered. "I'm so sorry. I'm sorry."

The old woman did not ask any details. She gently stroked Zuni's hair and held her. She began to rock and hum a lullaby.

"You are safe here," she soothed.

Zuni shook.

The old woman was named Sarah Britanga.

She was Matthew's mother.

The story she told Zuni was more terrible than any horror tale Zuni had ever heard, and it chilled her heart.

For centuries, the Britanga tribe in what had become the country of Uganda had been vicious, raiding warriors — the Vikings of central Africa — thriving on the excitement of ritual murder, taking members of other tribes as slaves, and living on the spoils of their raids. Plunder was a way of life — for the Britanga were not farmers or craftsmen.

Instead, they took the fruits of those foolish enough to toil. Cannibalism was a high ritual — roasting alive the bravest and strongest of enemies and slicing off their flesh before they were yet dead. To devour the heart, liver, and brains of a formidable opponent was believed to give the Britanga great courage, strength and wisdom.

That was not the only reason to devour an enemy. The Britanga liked the taste of human flesh — which is similar in texture to pork. Favorite captives for the pot were young enemy children and plump men and women.

Traditional Britanga taboos had considered anything new to be an insult to the spirits, explained Sarah. "As a result, we were quite backward. Our religion discouraged change of any kind. The demonic spirits wanted us to stay the way we were.

"That gave them free reign over us.

"They kept us in darkness. Matthew tells me that a popular idea among Americans and Europeans today is that traditional African spirit worship should be preserved as a cultural treasure — and that believing in Jesus Christ has destroyed our cultures and traditions. Nothing could be more absurd."

Sarah shook her head, amused. "In their broken-hearted search for anything but God, some people will say almost anything.

"In the 1840s, a missionary named David Livingstone came. The Britanga heard of him and watched in amazement as the white-skinned evangelist succeeded in convincing even the most brutal warring tribes to live in peace and coexistence. Amazed at his courage and unflinching determination to teach the story of Jesus, the principal chief and top witch doctor of the Britanga, whose name was Omo Awambe, took the new name of Paul Britanga.

"He proclaimed that the Britanga would become Christian and would henceforth live in peace. They applied their traditional skills of stealth and violence to hunting and became famous for their ability to stalk even the rhino and the lion.

"Gradually, they also learned the skills necessary to be farmers and herdsmen. The Britanga people took their place in a loosely confederated ethnic group that became known as the Baganda nation.

"Keeping us in the grip of spirit worship condemned us to the Stone Age. When Dr. Livingstone came to our people, the Britanga didn't even have the wheel. We had not invented an alphabet, calendar, or arithmetic. Cannibalism, sorcery, witchcraft, fear, poverty, misery, torment, ritual murder, war, and famine were the heritage of our old religion.

"Dr. Livingstone came with the message of a personal God desiring a relationship with you and me. It was the message of God's great love in sending His Son to die for each of us. It was the message of deliverance and freedom from the prison of witchcraft and sorcery. It was the message of the Lord Jesus Christ to each individual Britanga.

"Paul Britanga, who had been a powerful sorcerer, joyfully threw off his chains and ran into the light of God's wonderful love! The Britanga had never valued life before. Now each life was important.

"Paul Britanga had become not only a free and independent human being, but a close confidant of the very Creator of the Universe — who has complete power over all the old spirits, which were very real and evil — and angry.

"New life stirred within the Britanga. Paul sent

his sons to England where James Britanga was admitted to Cambridge University, then settled in Canada. He never returned, which greatly troubled the Britanga elders. Nevertheless, with the message of Jesus Christ, there was a joyous awakening of new possibilities. We knew what Jesus meant when He spoke to Nicodemus about being born again. There was no mystery in that message for the Britanga.

"With us, it was not so much being born again, as being born for the first time into life, abundant life, full and free, and secure from demonic attack."

"A terrible truth was learned. Not all white men were Christian—and many who claimed to be did not know as much about God as did the bush natives.

"More and more whites came and with them the terrors of the slave trade. Fortunately, because the Britanga were so far inland — and on the distant eastern half of Afrca — their people were not ravaged as badly as people along Africa's western coasts. There entire tribes disappeared to toil in Brazil's rubber plantations, Jamaica's sugar cane fields, and South Carolina tobacco farms.

"Slavery died in the wake of America's Civil War. But even more whites poured into Africa.

"They brought the confusion and slavery of colonial rule. The black, rightful heirs to the Great Rift Valley and the broad plains and deep jungles were declared lesser humans. Whites spread a lie that the black natives were not advanced enough to rule themselves. Even so, the whites' influence was mostly limited to the cities and plantations they established.

"After World War I, the British consolidated their rule over Britanga lands and Baganda territory and began imposing it over us. Invisible lines were established across the grasslands, mountain ranges, and rain forests. The Baganda nation found itself inside a territory that came to be called Uganda.

"After World War II, the British began to withdraw. Uganda was declared a nation. Because the Baganda were the most populous tribe, their principal chief, Edward Mutesa, was proclaimed king.

"A gentle Christian man, he preferred to call himself prime minister. In 1959, in recognition of his strong leadership and dedication to peace, he was knighted by the British monarch, Queen Elizabeth II, in a ceremony in London.

"Perhaps he should not have accepted her endorsement. His influence began to wane as he seemingly attempted to imitate white ways. Resentment grew among the two largest minority tribes — the Langi and the Kakwas — demanding a role in the Baganda-dominated government.

"Warfare broke out. In 1962, Milton Obote, a member of the brutal Langi tribe, overthrew Mutesa, executed him without a trial, and imposed what became an increasingly repressive regime. Oppression against Christian Bagandas began with a vengeance.

"Obote was Moslem. Anyone who admitted faith in Jesus Christ was deprived of property. A reign of terror began.

"It intensified in 1971 when a bloodthirsty Kakwa lieutenant, Idi Amin, deposed the Langi-run government and embarked on an orgy of bloodshed in which an estimated three hundred thousand Ugandans were shot, tortured, and battered to death.

"Amin, supposedly a Muslim, hated Christians, but also ignored the laws of Islam. He was believed to remove, freeze, and devour at leisure the vital organs of slain enemies — as had his ancestors — and worshiped their ancient idols.

"When Amin was driven out of the country in 1979, no one wept — indeed they welcomed back the murderous Milton Obote, leading a rebel army armed by neighboring Tanzania.

"Obote's rebel army and the invading Tanzanians did not liberate Uganda from violence. Instead, Obote took up where they had left off. His guerrillas laid waste to the land, terrorizing and killing uncounted hundreds of thousands of people. More than a half million refugees fled into Zaire and the Sudan. As many as a million Ugandans—predominantly Christians — were executed in wild sprees of ritual blood-letting.

"Matthew's father, Titus Britanga, was a village councilman in the town of Kyotera, on the shores of Lake Victoria. A Riwindi native of the town of Luwero, Titus was a successful tradesman who had a number of enterprises, including the only modern supermarket between the Ugandan capital of Kampala and the Tanzanian border.

"He had provided many jobs for his fellow Christians among the Britangas and the Banyankole tribe. He had been serving as council member for over a year when unrest broke out, led by Obote radicals determined to destroy all existing structures and replace them with their own. The Obote radicals demanded revolutionary government, revolutionary people's courts, revolutionary health services, and distribution of basic commodities exclusively through their own channels. Thus, their violence was directed at the community council members, outsiders, Christians, and businessmen.

"Titus Britanga was an obvious, easy target.

"The radicals demanded his resignation as councilman but he bravely refused. Death threats followed. The intimidation grew. A mob stoned his house twice and burned down one of his businesses, a coffee warehouse, but still he stood firm.

"Expecting the radicals to move against his supermarket one night, Titus and his four sons, fifteen-year-old Matthew, twelve-year-old Mark, eleven-year-old Luke, and eight-year-old John, spent the night in the store to protect it.

"Just before midnight, they were awakened by the frenzied roar of a mob surrounding the building and setting the warehouse next door afire with Molotov cocktails — beer bottle bombs full of gasoline. Although Titus and his boys were armed, Titus knew resistance was futile. He lowered fifteen-year-old Matthew out an alley window to go get help.

"Matthew crazily ran from house to house pleading with supposed friends, members of his church, distant relatives, and the town's lone policeman to come to the aid of his father and brothers. A few came, but were intimidated by the size of the furious mob.

"Flames from the warehouse licked the sky as Matthew watched the policeman stand atop a bus and fire his pistol into the air. Angry screams filled the air. The native officer was dragged off the bus and, amid hideous shrieks and laughter, was hacked to death with the axes, picks, and spades that the crowd wielded. Gasoline was thrown over his body and he was set on fire.

"The crowd surged, screaming for more blood.

"Appearing in the doorway of the supermarket, Matthew's father demanded the safe passage of his boys. The sneering, mocking mob leaders agreed to let them pass — but Titus would have to stand trial for his 'crimes.'

"Little Mark, Luke, and John Britanga appeared in the doorway. Hesitantly, hugging their father and bidding him goodbye, they stepped outside. Then, eight-year-old John balked, hanging onto his father.

"What followed was the stuff of nightmares.

"Mark and Luke were grabbed by the mob, thrown into the concrete wall of the supermarket, then brutally stoned, stabbed, and hacked to death.

"Friends stifled the screaming, weeping Matthew, stuffing the frantic fifteen year old into a car as the chanting crowd set the supermarket on fire. Friends rushed to the Britanga home and dragged Sarah to safety. Crazily, they rushed on back streets to the army garrison on the edge of town.

"In the hellish light of the blazing warehouse, the mob dragged Titus Britanga and little John outside. Auto tires were put around their necks and filled with gasoline. Terrified, the eight year old tried to wrestle his 'necklace' off, but laughing, chanting, and shrieking, the crowd roared its approval as the little boy's hands were bound with barbed wire.

"Titus was shoved to the ground.

"Lit matches were thrown at him. With a whoosh, the gasoline in the tire ignited. The crazed crowd cheered and howled. They chanted and danced as flames shot up billowing black smoke.

"Titus rolled in the dirt trying to put out the fire. He pleaded for mercy. But he inhaled fumes that quickly singed his throat and lungs. Hoarsely he struggled to scream. The mob howled its delight.

"To add to the show, one of the mob leaders unbound eight-year-old John's hands and shoved him toward his father. Desperately, the little boy shed his own tire and tried to save his daddy — rolling his father's writhing body in the dirt to extinguish the flames.

"The mob leaders knew it was too late. They laughed and offered mocking suggestions. The molten rubber was like boiling tar, burning the little boy's hands. It could not be extinguished or removed from Titus' scorched flesh although the weeping eight year old struggled to help him.

"For twenty minutes the child tried to save the man who had given him life. Then, as the mob howled, the boy was given a knife and ordered to cut his father's throat.

"The eight year old refused.

"They threatened him with the same fate.

"Weeping, John refused. He threw the knife away and clutched his father's charred body. But Titus Britanga was dead.

"Younger members of the mob continued to kick and stone Mark and Luke's dead bodies. In the light of torches and the raging warehouse, some began to carve off hunks of flesh, which they waved about and actually began to eat.

"It surely was a horrible way to die," Sarah whispered to Zuni. "But the real victim was my little John. They allowed him to live, convincing him he had killed his father.

"First, they put another tire around his neck and shoulders. They forced him to drink petrol. They poured the rest into the tire and all over him and acted as if they were going to set him alight, too. But then they said there was not enough fuel. Another tin of petrol was fetched.

"My little boy was screaming for mercy and crying that he was sorry. They set him free.

"The frenzied crowd carried the little boy aloft on their shoulders, proclaiming him a hero of the revolution.

"When the army got to the scene, the mob leaders were dishing out parts of my husband's body. Hundreds of them ate pieces. Before they would surrender my little boy to the army, the mob forced John to eat a mouthful — of his father's flesh.

"That night a massive crowd of 'mourners' danced around the bodies, now displayed in front of the burned-out police station. Someone chopped Titus's charred head from the body and hung it on a telephone pole outside the family home to the wild shouts of acclamation from the bloody mob. A truck stolen from another businessman was driven into the house and set afire.

"I lost everything," Sarah said. "My home. Our earthly wealth. My husband. My sons Mark and Luke. John was never right again. He disappeared at age eleven after he got into drugs and jungle voodoo." She sighed. "I think that he is dead. We heard that he joined Amin's guerillas, but later committed suicide."

The old woman looked at the sky. She smiled. "But God is good." She paused. Tears filled her eyes and the noises of the village filled her silence.

She touched Zuni's arm. "God is very good."

Zuni shuddered. "How can you say that? After what He allowed to happen? God is not good. If He even exists, He's some sort of — I don't know what — laughing at us, letting us die in pain. I can't believe in a God like that. A real God would not have let those ..." Zuni trembled in growing bitterness, "those ... evil ... morons just blow my Daddy's head away and ... and ... in their sick meanness ..." Zuni sank down, squatting, almost assuming the fetal position. Her eyes were faraway. "I hated them — and God who didn't stop them."

Startled at Zuni's words, Sarah bit her lip and looked down at the village. "My Matthew went through a terrible time, too, and said things like that." Her voice trembled. "We returned to our family hometown near Luwero. But John was no longer a little boy. He never spent another night under my roof."

There was another long silence. "Matthew could not accept that he had been permitted to live — and not even suffer a little. He could not understand why he had been spared. He wanted to die — heroically, taking hundreds of his father's murderers with him.

"I tried to show him that God knew that John and I needed someone to take care of us. But that was not enough. John had nothing but terrible, raging accusations against his big brother. Matthew took it all very badly. He rebelled. He took drugs with John's awful witchcraft friends. He became," Sarah paused, embarrassed, "like an animal." She winced. "After John disappeared, Matthew and Sarah escaped death again when Obote launched an offensive against the Baganda heartland. What followed was a long winter of death and terror that would come to rank among the world's worst atrocities.

"The army slaughtered a half-million Bagandas, many of them Britangas. Today, Britanga lands around Luwero are empty and perhaps cursed. I believe that God has decided to punish the evildoers in a way never seen before.

"I am too harsh," she quietly confessed. "I believe that the people who had given themselves over to depravity and violence and sexual decadence became themselves victim to the death in which their evil master takes such delight. Satan is never kind to his disciples. They suffer far more than those who refuse to follow him."

Zuni listened, but did not comment. She had heard of the Ugandan wars of genocide. She knew of the AIDS plague among tribal men and women — completely out of control throughout Central Africa. The Zaireans called it "SLIM" because of the skeletal appearance of the victims awaiting death.

"Here in our safe, hidden valley," continued Sarah, "we have been isolated completely from the terror sweeping the outside world. We have been here for almost twenty years now.

"Coming to the valley had been Matthew's idea. He said that we had to return to our roots and the ways of our ancestors — to the land. Civilization was vanishing from our country, he said — we must not be dependent upon it any longer.

"We could not be at the mercy of those who controlled the money. We would do without cash. We would form a society based on land, cattle, Britanga tradition, and the New Testament Church.

"At first, we attempted to be a commune. That didn't work. There were too many conflicts. No one wants someone else making decisions for them.

"We settled just outside the Bugungu Game Preserve, near Lake Albert, but there were problems with the Banyoro tribe. They did not believe the land could support them and us, too. We wandered to the highlands of Mount Nyiragongo — but by then there were too many of us, almost four hundred, and we were chased away by the Rwanda government which did not want what they called 'Uganda trouble.'

"We were forced to depend completely on the Lord. That was what changed all of us. We had no place to go, no resources, no answers — just our mighty God.

"One day when he was hunting, Matthew says that the Spirit of the Lord overtook him — like Philip in the Book of Acts. He was transported to our valley. The plateau above was rich with game. The valley was fertile. There was plenty of water.

"The entire area was completely abandoned. Up in the caves, there are thousands of bones from a civilization that once flourished here. But we have no clue about where they went or why they left centuries ago."

It was quite a story.

Zuni studied Sarah's face. The old woman had known terrible pain and heartache. Zuni touched her hand, comfortingly. Sarah glanced at her and smiled.

"And now, we must understand why God has brought you to us," said the matriarch. "Great warfare is taking place in the heavenlies over you. That machine you brought with you is . . ." Sarah shuddered. "I believe it was meant to do great evil. Even now, terrible people are coming here to take it away and . . ."

Zuni was silent. She remembered Patrick saying that a lot of people had been killed getting it out of Russia. And Molech Gordini was not known for being squeamish about shedding blood. When he spent money, he was expecting to make a lot of money — even if the bodies had to pile up.

"You are safe here," Sarah said. "I do not believe the Lord sent you here to let us be destroyed. That is not His way. He loves His children.

"It is He who has hidden us time and time again from our enemies. Only He could make us invisible to those who come our way. He alone ensures that we do not go hungry. We have learned to trust in Him completely and to trust totally in His Word.

"I remember the first time that someone was healed by prayer. Matthew and the older men searched the Bible for weeks — making certain that it was not sorcery. They became convinced that it, indeed, was of God. Just like in the Book of Acts, our young men began preaching with great power. Many signs and wonders came to pass.

"Now, we are beginning to send out evangelism teams back to Uganda and all the surrounding countries. We do not tell where we come from. We preach the gospel and many are saved."

Zuni shivered, although she did not know why. A wave of intense emotion shook through her. "Where exactly are we?" she asked.

Sarah smiled benignly. "We call this valley and this city only 'Britanga'," she said softly, putting her hand on the American gun-runner's. "I am not sure that even Matthew knows exactly where we are."

Zuni looked down at the village.

"Will you pray with me?" asked Sarah suddenly.

"What?" exclaimed Zuni.

"I am filled with an urgency that I do not understand," said the old woman, her face ashen. "Great evil is nearby. O Father . . ."

The old woman sank to her knees. Zuni knelt beside her, one hand on the old woman's trembling shoulders.

"Protect us in this hour of danger," blurted Sarah. "O Lord. Arise! Let God arise and protect His people. Let His enemies be scattered. But let the righteous be blessed, let them rejoice with gladness because God has triumphed mightily."

The old black woman stood, her hand raised to the sky. "Let us rejoice with gladness! God has triumphed mightily!" She was weeping, tears rolling down her face. "Father, confuse and confound the enemies! Give them chaos and terror! Turn them one against the other!

"Divert them from their evil plans! Confuse them! Let their hatred and anger be turned one against another, O Lord!"

In Poland, the little boy named Ladislav paused in the middle of a soccer match. As his coach yelled at him to go after the ball, the youngster squinted at the sky.

"O Lord," he whispered, obediently charging into the scrimmage. "Protect that boy You showed me. Confuse the evil people who are looking for him. Get them all mixed up like You did the Russians before they finally left us alone."

Then, putting everything he had into it, Ladislav slid into the ball and slammed it away from his goal. A team member snagged it and began tearing toward the other goal.

"Confuse the enemy, O Lord," prayed Ladislav, panting.

And then he charged back after the ball.

❖   ❖   ❖

A small helicopter sped across the African sky.

Inside, Molech watched Valentina as she moaned over the map.

"Listen," Molech said, his voice oily. He smiled at Valentina. But she was elsewhere. He cleared his throat and gently touched her shoulder. Irritated, she blinked and looked up at him.

"Say," asked Molech, "is your computer as powerful as you say?"

"Absolutely!" she declared. "In its crates, it is downlinking. Downlinking. Downlinking right now as we speak. Anything, everything that is transmitted, bounced off a satellite, sent over a telephone wire, sent to a hard drive — EVERYTHING — is being absorbed. Its memory is infinite. Infinite. And as its power source, it harnesses the energy of the earth's rotation."

"Yes, yes, yes," smiled Molech. "Can it tell the future?"

"What?"

"Can it project the future?"

"I don't understand. Of course, with the proper software, it can correlate probabilities and make conjectures based on whatever information you want. But that's not its purpose."

"I want it to tell me the future."

Valentina was absolutely taken aback. "Why?"

"Imagine the profits. Look at the possibilities. If I know that wheat is going to skyrocket, I can buy up wheat futures today while the price is low."

Valentina's cheek twitched. "Molech," she whined. "We're on the verge of taking over the world's monetary system. Wheat futures are nothing compared to that. What I'm about to give you is ..."

"Do not tell me what is nothing." Molech's voice

had an edge Valentina had not heard before. "I will tell you what I want."

Valentina blinked, trying to mask her anger. "My LORRD is not a crystal ball. This is not a carnival sideshow. I am going to shame the mighty! We are going to bring the world to a halt!"

"You will show me the future!"

Valentina clenched her eyes shut. Screaming her rage into the cosmos, she was hurled, flying and shrieking across the astral wildernesses. Then, she found herself surrounded by her dark counselors. Laughing, they showed her a program so simple and powerful that it took her breath away.

"I will show you the future," Valentina proclaimed to Molech. Her eyes were distant.

Gordini watched her carefully, then smiled with evil pleasure.

"The future?" he asked.

Valentina sneered in distaste, then smiled. "Yes. I'll give you a crystal ball like no other."

"Listen," whined Valentina as Molech's helicopter neared the plateau. She attempted to quell her growing frustration. "I don't think you understand."

Gordini glowered at her, then studied the map. "Understand what?"

"Look," insisted Valentina, "We're going to shut down world communications. We're going to take over everything in a massive shutdown. Then, we'll offer to restore civilian telecommunications and commercial broadcasting. In return, the world's financial services will have to channel everything through us. We will levy a 1 percent surcharge on all transactions. They'll have to pay us daily — and we'll take it in Tokyo real estate, German art treasures, Saudi oil fields — whatever pleases us."

Molech stared at Valentina in unbelief.

"Don't you see?" she exclaimed. "Look at the billions of dollars that change hands daily. How can we lose? Just the first hour will be far more profitable than your little scheme with wheat futures.

"It is so simple. If they refuse to cooperate, then we just open a few select communications lines and lob a few American nuclear warheads here, a few Chinese warheads, there and a dozen Russian or French warheads everywhere. The airbursts alone will wipe out every civilian computer system on earth — just the electromagnetic shock. Planes will fall out of the skies. No television manufactured since 1980 will ever work again. No car with electronic ignition will ever run again. We'll bring them to their knees. Maybe we'll wipe out a third of the world's population. No problem — fewer mouths to feed.

"Then we'll offer our services again. This time, we'll have the only operational backup system in existence. We'll have all their data — intact — and they won't. It'll be a choice of sending all their transactions through us or returning to the Stone Age."

Molech's eyes became steely. With careful patience, in a little pig voice, he whined, "I told you what I want."

"I know what you said, I just don't think you . . ."

His face began to flush. "I want to know the future," he hissed. "Can your silly little computer do it or not?"

"Sure," spat Valentina between gritted teeth. "But it doesn't . . ."

"Will it tell me when I am going to die?" shrieked Gordini.

"What?" exclaimed Valentina.

Gordini leered his most abusive leer. "I want to know the day and hour of my death."

His words pushed Valentina over the edge.

Out she soared across the cosmic abyss. "He is insane!" she howled to her spirit masters, her voice reverberating as a hoarse shriek. "He doesn't know the first thing about computers, does he? Any fool knows that sort of forecasting requires incredible variables and deals in data that just isn't mathematically organizable. This crazy man is talking about events that aren't reasonably predictable."

"Then you cannot tell the future?" hissed Gordini.

Furious at his intrusion into her private universe, Valentina imagined her fingers around his neck. She laughed as her spirit guides whispered descriptions of his painful and humiliating death.

"Yes, yes, yes," she oozed. "Listen to what this, this man who drugs small children wants. Yes, yes, with my LORRD's infinite memory we can deal in preposterous amounts of data. Supposing we can use as control data . . . no, let me think. Okay, if we factor the infinite details of every man, woman, or child whose life statistics are available, some interesting conclusions may be drawn." Her lip curled in murderous sarcasm. "Yes, yes, yes, we will do it for this impotent, gluttonous madman."

Molech's ears turned bright red. He peered at her, holding open her eyelids — although her eyeballs were turned back in her head. He waved his revolver in her face. "And you will foretell the sex of my third wife's unborn child."

"Yes, yes, yes," spewed Valentina, her voice thick with contempt. "The little liar man is also an idiot. We would give the fool his pitiful world and he tells us he wants to dabble in parlor tricks."

Molech calmly pulled back the hammer of his revolver.

"Yes, yes, yes," exclaimed Valentina. "We have seen his raging, insecure ego destroy the brightest and the most brilliant minds in the world. We have heard him lie to everyone who demands accountability of him. Oh yes, this is the man who bullies even his own children and traps them into lifelong servitude in his care while squealing in his pig voice that he loves them. Yes, yes, we can correlate seeming randoms and draw conclusions that allow projections. Of course." She began to shake as if stricken with palsy.

But Gordini would never see it, whispered her spirit guides.

"He would die first."

Painfully, they assured. *Horribly.*

"Yes, yes, yes," she crooned, her voice rolling up and down in contempt, "it may take us a while to work out the bugs. This deviant glutton doesn't seem to understand that all data may not be relevant." She paused, as if talking to herself. "No, that's the whole point, isn't it? All the facts are very important. This is the first time that a system has the capacity to process all the recorded knowledge of mankind."

Molech smiled. "And I wish to talk to God."

But Valentina no longer heard him. She was gone. The whites of her eyes stared blankly. She gasped for breath, then began to drool.

Molech shook her.

But she was completely gone, disappeared into her private cosmos — howling her vengeful contempt and revulsion. Molech slapped her across the face, once, twice, three times.

"What?" shrieked Valentina.

"Tell me your computer will let me talk to God."

"What?" howled Valentina. But before he could answer, she was at his throat. She bit him, clamping down onto his jugular.

Gordini's feet slammed into the instrument panel. As the blank-eyed Valentina held onto her toothy grip, she attempted to wrestle away his revolver.

Gordini squeezed off four quick shots.

Instead of killing her, the bullets shattered the windshield. In the sudden wind blast, a shard of plexiglass drove deep into the pilot's chest, killing him. Valentina fell into the floor — as if dead.

Cursing violently, Molech grabbed the controls and attempted to kick Valentina out of the careening chopper. Crazily she came to life and dived at his throat again, screaming and attempting to scratch his eyes out.

❖   ❖   ❖

"Look!" pointed Daniel.

The boys gawked into the sky.

An out-of-control helicopter twisted into view, speeding toward the boys like a runaway eggbeater.

Upside down not twenty feet off the ground, it suddenly collapsed into the high grass, thrashing madly, then grinding to a smoky halt, two of its great blades digging into the ground, one twisting crazily skyward.

As if oblivious to their precarious landing, two screaming figures scuffled out of the broken windshield and wrestled in the grass.

Silently, the boys crept near — disbelieving their own eyes.

"Talk to God?" screeched Valentina, spittle flowing down her chin. "Talk to God? You are a fool. A fool! There is no God. We are God. You insult us! You defile our vision. We could have given you *anything.*"

Stumbling to his feet, Molech Gordini held his revolver against her nose. "I want to talk to God," he croaked evenly. "You will assist me or you will die. Decide now."

Valentina's eyes again turned back in her head. She howled up at the sky, then violently began twitching. "We can talk to God. Anyone can talk to God. We are God. Or maybe the fool wants us to go find him a priest!"

"Valentina," whispered Molech, his gun point-blank in her face. "I want to hear His voice."

With a mad shriek, she fell on the ground, writhing, tearing her clothes, and cutting her skin on the small rocks. "We do not answer," she croaked. "We do not answer. We do not answer. We are God. The baby killer can talk to us."

"Valentina, my pet," soothed Molech. "Come, come now, help me. I wish to talk to Him. I want to make Him a deal that He cannot refuse."

She lay still.

"Valentina, my darling," he cooed.

She squirmed in rage.

She was then still. Far, far away in another spiritual plane, she was attended by hundreds of hideous, patient, soothing spirit guides. Her monstrous friends touched her and flattered her and whispered advice. If this crazy human Gordini wanted to talk to a god, then they could conjure one up.

Or several. Perhaps a whole crowd.

"One that would gobble up his liver?" she hissed.

Yes, yes, yesssssssss.

She opened her eyes.

"Okay," she said.

She sat up and began throwing dust in the air, showering herself and him with dirt.

He smiled.

"Of course," she said. "I can do it."

Watching the scene from the high grass, Patrick nudged Daniel. "I know that man. We gotta get outa here. He is the guy who is after my mom and me. Listen, he has to be one of the most evil people alive."

Transfixed by the bizarre theater playing before them, Daniel nodded. He whispered orders to the other boys. Silently, they slipped away. From behind a huge pile of boulders at least a half-mile away from the wrecked helicopter, they turned and watched the intruders again.

Shaken, Daniel knelt in prayer.

"That was Molech Gordini," said Patrick, his voice trembling. "I don't know who the crazy woman is, but they can't be alone. They've got to be part of an enormous search underway for me and my mom — or actually for that computer your dad stashed in that cave. We've got to warn my mother."

Around Daniel, the other boys dropped to their knees. "Father," prayed Daniel, "protect us from the terrible evil that we have just seen. Ours is not a spirit of fear, but of a . . . of a sound mind . . . not like what we just saw. Help us, Lord!

The other boys nodded their agreement.

Daniel stood suddenly. "I have to go tell my dad," he said.

In single file, the young boys set out running back to Britanga.

Patrick kept up with Daniel — offering new information about Molech — then fretting about the danger.

Suddenly, Daniel halted. "Look," he declared, his face grim. "Our people escaped Idi Amin. They hid from Milton Obote's army. How? The same way that the baby Jesus hid from Herod's soldiers. God protected us, hid us, provided for us, and kept us ahead of the ones who desired to murder us."

Patrick squinted.

"God will protect us," proclaimed Daniel. He turned and repeated his words to the boys of the village. Solemnly, they all nodded.

Andrew stepped up and put his hand on Patrick's shoulder. He grinned, completely unafraid, and yammered something incomprehensible. Patrick looked to Daniel for translation.

"He says that you will now see the mighty hand of the One who formed you in your mother's womb and who miraculously brought you here to be safe from the world to live here among the people. He wants us all to pray for you that you will not be afraid."

Patrick grinned. "Sure," he said.

In the tall grass, the skinny, black youth placed one hand on Patrick's head and lifted another hand to heaven. Loudly and with enormous confidence in his young voice, he prayed to the Great God he knew and loved. The other boys joined in.

Filled with an immense peace that he had never known before, Patrick bowed his head and prayed, too, overflowing with a feeling of belonging. Yes, God had sent him to this place, he knew. He sniffled and suddenly knelt in the dirt.

"God," he prayed aloud, lifting his hands to heaven. "Man, I know You are there. I know it. I feel You all around me. I remember how You grabbed me and Mom out of that volcano yesterday when I asked You to help us. I really thank You for all of these great guys, and I ask You to keep me and them safe from Molech and his soldiers."

Patrick stared up at the sky. He lowered his hands, then stood, and lifted his hands again. He turned around and around, suddenly laughing. Innocent and filled with great joy, he laughed and ran with his new friends.

Exhilarated, they raced back to Britanga with their incredible story.

As the boys trotted down the cliffs, Daniel shouted at a familiar figure. The boys gathered around Matthew. Excitedly, Daniel told of the helicopter crash and the wild rantings of Molech and Valentina.

Squinting, Matthew looked Patrick over, then smiled knowingly. "You seem to have gone native," he said gently.

Not understanding, Patrick looked down and for the first time remembered that he, too, like the rest of the boys had not dressed before scaling the cliffs to stalk the zebras.

At least he was still wearing his ripped-up shorts.

"Well, they have finally come," the mayor said wryly. "But we knew they would. Perhaps we will have the opportunity to speak to them about their relationship with Jesus Christ."

Patrick looked confused. Matthew was completely serious. "Look," exclaimed the American boy. "That guy kills people."

It was as if no one heard him.

Down the narrow trail the boys ran behind Matthew.

As they passed various fields, Matthew called out to men working there. Some of the boys fell out, running up to their fathers, and excitedly telling what had happened.

By the time Matthew reached the center of the village, a crowd had already gathered. The old men of the community formed a circle and sat on grass mats. Solemnly, they listened to Daniel's testimony, then began to question Patrick as Matthew and Daniel translated.

As well as he could, Patrick explained that he and his mother had been smuggling the computer to Mombasa. He related some of the stories he had heard about Molech. At the first mention of Gordini's first name, there was an audible gasp.

"Molech?" inquired Matthew, "like the great, evil demon that the Canaanites worshiped and to whom they sacrificed their babies?"

"I don't know," shrugged Patrick.

The men murmured among themselves. A debate began. Patrick nudged Daniel, who began translating bits and pieces. Basically, the old men were arguing whether Gordini came under Old Testament commands to utterly destroy evil and wicked kings who defiled Canaan. The counter-argument was that under New Testament teaching, they had no choice but to love their enemies and to pray for them.

Matthew reminded the men of the village that the Bible tells believers to be wise in dealing with evil — but that the apostle Paul begged to be allowed to preach to the mad Roman Caesar who was spreading persecution throughout the known world.

They talked on. Zuni made her way to the front of the group. "You're getting one heck of a sunburn," she whispered to Patrick. "What on earth is going on?"

"Gordini's here," exclaimed the boy. "We were swimming and then . . . well, we saw this helicopter crash and rushed back here to warn everybody."

Daniel nudged him. "We're going to have a continuous prayer vigil for Molech and his men," said the older boy. "We are going to pray that the Lord will change their evil hearts and that He will protect us from any weapon formed against us."

"Matthew," Zuni said loudly. "I think this has gone far enough. Just give me my cargo. I'll deliver it to him."

The mayor translated. The men of the village rumbled their disapproval.

"No," said Matthew. "There is great power in those crates. Power that must be harnessed for good. We cannot let it fall into the hands of ruthless men."

After more than an hour of debate, a plan was finally agreed upon. First, a non-stop prayer vigil would begin immediately, with at least three people praying at one time. Second, scouting parties would keep an eye on Molech and Valentina and do whatever was necessary to keep them wandering in circles — or at least away from the village and the hidden valley.

Third, in the night, a work party would hide the wrecks of the chopper and the Martin.

As they began enlisting volunteers, Patrick stepped forward. There was a unanimous rumble of approval. Daniel glanced back at him. "Do you know what you volunteered for?"

Patrick shook his head.

Daniel grinned. "You offered to show up for the 4 a.m.-to-dawn shift of the prayer vigil."

Patrick groaned. "It's okay," assured Daniel. "Andrew and I said we'd come, too, to help keep you awake. Have you ever prayed for two hours before?"

Patrick rolled his eyes.

Daniel laughed heartily and slapped him on the shoulder. "Not much of a Christian, eh? Well, we'll see what shape you're in come morning!"

"He is an idiot!" screamed Valentina to her spirit guide — pointing toward Gordini. Her face red, she leaned against a rock, her sides heaving. She was in no shape to be hiking across Africa. "He — HE! — HE got us into this."

"Watch yourself," snarled Gordini, collapsing against the trunk of a tree.

In the high grass, Britanga men and boys watched in total silence. Valentina and Molech had wandered almost ten miles from their crashed chopper and were nearing Mt. Matoke volcano, one of the world's few perfectly symmetrical volcanic cones.

Safely out of earshot, one of the old men pointed out to Patrick a tall column standing high above the grassy sea.

"That is Matthew and Daniel's miracle tree," he said softly, telling Patrick how three years before, Daniel and Matthew had been hunting in a forest when the volcano erupted suddenly. Caught in a firestorm of falling ash and pumice, the two had taken refuge in a hollow tree.

When the lava flowed down Mt. Matoke, it destroyed the entire forest, but miraculously parted before coming to Matthew and Daniel's tree. Even so, the intense heat had incinerated the top of the tree.

For two days, father and son had waited inside the trunk, praying and trusting God. They believed that God would keep them safe and protected. He did.

When they emerged from their sanctuary, they did not believe the scene. The forest was gone.

Now Patrick gazed over at Mt. Matoke, rising above them, beautiful, majestic, and powerful. "Wow," he breathed.

Darkness began to fall.

"How long have your people lived here?" asked Patrick, sitting against a tree. Squatting next to him, Matthew peered into the darkness. The main scouting party was camping a safe distance away from the intruders. Only three kept a silent vigil over Molech and Valentina's attempt to build a campfire.

"Ever since terrible persecution forced us to flee our homeland in Uganda," whispered Matthew. "You whites do not know what Africa has endured."

"Don't be so sure," said Patrick softly. "I have lived here all my life. My grandfather was killed by guerrillas. My grandmother and Mom were almost murdered."

"Really?" exclaimed Matthew in surprise.

"She was very little," Patrick said. "My grandparents were missionaries in what was Southern Rhodesia. When it became Zimbabwe and the whites no longer ran the government, things were very bad. My grandparents stayed and ran a hospital in Bulawayo. It was rough, but they hung in there. Then, when Mom was just old enough to go to school, there was a civil war. My grandfather was murdered. My grandmother and Mom were taken away, driven for a very long time across the countryside until they came to a French Catholic mission where the guerrillas had taken a number of nuns hostage.

"My grandmother and my mother were forced to stay there for a very long time. The guerrillas would come in at night and rape whomever they wished. Two of the nuns went insane. But Mom has told me about one named Mary Simone who gave in and actually would be . . . sexy, I guess. Mom told me that she was too little to know what was going on, but that nun was keeping the soldiers away from the rest of the women. Her shame was great, but she sacrificed the purity that was so important to her so that my mom and grandmother did not become their playthings."

Patrick looked up with tears in his eyes.

"Mom told me that she was too young to understand. Since the other, older women shunned the nun, she did, too. That nun was so noble, she did not see their stupidity. She only saw Jesus. Mom told me that He let himself be whipped and scourged and crucified for all of us, so that nun let herself be humiliated by her enemies and her friends . . . for my mother."

Patrick was silent. He offered no other details.

"Was your grandfather a doctor?" whispered Matthew.

Patrick nodded.

"The rebels killed off all our leaders, too," said Matthew. "First they murdered all the elected officials and the educated people. They then targeted anybody who showed any kind of leadership. One of my uncles was burned to death by a mob a week after he was elected chairman of a committee to build a new basketball court on our block."

"Why?" asked Patrick.

"Fear, intimidation," shrugged Matthew. "To destroy the human soul. To quench hope. To eliminate anyone with courage so that the masses could be led like sheep to the slaughter."

"How did you survive?" asked Patrick.

"God," said Matthew. "We learned to depend completely on Him. There were times when He made us invisible to our enemies. They passed right by us and did not stop. He provided us with food, too.

"When all the doctors were gone and all the medicine, we were forced to look to the Lord completely. I believe in medicine. We keep a stockpile of antibiotics and soon will send three of our young men out to go to medical school. God takes care of us."

Patrick looked skeptical.

"I remember once," reflected Matthew, "when I was very sick with coughing and fatigue. I just couldn't get over it. I was getting sicker and sicker, but I had to keep working.

"I thought it was my burden.

"Then Daniel got sick. He was only four years old. We had no doctor and no medicine. His throat was raw and he had white blisters in his mouth. He could hardly talk. He was having a terrible time talking. He just cried and coughed and cried.

"I realized that I had been so stupid.

"I had tried to do everything myself. Well, the time had come when I could do nothing. If I did not depend on the Lord to save my little boy, he was going to die.

"So, I anointed his head with oil and I simply asked the Lord to heal us both.

"The next day, we were both stronger.

"We improved daily.

"That's the way we have had to live here. We have no choice. The Lord sends us rain for our crops. He sends us the spring floods to fertilize our fields. He keeps the grassy plains full of game. He keeps the mosquitoes away that would bring malaria — and flies that would spread sleeping sickness. Our river flows strong and has plenty of fish. It is not filled with parasites — so our children can play and swim without fear.

"This is not the Garden of Eden. We have to work very hard. There is sickness and heartache. Our people get into disputes, but we trust the Lord and know that He alone is our Source and our Provider and our Protector. He is our mighty refuge, our mountain of strength. He hides us under His wing."

Matthew paused.

"Unless you have been one of our people, you cannot grasp what it means to be a heathen in Africa. But I have seen it.

"I made my choice.

"This is the only way that works."

Patrick accepted a gift of a banana from Andrew, who crawled up beside them in the tall grass. The boy grinned although he could not understand a word they were saying.

"As a boy," continued Matthew. "I heard it said many, many times that we Africans should return to our ancient traditions and abandon the white man's slave cult — Christianity.

"I was told that I was the noble savage — that I should return to the religion of my famous great-grandfather. His religion, alone, had the answers for Africans, not the slave cult filled with lies about a loving, murdered, forgiving God. Telling us to forgive your enemies was part of the white man's trick, I was told. It was to get us to put down our spears and surrender to the lying white man — and to forgive him whenever he betrayed us.

"He was our enemy, I was taught. Why else was he so intent on teaching that we should constantly forgive our enemies and be good to those who did evil to us? Why else, indeed! So he could enslave us!

"After my father and brothers were murdered, I turned my back on Jesus Christ. However, I didn't return to the ways of my ancestors, either. The sorcerers would have been glad to have me. They already had my brother, John.

"I didn't want to be one of them. I didn't want anything to do with Jesus Christ, either. Gods and spirits and all that hocus-pocus were for old, foolish people, I decided. I was too intelligent of a person for all that. I wanted to go to college and be a sociologist or a physicist in America or England maybe or the Soviet Union. I didn't particularly care. I just wanted an education. I didn't want to have to work so hard like my father had — grubbing for everything he had.

"When my only surviving brother, John, got into witchcraft, I had to see what it was all about.

"My little brother had become a member of a society where fear controls by day and by night — especially at night! You cannot imagine life under constant surveillance by countless spirits, using animate and inanimate mediators, some human, some supposedly half-human, to accomplish their evil purposes. You cannot sense the monotony of a life when you are never safe from attack from unseen forces. Health and happiness are liable to be snatched from you without warning.

"John's friends were into old jungle drugs that supposedly helped you find your spirit guide. John had been doing the drugs a lot and believed that he was able to turn into a scorpion in the night." Matthew shrugged.

"One night, I did their mystical powders with them and was dancing. I was carried away on the wings of the great fruit bat. I saw through his eyes. I heard with his ears. I was shown amazing things. The great fruit bat was to be my spirit guide. He would show me the secrets of the spirit world."

Matthew squinted, his eyes faraway. "I was seduced. I ripped off my white man's clothes and stood in the nakedness of my ancestors — and I was proud for the first time that I was an African.

"I was seduced by half-truths. I was given enough truth so that I would swallow the terrible lies of evil bondage that the witchdoctor has used for centuries to enslave my people.

"I renounced Christianity and underwent their bloody Ceremony of Purification to begin training as a witch doctor and in preparation for assuming the post of custodian of our sacred tribal relics, the post that our great-grandfather had held."

Over the next summer, eighteen-year-old Matthew was taught the sacred legends and closely guarded secrets of Britanga superstition. He was given the great relics and pronounced their protector.

One special holy night, he was summoned by the Britanga spirit-worshipers to help prepare a powerful curse that was meant to bring terrible death and revenge upon the murderers who had laid waste the province.

"The old witchdoctor, Omo Karianga, who had so intensely hated my father, stood atop a sacred high place," Matthew told Patrick. "A lion skin was wrapped round his wrinkled body. His blind eyes stared blankly into the night — his old body filled with vengeance and hate. He was given a drugged holy potion, which he drained — then fell to the ground, writhing, and convulsing. He shrieked again and again, then was silent.

"Suddenly, he put his hands to the back of his neck, his face contorted. 'Ohhhhhhh!' he wailed, then was horribly sick, vomiting onto the ground.

"Collecting himself and struggling, very slowly, to his feet, Omo Karianga began a powerful stamping to and fro, his arms bent above his head as if carrying the whole world which, but for his support, would crash out of the sky. His blind eyes unfocused, his ancient lungs struggling for breath with desperate spasms, he summoned his spirit guide in a deep chant. After several minutes, drained and faltering, he sat down, withdrew to himself and became silent again.

"The crowd gathered at the bottom of the hill and murmured a chant to their own spirit guides to gather around and give them their revenge. Slowly, the old sorcerer began to move again.

"He trembled, his eyes turned back in his head. He leaped up, dancing convulsively. He shrieked over and over, his old voice rising into the heavens.

"We were all supposed to take the same potion," said Matthew. "It was really nasty stuff. I tried to back out, but they held me down and poured it into my mouth, forcing me to swallow. It was as if someone had hit me in the chest with a burning log. I put my hands to my throat and could feel my head come off in my hands.

"Amazed, hallucinating, of course, I believed I was holding my head in my fists, watching my headless body writhe in the dust. I felt as if someone had eased a burning stick down my throat. My lungs were filled with burning ashes. I reeled, unable to breathe. I passed out completely.

"Excitedly, the crowd chanted, passing around gourds filled with the same potion. Shrieks, howls, then groans, and the sounds of vomiting and convulsions filled the night. Hundreds of bodies twisted in the dirt, writhing blindly — in terrible pain as the drugged drink inflamed their chests and sent searing pain through their heads.

"But as a single body, they rose, writhing, dancing, chanting, cursing, and demanding the blood of their enemy. It was as if they were possessed by the same terrible evil — twisting their bodies like a great snake that exulted in their pain and hatred.

"Up on the hill, Omo Karianga began to chant a sacred blood oath — an ancient spirit curse on the fertility of the enemy's women, the masculinity of their sons, and the wisdom of their old men. It visualized violation of the enemy's ancient holy graves — that the old tombs would be buried under many feet of water so that the bodies of the honored dead would become food for worms and fish.

"Then he declared a holy war of extermination against every soldier who opposed a single member of the Britanga.

"As the old man waited, the moon rose. There was a rustling in the forest at the base of the hill on which the old man stood.

"Witch doctors dressed as skeletons, ghosts, and corpses emerged and started crawling up the hill, shrieking a song reviling the enemy's dishonored dead. Clawing their way up the turf, they wept their anger and revenge against the enemy who had raped their young girls, hacked to death the old women, necklaced the young men, and humiliated the elders, making the old men serve as latrine servants in the guerrilla armies.

"A goat was sent running up to Omo Karianga. On its back was a scarecrow-looking rag-doll figure of a soldier, complete with shoulder bars, chest ribbons, and brightly colored belts. In a rage, the old man lashed out with his spear. Although he was completely blind and had been for years, his single blow decapitated the goat. It fell, kicking and gasping, headless, bleeding all over the 'soldier' on its back and all over Omo Karianga.

"A man, daubed all over in hideous white and yellow with brown circles, ran up to the old man. Clutching the old witchdoctor's thigh, he shrieked hideously, 'They have killed me, Omo Karianga! They have killed me! Will you not avenge my blood? They have scattered my bones so my loved ones cannot bury my body. My soul cannot rest! Will you not avenge my eternal misery, Omo Karianga? Will you not avenge my torment?'

" 'Will you not avenge him?' called Omo Karianga into the night.

"From the shadows, the writhing, drugged worshipers danced. 'We will avenge him!' they chanted.

" 'Will you not avenge him?' repeated Omo Karianga.

" 'We will avenge him!' they chanted.

"Horrible shrieks filled the air. Dramatically, with his hands covering his loins, then sweeping to cover his face, Omo Karianga knelt and placed his head on the ground, then stood, his voice loud in a chant invoking the protecting, watchful Britanga spirits of the dead. 'Avenge him,' he screamed.

"Perspiration ran down his wrinkled face. His whole body trembled as he stretched his hands high over his head. He began to cry out terrible curses upon the enemy. He described terrible things — an epidemic of the birth of twisted freaks, the filling of wells with poisons that destroyed the mind and the vital organs, the onslaught of a new and horrible plague that would sweep through the enemy's camp.

"He shivered as he described this hideous disease that would subject its victims to the most painful and humiliating of deaths — years of wasting, rotting, withering away while the victim became hated and scorned by all mankind.

"He described innocent children falling, writhing, and dying with wretched pleas in their mouths, their flesh melting from their bones. He pictured young girls giving birth to serpents. He shrieked and described old women weeping over a nation turned into walking, babbling corpses.

"Then, with an animal-like cry that ripped the darkness, Omo Karianga fell to the ground as if he were dead. He writhed, then was motionless.

"A terrible chant of revenge and hate echoed around him.

"I remember regaining consciousness," said Matthew. "I was wearing the bloody corpse of the goat. Around me, everyone had begun a savage, silent, stamping dance to the accompaniment of clapping by the women. Before me old Omo danced — and while he danced he became as mad as a demon. He turned his spear's sharp head in his hand, stabbing his thighs until blood ran freely. He leaped high into the air and hurled himself to the ground. Finally, he jumped a full four feet into the air and as he landed he seemed to attack me. He slashed the belly of the goat draped over me and dragged out its intestines with his teeth.

"He continued to dance in front of me, tearing the guts of the goat to pieces with his hands and teeth and spitting pieces all over the place. I suppose his mad and gory dance was symbolic of the curse he was wishing on the soldiers. He wished they would go mad and disembowel their own children.

"At this stage the four boys, one of them my little brother John, hurled themselves upon the hill and danced wildly around the old man. They spat on him and pretended to gouge out his eyes and tear his ears from his head. Then the youngest leaped on my back and fastened his arms around my neck, forcing me to the ground in a symbolism of final, disgraceful, and horrible death.

"Other goats were hurled alive onto the hill. The other witch doctors were in a frenzy, strangling the goats, beating them with their bare fists, kicking, and abusing the animals.

"Then, a thoroughly maddened Omo cut the belly of the largest goat and dragged out its entrails. He then grabbed the youngest boy who had run up with John and pushed the child, still alive, into the stomach cavity of the gutted goat, which the other witchdoctors closed quickly by a thong tied around it like a saddle.

"The dead goat with the living boy inside — who was now screaming and fighting to get out — was brought before Omo Karianga. He raised his hands to the skies. His voice was harsh when he said, 'Grant that their women die at childbirth and their young never see the light of day, Oh Ancient Ones of Britanga!' He then began to stab the goat with his spear.

"Crazily, the others joined in until blood was dripping from it and the boy inside was still."

Matthew looked at Patrick, his eyes filled with tears.

"The boy was dead. They had killed him and thought nothing of it. Human life was nothing. It could have been John. Very easily, it might have been my little brother."

Matthew told of rushing away from the scene, horrified and ashamed that he had taken part.

"Throughout that night, I could hear the orgy going on up on the hill. I fell to my knees and asked my Heavenly Father to forgive me for being a part of something so horrible, so evil, so demonic. I prayed for the safety of my little brother."

Matthew sighed. "The Lord heard my prayer. He forgave me. He delivered me from the evil that had filled my body that night when I drank that potion. I honestly believe that I was possessed by a wicked spirit. But the anointing of the Lord was upon me, although I had renounced Jesus Christ." Matthew's eyes were filled with tears.

"I had broken the heart of the Saviour who loved

me so, but still He had not left me. He was protecting me. He let me see the terrible evil that I was choosing. He welcomed me back with open arms when I ran to Him in repentance.

"He let me see that I could be an African without being a heathen. I can honor the traditions and customs of my forebears without apology — but I do not have to be a savage, too. I am an African. I can stalk the giraffe in the high grass and run like the wind or go fishing in the river or gather turtle eggs. I am an African. And I love Jesus Christ."

"What about your brother?" asked Patrick.

Matthew shook his head. "I do not know," he said softly. "I have not seen him again since that night. I believe my brother is dead."

Looking around for his little brother, José Chimon, Miguel tried to sit up. He was in a hospital room, his head sheathed in bandages. He squinted through his blurry good eye.

His bed was surrounded by young Lions.

Where was José? One kid leaned against Miguel's bed, a shotgun resting against his thigh. Like some kind of movie Mexican bandit, the kid wore an ammo belt. He was watching Miquel's TV — the "Oprah Winfrey Show."

"Hey, Dude!" greeted José, leaning over into Miguel's face. "What you think, Blood?"

Miguel was in pain. "Chimon," he whispered. "There you are. Man, what happened?"

"Hey, Man, your Jesus Christ stuff didn't do you much good. Them Dukes, they tried to take off your face. They wasted Ochoa — sent him to the devil. But we hit 'em. We hit 'em hard. It's war, Man. Last night, we burned out their building — then shot maybe twenty of them as they ran out like rats. It was beautiful. We got Roberto Elegante, that . . ." José's obscene description of the big Dukes leader was vivid and profane. He grinned proudly at Miguel. "We takin' care of you, Bro'. You just rest and know that your colors are watchin' over you."

Miguel moaned. "Don't do that, Man," he spat at his brother. "I forbid you to kill anybody, Man."

"Too late," laughed José. "They dead, Man. Bunch of 'em. All fall down, too bad, bro. Wish you'd said something earlier." He and all his buddies roared with laughter, brandishing their weapons, and pretending to shoot at each other. A nurse stopped in and looked quite worried for her own safety.

She gave Miguel a pill that put him back to sleep. In the night, the former addict awoke. A matronly attendant was changing his sheets, rolling him over rather roughly.

"Hey," protested a sleepy kid sprawled out in a chair beside Miguel's bed. In his lap was an automatic pistol.

"You just keep out of the way," thundered the woman. "Lazy punk kids."

"Hey," whispered Miguel. "I'm not like that."

The woman flashed a withering look at him. She finished making the bed and stomped out of the room.

Miguel frowned.

In the darkness of the hospital, he wondered just what God was up to. Why had he almost been killed? What was God doing?

In his bed, Miguel clenched his eyes shut.

"Lord," he prayed, "I don't understand. I really don't understand at all. Man, what is all this about?"

In the darkness of the room, he began to realize that it was about José Chimon. The Lord was answering Miguel's repeated, fervent prayer that the boy would accept Him as his Saviour.

"Why this way?" Miguel prayed. Deep within him, he had a stunning realization, as if a complete thought had formed from outside: "My Son died for you. Are you willing to die for José Chimon?"

Of course he wouldn't mind dying if that's what it would take.

He realized that he would not have to die. Jesus had died for José. That was enough. Ours is not a God who asks for human sacrifice.

"Father," prayed Miguel in the dark night, "I don't know what You are doing here. I'm not very experienced in all this stuff. But, Father, I pray that You will touch my little brother. I sure love him. I want him to know You, Lord. Father God, protect and love my brother. Open his heart to You. Open his ears to Your truth."

Miguel sighed and then knew everything was going to be okay.

He silently praised the Lord and suddenly, he was filled with a vision. He saw ten million people across the world praying for the gangs, the druggies, and the crazies.

Five million of them would be kids.

"Wow," whispered Miguel. "Wow."

He saw a revival sweeping across Los Angeles and transforming San Diego, San Antonio, Detroit, Cleveland, Miami, and — his breath was taken away — he saw the millions fervently praying for New York.

Miguel clenched his eyes shut. "Father," he prayed, "what are You trying to say to me?"

He saw lonely people dying every day in the filth and horror that fills America's great Sodom and Gomorrah — New York City. He saw the thousands of runaways selling themselves for cheap sex. He saw thousands dying of AIDS on the curbs and filling the subway stations.

He saw a new, terrible drug sweeping through the city.

He saw ten million Christians praying that the plague would be thrown back into the pit of hell from which it had come.

"O Father," prayed Miguel, "why have You shown me this?"

"Go tell them to pray," came the message deep in his heart.

"Me?" exclaimed Miguel. "Man, I'm a junkie. I've got my head half-blown away. I'm sitting in a hospital with no home, no job, no money, nobody but my gangbanging little brother out on the streets killing people because of me."

"Go tell them to pray," the Father spoke again.

"Father," pleaded Miguel, "who is going to listen to me?"

Miguel squinted. It sounded like a line out of a baseball movie.

"If you tell them, they will pray."

❖   ❖   ❖

In the night, an old missionary was on her knees.

"Lord, protect Zuni and Patrick," she prayed. "I do not know where they are. I do not know why I feel such continuing concern for them, but . . ."

She paused, stunned.

"What, Lord?" she whispered.

"Five million kids praying."

"What?" she asked silently, her lips moving without sound.

"I am calling five million kids to pray," the voice spoke again.

Johanna Graham trembled under the power of the message. It was as if a branding iron had touched her spine. Its incredible electricity swept through her, stunning her with its intensity. Goose bumps covered her arms.

"Father," whispered Johanna, "will my grandson be one of them?"

She exhaled in the darkness.

"O Lord," she whispered, "such a vision. To see my grandson on his knees with five million other kids burdened with heartache for the violence and greed defiling great, wonderful America. O Lord . . ." She sank to the floor, her face pressed against the linoleum. "Yes," she murmured. "O Lord, I thank You for this vision. Now, I ask that You would awaken these young hearts across America. Let this be a mighty move of Your Spirit as they are filled with concern for their nation.

"Demonstrate to them, O Lord, Your mighty power and love. Yes, Lord, I see this vision. I see it, Father. Lord, I just plead the blood of Jesus Christ on this vision. Raise up these young intercessors with their young hearts tuned in to Your heart, listening and seeking Your guidance. Thank You, Lord. Thank You, thank You."

Suddenly, Johanna Graham saw another vision — of Noel and Zuni and Patrick running through a sea of high grass, laughing, and enjoying each other just like a real family.

Then the scene was gone.

Stunned, the old woman blinked.

She had never particularly liked Noel. He was a rather boring, quiet type — not a bold risk-taker like her daughter.

Had the Lord said that he and Zuni would get back together?

No.

Had He told her to pray that they would? That Patrick should go through adolescence with his dad at his side?

Johanna winced and tried to understand.

She trembled — and began to pray.

✤   ✤   ✤

In Australia, Aborigine hotel maid Helen Kalgoorlie stood outside her room and gazed up at the stars. "Oh, Lord," she proclaimed in the language of her ancestors, "I see ten million intercessors on their knees. Yes, Lord, let it be! And five million of them kids. America has been such a blessing, and now it is filled with such misery.

"Father, I lift up America. Father God, in the precious name of Your Son, the Lord Jesus Christ, I present before You their violence and perversity. America's people do not remember You. They are so proud — believing foolishly that they are responsible for their great blessings. Let them see how terrible things are. Let them see that this may be America's final generation. Hear my prayer, Father."

In Gdansk, Poland, eleven-year-old Ladislav sat up in bed. "Our Father," prayed the little boy, "five million American kids?" He stared out his window. "Let them know You. Let them see Your mighty power. You have delivered Poland when all was lost. You can do it for America if they will just ask."

The youngster paused, filled with exuberance. "Five million American kids," he murmured. "Is that Your desire, O Lord?"

"Do You want me to go to America and tell the kids to pray?" he prayed.

"No," came the answer. "I want you to pray and I want you to learn about spiritual warfare.

"I want you to see My power and what happens when you seek Me."

"Yes, God," whispered Ladislav, shivering with excitement.

✤   ✤   ✤

In the hospital lobby, Miguel leaned against the

shoulder of his little brother. A crowd of kids from church were gathered around him. A TV camera's lights illuminated the scene.

It was a prayer meeting. The hospital officials wouldn't let all the church kids come up to Miguel's room. So, he had gotten permission to come down and visit them.

A passing TV camera crew had paused — after doing an assignment on malpractice insurance. Now, the cameraman focused in for no particular reason — except for the interesting sight of a bunch of mixed-race street kids having a prayer meeting in the middle of a fancy hospital lobby miles away from their barrio.

Then, out of nowhere, armed Dukes were swarming everywhere. Young Leones took cover and opened fire. Girls screamed. Civilians scrambled for cover as Miguel stood, bellowing his disapproval.

As automatic gunfire sprayed the walls, as nurses ducked under the registration counter, as a security guard dived under his desk, as the TV cameraman recorded the entire chaotic scene, Miguel climbed up on a sofa and began to pray: "In the name of Jesus Christ," he shouted. "I say that your weapons will not fire, your bullets will not injure. I come against this violence in the name of Jesus Christ and I order it to stop."

There was sudden silence.

Right in front of the TV camera, a Duke and a Leone leveled their handguns point-blank at each other and repeatedly squeezed triggers that did not even click. In front of the elevators, a Duke leaped into the ornamental fountain and played his South African assault gun over the crowd. But it did not fire.

The anger and disbelief on the faces of the combatants could not have been faked, and the TV camera caught it all.

With a yell, the Dukes retreated down a hallway. Howling, the Leones tore after them, their guns mute but waved in the air.

In front of Miguel, José Chimon banged his German pistol against his palm and stared in absolute amazement at his big brother.

"Hey, Bro," declared Miguel, "you are no match for God."

José threw down his gun. "Man," he exclaimed, "we were just protecting your hide."

"God will protect me if I need to be protected," proclaimed Miguel.

The stunned church kids picked themselves up off the floor. Young spiritual giants that they were, they had not been prepared for what they had just witnessed.

As they scattered, they whispered among themselves, unsure exactly what had happened. All sorts of versions emerged. The Dukes and Leones had their own stories.

It all would have been forgotten — or fogged by explanations — except for the TV footage. The cameraman arrived back at the station with some of the most dramatic video ever shot.

By that evening, it was playing on the networks.

Cable News Network played and replayed the entire clip. "Street gang conflict took an interesting turn this afternoon in Los Angeles," intoned one of America's most well-known newsmen. "Watch this dramatic footage. What you are seeing are factions of the Bloods and their nationwide arch-rivals, the Crips, interrupting a religious meeting at a Los Angeles hospital. What happened next you will just have to explain for yourself."

There, on the tubes of one hundred million homes was Miguel, ordering the guns not to work — in the name of Jesus.

There, in incredible testimony to news viewers worldwide, gawked the Dukes and the Leones, squeezing triggers that would not squeeze, firing pistols and assault rifles that refused to fire. The fear and bewilderment on their young faces could not be contrived.

It was real.

Overnight, an ex-addict from the barrio was in demand.

Newspaper reporters wanted to interview him.

Women wanted to touch him.

Talk show hosts demanded him.

News crews filled the lobby of the hospital. Crazies stood on the lawn with placards and megaphones.

Miguel was an instant super-star, although he did not have the slightest idea what he had done — or why anybody wanted to talk to him — or what he should say to them.

In his hospital room, Miguel stared out at the dark sky. He gently touched his bandaged eye. It was still very tender.

He glanced down at the parking lot. Security guards were at triple strength. A mob of reporters, cameramen, photographers, and media groupies stood on the lawn. Network newsmen were demanding details about Miguel's treatment and progress from the hospital administrator, a short, mustachioed doctor who always looked irritated.

Miguel sighed and stayed back from the window.

He had turned on his TV and watched an old movie for a while, then clicked over to the religious channel.

There, a tall black man was talking with the talk show host about a famous evangelist — who apparently had died recently.

"Wasn't it hard being the son of such a famous preacher?" asked the host. "Just look at what your father did. He's credited with being the tool God used to bring about one of the greatest moves of the Holy Spirit in years. He founded the largest black denomination in America. His books are published in 107 countries and 35 languages. His Bible colleges send thousands of missionaries worldwide every year. Yet, he always returned to Los Angeles, to Watts itself, one of the worst ghettos in America. What did that do to you as a boy?"

The skinny black preacher smiled patiently.

Miguel sat up with a start.

He knew him.

It was the skinny preacher from the abandoned apartment building.

"I have had to be my own man," the preacher said. "That's not easy. To be truly at peace, I have to be God's man. I have to be what He wants me to be. But, at the same time, I have had to deal with a very strong sense of rebellion — an urgency not to be a clone of my father."

"Praise God," nodded the host. "But how did you feel?"

The preacher looked uncomfortable.

"I felt as if I was not in control of my life," he said. "I could not stand up in front of people and do an impression of my father — even though they would love it. I'm not an Elvis Presley impersonator. Nor am I an impersonator of my dad, although people would be delighted for me to get up and tell all his great old stories and re-preach his thundering sermons. But that's not who I am. So, I am working with addicts in East L.A. They don't give a hoot who I am. Most of them never heard of my dad."

"Were you a normal kid?" asked the host.

"Sure," said the preacher, "but it was hard for me

to be a normal Christian. When I came out of my rebellion at age eighteen, I couldn't just come back to the Lord. No, when I responded to the altar call at one of my father's crusades, he wept and pulled me up on the stage and they all prayed for me and laid hands on me and announced that I was going to be the next Billy Graham.

"The video they made of my return was sent out to thousands of homes as a premium — a gift when people sent in a donation.

"Naturally, I was sucked right into it. I thought I was going to be some great prophet. A super holy man. People were calling me up, wanting me to say profound things — to hold crusades and speak to stadiums full of high schoolers. I wasn't ready for that. I didn't have that much to say. I was just a kid who wanted to serve Jesus."

Miguel gawked. He understood exactly. Two book publishers had already tried to sign him for a book. A bunch of college kids from a film school had sneaked upstairs and presented him with an idea for turning his life into a made-for-TV movie.

"José," Miguel said, watching another TV station van pull into the parking lot. "I got a problem. I don't have nothing to say to these people."

"The security guards will keep them downstairs," said José. "Listen, this friend of mine wants me to show you this contract. He says that we can really make a bunch of money on T-shirts with your picture on them. He says that he just needs you to give him this exclusive on the licensing of your image and name for marketing purposes. I think it's a good idea. He'll give us 10 percent of the profit on every dollar he makes."

"Yeah?" exclaimed Miguel. "That sounds really good. Man, me on T-shirts? What a wonderful witness for the Lord."

There was a knock on the door.

Warily, Miguel looked up. The last visitor to slip past security had been a reporter from the *National Informer* offering him $10,000 to sign a release for a first-person article on his life that they would write for him. However, Miguel had read the scandal sheet tabloids when he was working at the convenience store. He refused.

Even with his limited education, he could tell the stories were mostly fake.

José stood and opened the door.

In it was the black preacher from the abandoned apartment building, but dressed in a double-breasted suit straight from the men's fashion magazines at the barber shop.

"Hey," said the preacher.

Miguel stood, grinning, delighted to see him. But he realized uncomfortably that he did not know the man's name.

"Can I come in for a minute?" asked the preacher.

"Hey, I don't know, Bro," said José, all 5' 4" and 135 pounds of his fifteen-year-old physique blocking the doorway.

"It's okay," called Miguel.

The preacher stepped into the room.

"How are you doing?" he asked Miguel.

Miguel tried to grin. Why didn't he know the guy's name? Awkwardly, he motioned at the room's only chair.

"Hey, my name is Barry Antioch," said the preacher, offering his hand to José.

"Eh, Dude!" greeted the kid. "You're from Africa, right?"

The preacher winced. "No. Watts. My great-grandfather was from Africa, though. Uganda. His last name was Britanga, but no Anglo could pronounce it, so my dad changed it to Antioch."

"Whoa," grinned José, "sorry, Man."

"No problem." Barry extended his hand to Miguel. "I think you probably remember me from the rehab center."

Miguel grabbed his hand. "I seen you on TV," he exclaimed. "Last night, I couldn't sleep and I was watching Christian TV and you were on with — what's his name."

"I have seen you on television as well," said Barry. "That is a mighty testimony of the Lord's power. How do you explain it?"

"Well," shrugged Miguel. He glanced uneasily at José. "I've got a theory." Behind the boy's back, he made a motion toward the door. Barry caught on immediately.

"Say, José," exclaimed Barry, "where can I get a can of root beer around here, Man? I am dying of thirst. If I have to drink another drop of water, I am going to gag."

"Root beer?" perked up José. "There's a machine downstairs in the employees' lounge. We're not supposed to go in there, but I bet I can pull it off, Man. I'll be right back." He paused. "You gonna be okay, Blood?"

Miguel waved him on.

Barry sat down on Miguel's bed.

"Here's my theory," said the ex-junkie. "I have been praying like crazy that my brother José, who is really involved with this drug-dealing, murdering gang in our 'hood called the Lions — or the way we say it, Los Leones — I been praying like mad that he will become a Christian and get out of the gang.

"So, I was praying really hard for José and I felt the Lord giving me this really incredible vision for ten million people interceding for America — half of them kids. So, I asked the Lord why He was giving me this vision and He tells me that I'm supposed to tell people to pray.

"I don't figure how I am going to tell anybody, and then this thing happens in the lobby."

Miguel squinted, nervously watching Barry's reaction.

"How did the Lord speak to you?"

"Well," remembered Miguel, "I was praying and asking the Lord to touch José. I sure love him. I was asking the Lord to help open José's heart to Him. Suddenly, I was filled with a vision. I seen these 10 million people across the world praying for the gangs and the druggies and the crazies. Five million of them would be kids.

"Wonderful," whispered Barry.

"I saw a revival sweeping across Los Angeles, San Diego, Detroit, Miami, and I saw the millions fervently praying for New York."

"New York City?"

Miguel clenched his eyes shut. "I asked the Lord to show me what He was trying to say to me, and I saw lonely people dying every day in the filth and horror that fills New York City. I saw the thousands of runaways selling themselves for cheap sex. I saw thousands dying of AIDS on the curbs and I saw a new, terrible drug sweeping through the city.

"But I saw ten million Christians praying that the plague would be thrown back and defeated."

"O Father," whispered Barry, "why have You shown us this?"

And the two were kneeling in the hospital room.

"Help Miguel proclaim his message: *Tell them to pray,*" came the message deep within Barry's heart.

Barry trembled.

"Go tell them to pray," again came the message.

"Father," Barry whispered, "who is going to listen to him?" But he knew the answer.

They were looking at a rare window of opportunity.

While people were still amazed about the videotape playing on the networks, they had to move quick.

"Have you signed any contracts with anybody?" asked Barry, his mind a whir. "Anything?"

"No, Man," exclaimed Miguel. "But people are wanting me to sign stuff. And you seen that mob of reporters down there on the lawn. They all want me to come out and say something righteous."

Barry nodded.

"Okay," he said, "here's the deal. My dad's attorneys are going to set up a trust for you." Barry dug in his suit pocket and dug out a miniature cellular phone. He started to punch numbers, then paused. "Miguel, I don't want anything from you. But you have a message that needs to be heard. I don't think it's any coincidence that God put you and me together. I know how bad it can be with people pulling at you and taking advantage of you so that they can make a buck."

Barry punched the buttons of the phone. "Olga," he said, "this is Barry." He listened. "Mom's fine. She's having trouble with her arthritis, but it's under control, praise God. Listen, Olga, I have a big favor. I need you to come out of retirement."

He listened. His eyes glistened with emotion. He grinned. "Olga," he interrupted. "Have you seen the kid on the news who prayed that the gangs in the hospital lobby would be unable to hurt each other?" He listened. He nodded impatiently.

"Olga," he said, then listened. He nodded. "Olga," he interrupted, "listen, I need you to get up here to the hospital. He has a powerful message that America needs to hear." He listened, then winced. "Olga," he whispered.

Miguel could hear loud talk on the other end. "Olga," Barry interrupted. "Olga, he is just a kid. A street kid. He doesn't have any idea of what he's up against. He is street smart, but..." Barry glanced at Miguel uncomfortably.

"Stupid," offered Miguel.

"He's naive. He doesn't know what's waiting out there to suck him dry," said Barry. "We need to protect him." He listened. He nodded, then grinned at Miguel. "Okay."

He hung up. He sighed and shook his head. "Olga Morgenstein was my dad's secretary," he offered. "She knows everybody and has seen everything. Miguel, Christians are not perfect. There are some out there who are going to try to take advantage of you. That hurts. It hurts much worse than when non-Christians try to exploit you."

Miguel grinned. "You gonna be my manager?"

Barry sighed. "I guess, but, we've got to get a few things clear. The minute you decide to try to get rich off this thing, I'm gone."

Miguel looked confused. "Get rich off Jesus? Come on, Man. Nobody would ever want do that, Man."

Barry sighed. Miguel had a lot to learn. "People do it, Miguel," he said. "The Bible has truly terrible things to say about them, but it's like in this day and age nobody can hear those warnings from God anymore."

Miguel grabbed a paperback Bible off the stand beside his bed. "I was reading this last night." He fanned the pages and read. "My dear Timothy, know this to be true that in the last days of the earth, some Christians will be lovers of themselves and utterly self-centered. They will love money more than Jesus Christ. They will be ungrateful, unholy and profane

—sneering at God—hard-hearted, liars, giving in to all kinds of immorality. They will pretend to be righteous, but theirs will be a terrible form of legalistic, lawless religiousness that denies the power of God. From these kinds of Christians, turn away. Avoid them completely."

Barry glanced at the Bible. "That's 2 Timothy, third chapter. I've never heard that paraphrase of it before. But that's what I'm trying to tell you."

"Man," breathed Miguel, "God musta sent you, Brother."

Barry squinted at him. He was filled with a peace. Yes, the Lord had sent him. This kid with the bandaged eye just might be the reason that God had put Barry on earth.

He sighed.

José pushed into the room with three cans of soda pop.

Barry raised his cellular phone. Carefully, he punched out the number of his father's attorneys. By noon, they had transferred Miguel to a ten-story nursing home run by the massive Watts church that Barry's dad had called home for three decades.

Olga was on the phone, booking Miguel onto local Christian TV shows, then arranging for the kid to make a short appearance on the "Tonight Show" that evening.

"Oprah Winfrey wants him tomorrow," she told Barry. "They'll come here for a live hook-up. What do you think?"

"I trust her," said Barry. "She was very fair to me. She can spot fakes. She appreciates genuine people."

"What about Geraldo?"

Barry winced. "He's an interesting guy. He's got this on-camera persona that is a little thick, but I believe he's genuinely interested in the truth."

"We gonna be on his show?"

"Hey, let's see how you do on 'Tonight' and 'Oprah'."

❖ ❖ ❖

That night, as Miguel walked out under the lights and shook hands with the "Tonight Show's" guest host, Barry was backstage in the dressing room, on his face before the Lord.

"Father," he prayed, "awaken our intercessors. Fill them with an urgency for this boy. Surround Miguel with your angels. Fill him with wisdom. Let America hear his vision. Open their hearts."

❖ ❖ ❖

"Well," chuckled the guest host as Miguel fidgeted on the sofa next to a movie starlet, "I've been told that I was going to meet a true saint tonight."

"Who?" grinned Miguel.

"You!" laughed the host. "Man, I have seen that tape and I'll have to admit that I was touched. I don't know why. I'll just have to tell you that it struck something inside of me that I don't understand. So, do you heal people?"

"Me?" grinned Miguel. "No way, Man. I just pray, just like you can."

"Well," smiled the host, grinning out at the millions watching, "I really don't do as much of that as I probably should."

"It's easy," exclaimed Miguel. "You just tell God everything that's tearing you apart. He listens, Man. Hey, if He listens to me, He's going to listen to you."

"When you put it that way," wisecracked the host.

"Yeah!" grinned Miguel.

"Why didn't those guns fire?" asked the host.

"Because I love my little brother more than anything. Those were Dukes, Man, and my bro, he's the big jefe of the Leones. They would have just blown each other away right there."

"Okay, so there's a feud in your neighborhood?"

Miguel chuckled. "It's a little more than that, Man. You ever heard of the Bloods and the Crips? That's what this is, Man. They all hate each other bad. To be a full-fledged member of the Leones, you have to kill somebody in one of the rival gangs."

"Are you a gang member?"

"Well," Miguel squinted, "yeah. I'm not exactly active now, but once you're in, it's for life. But I don't run with the gang no more."

"Did you ever kill anybody?"

Miguel got very serious. He glanced uneasily at the host. "I don't think I better answer that question, Man."

"But you were a member, so you must have killed somebody to get into the gang."

"Well," hedged Miguel, "those are the rules."

"So, here you are, an admitted murderer who has never been prosecuted — and you're preaching to me?"

"Saint Paul was a murderer who was never prosecuted," said Miguel. "He was on his way to Damascus to murder more Christians when God called him to preach."

"Did God call you?" asked the host.

"You did," grinned Miguel.

"What?" exclaimed the host.

"You called me," snickered Miguel. "You said you wanted me to come down here and be on TV."

The host grinned at the studio audience and flipped a pencil into the air. "You're right. I did," he said, rolling his eyes. The crowd roared. "So, God called you, then I called you, and here you are. What do you have to say to us tonight?"

"Well," said Miguel, "I was praying and asking the

Lord to touch my little brother José. I sure love him. I was asking the Lord to help open José's heart to Him. Suddenly, I was filled with a vision. I seen these ten million people across the world praying for the gangs and the druggies and the crazies. Five million of them would be kids."

"Ten million people praying," murmured the host.

"I saw America being changed as a result. I saw a new day sweeping across Los Angeles, San Diego, Detroit, Kansas City, Miami, and I saw the millions fervently praying for New York."

The host grinned. "New York City?" he exclaimed at the studio audience.

Miguel nodded. "I saw lonely people dying every day in the filth and horror that fills New York City. I saw the thousands of runaways selling themselves for cheap sex. I saw thousands dying of AIDS on the curbs and I saw a new, terrible drug sweeping through the city. But I saw ten million people praying that this evil would end."

"Incredible," said the host. "So that's your message. That we should all pray."

Miguel grinned. "I saw ten million people praying, Man. I believe it will happen. Ten million people on their knees, asking God in the name of Jesus Christ to save our great, beloved America."

"We've got to take a station break, but I really want to thank you for coming tonight. That is quite a vision you've got. I wish you the very best with it," said the host.

"Will you pray?" asked Miguel.

"What?"

"Will you pray for America?"

The talk show host stared at Miguel, stunned. Then, he flipped another pencil into the air. "Yes," he announced, grinning. "I will pray for America." He stared out at the millions watching on TV. "And,

Miguel, I believe that a lot of other people will, too."

Off camera, somebody made a wisecrack.

The talk show host looked wounded. "Come on," he said. "I'll do it. I mean, what the heck! Don't you bozos think I know how to talk to God?" He rolled his eyes. The studio audience roared its approval.

As America watched a commercial on dog food, Miguel shook the starlet's hand.

"Thanks," said the host. "You're going to come back sometime?"

"If you call me," grinned Miguel.

The studio audience applauded.

In amazement, the men and boys of the village watched Valentina and Molech head straight for the volcano.

The two had experienced a miserable night. Mosquitoes had swarmed. Matthew had given Patrick a sip out of a small bottle. "Mosquitoes will leave you alone, now," he said with a grin.

"Why?" exclaimed the boy, wishing he had brought his sleeping bag.

"Now you smell too bad for them to bite."

Patrick laughed.

Around 3 a.m., a heavy thunderstorm rolled into the area. Molech and Valentina lay under a tree — hot, soaking wet, and totally unable to sleep.

Their unseen observers, on the other hand, watched from a breezy rock outcropping. The rain had been refreshing. Now, the scout party dried in the moonlight. Around 4 a.m., Daniel nudged Patrick. "Come on," he said. "It's time."

With a sinking feeling, Patrick knew what he was talking about.

It was time for his prayer vigil. Sighing, the fourteen-year-old American followed the tall African sixteen year old.

He and Andrew and Daniel ran for a mile or two before they stopped at an enormous baobab tree. "Here," announced Daniel.

Patrick stopped and looked around. All about them, herds of wildebeest and zebra grazed. A flock of crowned cranes slowly winged toward a small lake.

"Lord," prayed Daniel aloud, "You are my Father. I honor Your holy name. You alone are God. I turn from all others. I look to the heavens and know that You alone are God."

Andrew began praying, but in his native language. Patrick glanced around. A herd of wildebeest not far away boiled into a frenzy. A large bull broke and galloped away from the commotion. Patrick strained to see what was happening.

He could see a hyena running at full speed on the wildebeest's heels. The stocky little hyena had little trouble keeping up with his longer-limbed quarry. Every now and then, the hyena would leap up and nip the hindquarters of the fleeing bull.

Patrick exhaled in excitement. Then, he realized that Andrew had fallen silent. Giggling, the younger boy elbowed him.

"Uh," said Patrick. "Now I lay me down to sleep." He stopped. That was hardly appropriate. He chewed his lip and glanced at Daniel, who did not betray any impatience at all. "Well, uh," whispered Patrick, his eyes clenched shut, "I'm pretty new at this stuff. I know that You got Mom and me out of that volcano and that was pretty good. I just know You did it and not some fluke of an updraft. Mom says it was just a — what do you call it — one of those hot air deals, but I know that even if that's what it was, You sent it, because I asked You to."

Patrick took a deep breath. He glanced at the horizon.

The wildebeest and hyena were gone.

He winced in disappointment. "And, uh, I am supposed to be praying for . . . well, something about keeping Molech and that crazy woman away from the valley.

"I want You to do that. No, that's not how I'm supposed to talk to You, You being God and all that." Patrick glanced around self-consciously. "I mean," he sighed, "take care of the hidden valley and all the people there and my mom."

Then he was silent. He glanced at Daniel, who did not even look up. Patrick cleared his throat and elbowed Daniel.

"Father God," prayed the African. "I look forward to the day that Your mighty kingdom will be established — whether I will see it on Earth or in heaven, it does not matter. I only pray that I will be wise enough to accept Your will. You are wise, Lord, and I am not. I try to be and I think that You give me wisdom lots of the time, because I really am not too wise yet. Thy will be done." He paused.

"I ask that it would be Your will that those evil people stay away from our beautiful, hidden valley. Lord, back in the Old Testament, You hid Elijah and You hid the hundred young prophets, (I think that's how many it was). You hid the baby Jesus from Herod.

"My dad has that *Reader's Digest* where the American J. Russell Morse hid Christians in Burma during the terror of the 1960s in a secret valley where You kept them safe until the evil government was overthrown.

"So, I thank You, Lord, for how You have hidden my family and my uncles and aunts and all the kids who have been born over the last twenty years in our village. I thank You for healing me when I got sick last year. Now, I pray that You will spread Your great, mighty wing over our valley and blind the evildoers who are searching for their wicked machine.

"If they find us, let them not see us. Let them come and go in darkness, unaware of where they have been. Thank You, Lord. I ask for great confusion for the enemy. Baffle them with foolish problems that they cannot understand. Send them in circles, irritated, and fighting one another instead of us. Thank You, Father."

He was silent.

Andrew began praying aloud, again in his own language — or maybe French this time. Patrick couldn't tell.

He felt Andrew's elbow in his stomach.

"Oh," the fourteen year old said. "God, I, uh, am real glad You saved me from that volcano and, uh . . ." He peered out at the lake and the frustrated hyenas pacing the shoreline. "God, I pray that You will protect us from any evil people. I mean, You can do anything, so I ask You to let those stinking hyenas that are chasing Mom and me and the LORRD computer just go crazy.

"I've been watching them with everybody else, God, and You're already doing it. I mean, they are really nuts. Wrecking their helicopter like that and yelling all those insults at each other — they have real problems. Well, I thank You for keeping them away from us. It's been really incredible . . ."

And so went the boys' prayers into the early dawn. They were certainly no Psalmists or John Wesleys. Not yet, but God heard them.

"Watch," pointed Matthew as the trio rejoined the scout party at sunrise. "Those two are absolutely nuts. They're climbing the volcano."

Patrick peered over the tall grass. A mile away,

Molech and Valentina were yelling insults at each other again as they began to scale the slopes of a long, black fissure.

"They're going to stumble into the pits," whispered Daniel.

Indeed, the arguing hikers carefully approached the bubbling waters of a hot spring. Patrick peered through the haze.

"It is salt water," whispered Daniel. "My dad thinks that it comes from the ocean. The water evaporates, leaving deposits that look like cauliflowers. This is where we come for our salt. In the shallow water, it floats on the surface like fine snow in the winter. The water is too hot to swim in."

Molech and Valentina did not pause. As the sun rose into the morning sky, they began to argue more loudly. At one point, Valentina sat down on the ground and seemed convinced that she had found a Mexican restaurant in which to eat breakfast. She loudly ordered scrambled eggs, rice, and refried beans. As Molech fumed, she exclaimed aloud at how good the hot coffee tasted.

Then, she stood, pointing straight at the imposing volcano. It was as if she were possessed by great evil. She shouted absolute babble. She stalked across the barren lava, describing aloud how she and Molech would have to cross a crocodile-infested lake that only she could see. She suggested that he get a net and catch some fish.

"Have you ever seen a Nile perch?" she called, her voice high.

The scout party stopped at the hot spring — but were unable to follow any farther under the cover of the high grasses. Patrick peered into the water, his feet sinking into the foul-smelling, hot muck at the edge. He touched the water and agreed that it was much too hot to wade in.

He was surprised to see that his touch startled a school of tiny fish. He was amazed that something could survive in such a scalding, salty pool.

"We will wait here," motioned Matthew.

Patrick peered at the enormous cone rising straight out of the ground. The circumference of the base stretched for miles, sparsely covered with rocks and boulders. The incline wasn't all that steep.

As the sun rose higher and higher, so did the temperature. The sky was clear. The sun beat down on the climbers and the watchers. When the heat became intense, Matthew sent the three boys for water.

Patrick, Andrew, and Daniel set off running. As fatigue quickly set in, their enthusiasm faded. Around ten o'clock, the previous night's lack of sleep and the morning's lack of breakfast began to take their toll.

Patrick developed a severe case of stomach cramps, then loose bowels. Embarrassed, he knelt in the grassy sea. Daniel and Andrew politely looked the other way — exclaiming hoarsely about a herd of gazelles.

Patrick's diarrhea, combined with his worsening sunburn and excessive perspiration from the heat, began to dehydrate the boy rapidly. He was getting weaker by the moment when the three burst into the shallows of the lake.

Weakly, Patrick plunged in, wishing he had not left his boots and cap back at the village. Sitting down in the water beside him, Andrew gently touched his blistering skin and commented. He grinned broadly.

"He wants to know what is the matter," asked Daniel. "You are turning red like a parrot. What is wrong with your skin?"

"I am not a black man," muttered Patrick. Apologetically, he squinted at Daniel. "Tell him that it will take me many weeks to darken my skin so that I do not burn so badly in the sun."

Daniel looked very surprised, but repeated his words.

Andrew looked amazed. He yammered an excited question.

"He wants to know if your hair will get healthy, too."

"What?" exclaimed Patrick.

"Andrew has seen people die of starvation," said Daniel. "One of the last things that happens is that their hair turns red and sometimes white. He thinks that your hair is sick and wants to know if it will turn dark and get curly like it is supposed to be."

Patrick rolled his eyes. He snickered. Both African boys watched him, waiting for an answer.

"No," said the American, irritated. "My hair will get lighter, but my skin will get darker."

"How dark?" asked Daniel after he had translated for Andrew.

"Real brown if I stay outside all the time with you guys."

Daniel translated, then asked, "Will you be as dark as Andrew and me?" The two were as black as Matthew — almost ebony.

"No," said Patrick. "I'll just get really tan. Like a hyena or a lion."

Andrew asked something else. Daniel looked uneasy and answered something back in sharp rebuke.

"What did he ask?" demanded Patrick.

"Nothing," snickered Daniel. "He is just a boy, as you can see." Although he was quite tall, Andrew had not yet entered adolescence.

Patrick squinted at Daniel, not understanding. "Tell me what he asked."

"No," refused Daniel. He was sitting up to his waist in the water. He tossed a rock out into the water.

Patrick glanced around and spotted a flat rock. He held it carefully and spun it out over the water. Both Andrew and Daniel exclaimed their admiration as the rock skipped multiple times.

"What did he ask?" repeated Patrick as he held Andrew's wrist, trying to show him how to hold a rock for skipping.

"He is stupid," snorted Daniel, unsuccessfully throwing a flat rock out across the water. It splashed once and sank.

"Tell me."

Daniel sighed, then grinned, embarrassed. "He wants to know if you are a man or a boy."

Patrick looked at Andrew quizzically. "Huh?"

If Daniel had been capable of blushing, he would have. He giggled like a girl and splashed out into the water. "You figure it out, white guy." Then, he began attempting the Australian crawl that Patrick had taught him the day before.

Patrick squinted at Andrew. The kid was stalking a fish.

Embarrassed, Patrick fidgeted with the waistband of his ragged pants. Then bravely, he yanked them off and tossed them up onto the bank.

As nonchalantly as possible, he stood, intently studying the clear water. He was startled by sudden, wild laughter.

He spun. Both boys were pointing at him and howling with glee.

"What?" he demanded.

The two roared, yammering back and forth in their language. Crossing his arms self-consciously, Patrick gathered all his fourteen-year-old dignity and glared at the Africans. "What's so funny?" he demanded.

"The moon is full," answered Daniel. He grinned, but tried to be respectful. "You really are a white man." He chortled and pointed.

Patrick peered down and around at his posterior. His seat gleamed quite white, unlike his back and legs, which were tan from the beach and red from his recent adventures.

"Dumb niggers," growled Patrick. And suddenly he was filled with guilt, enormously ashamed of himself—even though neither of his friends had ever heard the insult before. Hiding his shame, he dived into the water and coasted under the surface, trying to sort out why he felt so irritated with them and himself.

Why he had uttered such a powerful insult so easily?

It was simple.

He didn't like being different.

They were his friends. They were good friends. He knew he could depend on them for anything — although he had known them only a very short time.

He wished he, too, was a black African boy, able to run across these beautiful grasslands forever, stalking the wild game, watching the lions, and marveling in the beauty of creation.

But he was just a white boy.

An American.

A stranger in an awesome land.

He could try to fit in, but his skin would never be as dark as Andrew's or Daniel's.

If he ever took them to the city, the roles would switch.

As he glided through the water, he knew how people would stare at his ebony friends, carrying their spears, speaking in their native tongue. People back home would not understand. They would think that Andrew and Daniel were stupid.

Patrick surfaced, gasping.

He treaded water and realized that Daniel and

Andrew were calling to him from the shallows — urgently, pointing.

Patrick looked up, not understanding. Then, he looked around.

Not fifty yards away, the unmistakable knobs of a crocodile's snout and eyes were moving straight toward him.

Patrick gasped.

He fairly skimmed the surface of the water as he ripped into his best freestyle stroke. He didn't look back, but whenever he looked up, he kept his eyes on the yelling, whooping Daniel and Andrew.

Suddenly, Patrick's knees scraped the rough bottom of the lake. Gasping, he splashed out into the shallows. As Daniel and Andrew yelled and laughed, he ran up on the bank, then turned and started shouting his mom's familiar Japanese insults at the croc. He hurled rocks at the big reptile.

It turned and headed back toward the distant shore.

"You are a crazy man!" bellowed Daniel, slapping Patrick on the back. Loudly yelling in his usual garble, Andrew whooped and aped Patrick's sudden flight, imitating his wild paddling.

"If you lived in the days of our ancestors, he says, they would have decided your spirit guide was the water bug!" translated Daniel, laughing. "Andrew says he never saw anybody run on water before!"

Yelling and reliving the excitement, the three began gathering gourds. Daniel showed Patrick how to pick out dried ones hanging on the trees, avoiding ones that were rotten or still green.

Soon, laden with the hollow squash, the boys knelt at the lakeshore and began shaking out the seeds. Daniel made vine harnesses as Patrick and Andrew filled the vessels with drinking water. Patrick paused and put on his shorts.

"What kept you?" asked Matthew as he accepted a large gourd from his son.

"I got chased by a crocodile," muttered Patrick, passing out water to the others.

Why were Molech and Valentina climbing the volcano?

She was convinced search parties would find them much more easily if they were waiting on high ground.

That might have been true, except that they had filed no flight plan, so nobody knew where to look for them. Their chopper had been flying too low to show up on radar.

The trail began to narrow. Molech and Valentina could still follow it, but it wasn't as clear as it had been before. Long ago, the grassy plains had given way to a lunar landscape. Both were hungry, exhausted from a lack of sleep — and desperately in need of water.

As Matthew and the men from the village watched from down below in the high grass, Molech and Valentina reached a twenty-foot-wide crater on the side of the cone. Valentina sat down beside a steaming vent. Suddenly, a different volcanic vent hissed loudly. No mere crack, it reached down into the very bowels of the mountain and spewed out a fountain of black lava that looked more like boiling tar than the scarlet lava flows Patrick had seen from the plane.

The ground rocked and another fountain burst through another vent. Shrieking, Valentina jumped up and began weeping.

"Listen," whispered Molech. "Beneath our feet, a lake of fire is seething."

Valentina did not listen.

"Don't worry," Molech spat. "This lava is black.

That means it is much cooler than most lava. This crust is probably a couple of inches thick. If you fall through, you'll have plenty of time to scream before you die."

As he spoke, his own foot broke through the brittle ash and he sank up to his knee in the crust. There was a puff of steam and he yanked his leg free, cursing in Italian. He looked up at Valentina in disgust. His shoelaces were burned away. His pants cuff was charred.

The two scrambled out of the crater and made a wide circuit around it as they continued up the mountain.

Watching from the hot spring, Patrick shook his head. "They made it through the crater. I don't know where they are going."

"They are possessed," mused Daniel.

Patrick grinned at him, amused by the insult.

"No, I mean it," said Daniel.

"Possessed?" laughed Patrick. "Like in the movies? Possessed by Satan?"

"It happens in real life."

"Give me a break," scoffed Patrick.

"I have seen it."

"Come on." Laughing, Patrick looked at Matthew.

Daniel's dad smiled gently at the American boy. "I have seen the great evil that walks the earth. The Bible tells about a great war in heaven."

"A war?" exclaimed Patrick, watching the volcano's slopes. "Yeah, I've heard about that."

Matthew studied the mountain. "Renegade angels rebelled against God. They lost, of course, and managed only to bring punishment upon themselves. The Bible doesn't give a detailed account of their surrender or how God kicked them out of His life-giving presence.

"It tells that for now, they infest the air and

torment mankind."

"Why?" exclaimed Patrick.

"They hate humans, mostly since God loves us so much. They can get to Him by hurting us. They take terrible delight in our defeat, our depression, our destruction, and our death."

"Why?" asked the boy.

"Because the Father loves every one of us like His own son or daughter. Each one of us is important and wonderful in His eyes. No human who has ever lived did not have the watchful love of the great Master of the Universe."

Matthew nodded. "Such love incites the renegades to rage. They know that whenever God decides the end of time has come, they will be cast forever into a great lake of fire, like the one your two friends were tip-toeing across."

"They're not my friends," shouted Patrick. "I don't know that crazy lady. Molech is more a friend of my mother."

Matthew smiled, watching as the two on the mountain traversed a ravine.

"So, devils and stuff like that cause everything bad in the world?" asked Patrick. "Like in storybooks?"

"No," answered Matthew. "In the little time the evil ones have left, they spend all their time trying to hurt God the only way they can. They torture us, His beloved sons and daughters.

"They seduce us to self-destruction. They turn our hearts against the One who is our greatest source of joy, contentment, certainty, and knowledge. The power of evil spreads sadness, discontent, doubt, and ignorance."

"How?" asked Patrick, peering up at the mountain and wishing he had his mom's field glasses.

"By removing us from communication with God," said Matthew. "The devil did not want you ever to learn that you can ask anything you want from your Heavenly Father. But now you know the truth."

Patrick pondered that. He had always been taught that you weren't supposed to bother God with unimportant, daily things.

"Satan can never win any victory over you, Patrick, if you will listen to the gentle, inner voice of your Creator and compare what you think you hear to the great, written-down truths of His Holy Word: 'The Name of the Lord is a strong tower. The righteous runneth into it and is safe,' says Proverbs 18:10."

Matthew stood. He could not see Valentina or Molech. Then, they emerged from a small rift in the side of the mountain.

"In the Garden of Eden," said Matthew, "the first thing the devil said to Eve was that God had lied to her.

"After putting in her mind the terrible idea that her mighty Father could lie — and would lie — and had lied, the devil made her doubt God's goodness. God is good." Matthew stood and picked up a water gourd. "He wants only good for us. He delights in us." Matthew took a long drink. "It is a lie straight out of the pit that God is not our loving Provider and Protector.

"The biggest thing that Lucifer did in Eden was to get man to declare his independence from God. 'God knows that in the day that you eat the fruit,' said Lucifer, 'that your eyes shall be opened. You will be like gods.' Eve was deceived into thinking that if she would disobey God's firm command, she would be far better off.

"So, Lucifer detached her from believing God's word is always true. He detached her from the absolute truth that God is good. He got her to divorce herself from dependence on God. For the first time, a human went off alone, out of God's will.

"Satan was delighted!"

"Now he had company!" offered Patrick.

"Right," agreed Matthew. "Once before, there had only been one will in the universe. Then Satan rebelled and there were two.

"Now, there would be millions — all fighting and conflicting and pulling their own way. 'All we like sheep have gone astray,' lamented the prophet in Isaiah 53:6, 'we have turned every one to his own way.'

"Satan achieved a magnificent feat: he turned the apples of God's eye against Him. The next victim was easy. Adam didn't even have to hear Satan's lies. At Eve's mere suggestion, he, too, disobeyed.

"What followed was banishment from the Garden and murder. Adam and Eve's own sons could not get along. In a fit of jealousy, the eldest killed his brother, then lied about it.

"Imagine, Patrick, the pain that filled God's heart — and the delight that filled Satan's.

"He — the ultimate evil — had deceived man into believing that God is not good. He got man to disobey. Then, he won mankind away from total confidence and dependence on Him for everything.

"Instead, mankind went off on its own."

"Yeah," exclaimed Patrick, "with a bunch of rebellious ex-angels thinking they can keep us from depending on God. They're stinking wrong."

Matthew smiled.

"They are powerful, Patrick. It is they who have masqueraded as gods, genies, spirits — the false gods and bogus bearers of truth throughout history. They are the false 'spirit guides' who whisper alternate paths to immortality and false promises of New Age godhood. It is they who guide foolish men into astral plains and use, for their own terrible and evil purposes, such disturbed people as that woman up on the mountain."

Patrick peered up at the volcano.

❖   ❖   ❖

On the side of the mountain, Valentina and Molech were shrieking at each other again.

"Fool, fool, fool!" howled Valentina.

Exhausted, Molech growled darkly, then spat on the ground. The two sat on warm boulders and glared at each other.

"Witch," muttered Molech. "We're two-thirds of the way up the volcano, out of water, and with no guide. There's no way we can make it without water. I'm so thirsty that my throat feels like sandpaper."

Without a word, Valentina stood and began walking back down the ravine in the direction they had come. The two were quite a sight. Valentina's whole body was covered with cuts and bruises. Her clothes were soaked with mud and blood. She could barely walk.

Molech's clothes, too, were ragged. "Now where do we go?" he demanded hoarsely.

Valentina sat down and groaned, her eyes closed. She was far, far away, soaring in the white heavenlies of her spirit guides.

"Where is my computer?" she wailed.

Beside her, a great demonic prince laughed at the very idea of a primitive Christian tribe trying to hide the LORRD computer.

In evil glee, he pointed.

Airborne in the spirit realm, Valentina and her evil companion sped over a great gorge. Along its valley wound a pretty little river, feeding Lake Nyamulalengai.

Zooming along the high cliffs, Valentina saw the caves to which she had been taken before.

"Come," whispered the demonic guide. "Let us get

this underway."

"What?" gasped Valentina.

"The final confrontation," whispered her hideous host.

"The final battle," she smiled.

"Yes," said the spirit guide. "Armageddon."

In delight, Valentina returned to Molech.

"Come," she howled, running down the slopes. "We shall bring about the Battle of Armageddon tomorrow morning."

"Where are you going now?" he demanded. "What are you talking about?

"Come!" she screamed. "We are going to start the beginning of the end."

❖   ❖   ❖

Across the globe, there was a darkening of spirits. Johanna Graham looked up from her daily correspondence.

"Oh, Lord," she cried out in despair. "I sense great and terrible things."

In East L.A., Miguel Rodriguez paused in the middle of a live interview with a Canadian Christian talk-show host. "I . . ." he mumbled, looking confused.

"What is wrong?" asked the enthusiastic Canadian.

"I believe the time has come for us to pray," exclaimed Miguel.

Suddenly, he was on his knees.

"Father," he exclaimed, "awaken Your intercessors. Stir them awake. I sense a truly evil . . . evil . . ." Searching for words, Miguel faltered, staring right up at the TV camera.

In thirty million homes worldwide, his words echoed true. "My spirit confirms what you feel," said the Canadian host, his face white with concern. "My brothers and sisters across Canada and in the United States and wherever else satellites are taking this broadcast, I ask you to fall to your knees right now.

"Father God, we do not know why we sense this urgent need for Your people to pray, for we do not truly understand Your ways or the specifics of true spiritual warfare," proclaimed the Canadian.

"But we know this, O Lord. We know that You are Lord! You are Lord. You are Lord! To the glory of the Father, we declare that You are Lord. You are the everlasting Father! Jesus Christ is Lord, the King of kings and the Lord of lords! God, You have filled the earth with Your glory and the earth now shall be filled with the knowledge of Your glory just like the waters cover the sea!"

Across the world intercessors were, indeed falling to their knees. In Melbourne, Australia, the hotel maid Helen stood in the middle of a large prayer group she held each week in her apartment.

"Why have You called us to pray?" she wept with all those kneeling on the floor beside her. "Why? Because we have been ashamed to proclaim Your name? Because You desire for the truth of Your goodness to be proclaimed to the very ends of the earth?

"Or is there something else, O Lord? Is there terrible warfare underway above us in the heavenlies and all around us in the spirit realm? Father, we proclaim to the evil that Jesus Christ is Lord! We proclaim it! Jesus Christ is Lord."

In Poland, a little boy named Ladislav knelt with his parish priest. The two clasped hands, their heads bowed. "By the blood of Jesus Christ spilled when evil men killed Him on the cross two thousand years ago, we are set free! He paid the price for our rebellion!" proclaimed the clergyman.

"Yes," agreed the boy, "we proclaim that Jesus

Christ is Lord! The earth is the Lord's and everything in it! God, Your mercy is without end and Your power, without measure. Your holiness establishes Your throne!"

In Canada, "You are Lord, Jehovah, the Lord our God. You are Lord, El Shaddai. Your ways are forever and ever the same!" wept the talk-show host. "Your mercies are without end. Your power is without measure, and holiness establishes Your mighty throne, O Lord God!"

Exhausted, Miguel Rodriguez rose to his knees. "Holy, holy, holy is the Lord!" he proclaimed. "Holy is the Lord! Holy, holy, holy! Holy is the Lord. Holy, holy, holy. Around Your throne, we bring You praise. We praise Your name! Holy is the Lord! Holy, holy, holy!"

On the African plain, Matthew knelt in the high grass, the scouting party gathered around him. "You are our refuge!" proclaimed sixteen-year-old Daniel. "You will not let us down! Lord, we ask You to save us from our enemies, for You are just and You love us so!"

"Rescue us, O Lord!" cried Matthew, putting his arm on his son's bare shoulder. "Throw back the evil devices of the wicked! Bend down Your ear and listen to our plea! Save us, O Lord! As You have so many times, be to us our great protecting rock where we are always welcome, safe from all attack."

In a cornfield in Iowa, a farmer stood atop his tractor, a fist raised to heaven, and proclaimed, "You are the One who unleashed all the angelic powers of heaven to protect us frail humans. You issued the order long ago to save us! Rescue us, O God, from these unjust and cruel forces. O Lord, You alone are our hope."

"Throw down the evil devices of the wicked!" wept Johanna Graham in her room. "O Lord, You alone are my hope. I've trusted You from childhood. You have been with me from birth and have helped me constantly! Now, in my old age, don't set me aside. Don't forsake me now when my strength is failing."

On TV in Florida and California and Indiana, Christian talk show hosts interrupted their guests.

"I don't know what to tell you," drawled one familiar face broadcasting from Virginia Beach, "but ladies and gentlemen, I've just got to tell you that it is time for us to pray. Something great and terrible is occurring in the heavenlies. That's all I can tell you."

"My spirit testifies exactly the same thing," agreed his attractive co-host, her Scottish accent stronger than usual. She smiled, her eyes troubled. "I feel that we need to pray this: O Lord, don't stay away! Come quickly! Help! Destroy our enemies! They are whispering that You have forsaken us — well, destroy them! Cover them with failure and disgrace and confusion and terror!"

Beside her, his eyes clutched shut, the host proclaimed, "I cannot count the times, O Lord, when You have faithfully rescued Your people from danger. O God, You have helped me from my earliest childhood. Your power and goodness, Lord, reach to the highest heavens. You have done such wonderful things. Where is there another God like You?"

On the volcanic slopes, Valentina stood, her eyes an evil slit. She turned to Molech. It was as if she knew something incredible, unseen was happening.

In the dark and spirit-infested heavenlies over the earth, great spirit entities reeled under the onslaught, shrieking their defiance, but unable to defend themselves except in retreat.

One of the greatest princes of the darkness cowered, his fanged hands covering his hideous face.

"What have you done?" hissed a great and terrible voice.

The demonic prince stared into the livid and violent face of his great and evil lord. "Sir," he gasped.

"You have yanked the lion's whiskers," shrieked the great and ancient leader of the rebels. "You have pulled the sleeping tiger's tail. You fool!"

"No," denied the prince, his face full of defiance. "I have set the stage for the final assault. I grew tired of waiting. Now, it is time. We will, indeed, have Armageddon by next morning."

"Fool!" shrieked the terrible voice of the truly evil one. "We do not want war!"

"What?"

"I do not want any Armageddon by tomorrow morning!"

"Why not?"

"They're defending themselves!"

"So?"

"They were like untended sheep. They thought they were rich with everything they could possibly want. We had them the way we wanted them: spiritually wretched and miserable and poor! They were easy picking, sleepy, content, blind. Now, look at them! What have you done?"

"It is time for battle!"

"I do not want battle!"

"What?"

"Fool! Fool! Fool! Stop everything. Pull back. Retreat. You have undone centuries of work."

"We can be victorious by morning!"

"Fool!"

For the first time, the great and powerful prince saw the terror of his dark lord. No, he did not want to begin the final battle.

He did not want the inevitable final confrontation.

Satan's is a war fought quietly.

For centuries, the legions of evil have sniped at mankind, silently seducing, building great strongholds that humans deny even exist.

Satan's war is fought under cover of darkness. Its purpose is to turn God's beloved humans against Him, to stop them from turning to Him for help, adoring Him, praising His name, and communing with Him as His children.

And now the evil angelic prince saw his error.

Millions were now worshipping the Lord their God. Obeying Him. Loving Him. Depending on Him.

Just like it had been in Eden so long ago.

The evil prince knew the horrible truth.

They could not win the final battle.

They would lose.

They would, eventually, be thrown into the great lake of fire for all eternity.

No longer would they roam the earth, picking out victims for subversion.

Only terror and punishment would be theirs. No one would reign in hell. All would be horribly and vengefully equal. Tortured and punished without mercy — without a chance that they would ever again see the mighty, life-giving face of God — screaming and clawing and accusing amid their great pain.

"Fools!" screamed the occult prince at his subordinates. "Fools! Fools!"

❖   ❖   ❖

In New York City, a network advertising executive slammed down his phone. He ran out of his office.

"I don't believe it," he raged at his secretary. "Get me legal. And call corporate. The entire ad campaign for SuperRich has been cancelled. They're our primary sponsor for the Olympics. They can't do it. This will ruin me. I'm finished!"

His secretary tapped buttons and handed him her phone.

"Perry!" yelled the executive. "SuperRich has yanked everything. Apparently some lab rats in Indiana or Ohio or somewhere were given massive doses and have gone absolutely nuts. Something in the stuff builds up in the bloodstream and causes hallucinations. Can they cancel their sponsorship of our Olympic coverage?"

Loosening his collar, he mopped his forehead with a tissue from his secretary's desk. "I don't believe it."

He slammed down the phone.

"They can cancel," he roared.

"SuperRich causes hallucinations?" gasped his secretary.

"And it's addictive," bellowed her boss.

Within minutes, the news was on all the wires. Live in Springfield, Missouri, a Cable News Network camera team broadcast a news conference.

Kids from the three local colleges delightedly revealed they had been given federal grants to test SuperRich, but that their alarming discoveries from testing the sweetener on rats had been ignored.

"So," said one kid from a small Christian college, "we put it out on the nationwide computer networks last night. That stuff is poison. It's a drug! Last night, we dumped all our findings on all the major computer networks — Compuserve, Prodigy, Genie, everybody. Then, we played hacker and fixed it so that anybody who signed on at the Pentagon or NASA or the Associated Press got our findings instead of their usual start-up screen."

Proudly, he grinned at the cameras.

On Capital Hill, the U.S. congressman from Springfield was applauding the hometown kids and demanding a congressional hearing into their allegations that SuperRich was deadly — and that somebody had bought off the Food and Drug Administration.

"This, my fellow Americans," the congressman was declaring, "is bigger than Watergate. This is far bigger than BCCI. Someone or something put a major protective agency of the United States government in his pocket — for financial gain — and was on the verge of poisoning American consumers!"

It was as if a spiritual Star Wars was raging over earth's cloudy globe. Unseen to human eyes, great and terrible forces of evil and power were being thrown back by mighty angelic warriors who had not put on their full armor since Lucifer's expulsion from heaven.

In Iceland and Swaziland and Siberia, Christians were on their knees. In Poland and Australia, intercessors were consumed with concern for Patrick and Zuni.

In the inner cities of East L. A., Chicago, Detroit, Houston, and Newark, kids were praying.

On Christian TV, hosts were in tears.

On the Cable News Network, a Christian afternoon news anchor trembled with an excitement that he did not understand. Professionalism kept him from lifting his hands to heaven.

He knew something monumental was happening — and was not being reported by his network.

"Frank, are you all right?" barked a voice in his earplug.

In East Los Angeles, Miguel Rodriguez stood, waving his hands in the air. The Canadian TV host, too, was standing, proclaiming God's goodness.

"Hallelujah!" yelled Miguel. "Hallelujah!"

As prayer spread worldwide, great battles were being won. Terrible princes of evil who had long reigned over great earthly territories were thrown back.

The demonic counterattack was mounted. In the dark heavenlies, great and evil princes of wickedness looked for weaknesses in the defenses of the enemy.

Filled with terrible fear and dread, Johanna Graham fell to her knees in prayer — pleading for the lives of Patrick and Zuni.

Unexpectedly, she was filled with enormous joy and thanksgiving. She stood, delighted, but not understanding.

She was to rest in God's goodness.

The old prayer warrior trembled.

"What?"

"Rest in His goodness."

"Whatever happens? What? No," she refused, "Lord, I cannot give them up. I claim them in Your holy name."

"Rest in My goodness," repeated the assurance.

"But they are not yet safe!" she wept. "Where are they?"

"Give them up."

"What?"

"Give them up."

Like Abraham on the mountain, she must be willing to put them on the altar and give them to God.

"I gave You my husband," she whispered. "What more do You want?"

"You must have no other gods before Me."

Stunned, Johanna protested.

"I love them!"

"You must let them go."

She refused.

❖   ❖   ❖

A great sense of false peace settled across the Earth. A few intercessors were not fooled.

Millions breathed a sigh of relief.

The battle was over.

They exulted.

"Yes," wept a familiar evangelist-host hugging his wife. "Thank You, Jesus. Thank You, Jesus. It is over. We are the victors."

Across the globe, other shallow leaders proclaimed the same false hope. They opened their Bibles and returned to the same divisive and argumentative doctrines that had kept them at each other's throats for centuries.

In the dark heavenlies, the powers of deception screamed their delight.

In a dark cliff's caves, great evil brooded. Its lights flashed silently. Across emergency monitors worldwide, it announced its coordinates and pleaded for help — on behalf of Zuni and Patrick.

❖   ❖   ❖

Simon and Huck both heard the helicopters.

Huckleberry had been in his tent, praying. He had not understood the sudden urgency that had gripped him, but obediently had sunk to his knees, worshipping God.

Simon had been translating one of the Epistles. He had glowered at his keyboard, irked that the kid had erected the satellite dish.

"We advise you to pause for a moment in prayer," had flashed a message across the bottom of his screen.

"Right," Simon snarled. He reached over and yanked the cable that connected him to the dish. No more stupid messages would defile his screen. He continued his work, uninterrupted.

In the next tent, Huck tapped out a message of concern to Amsterdam. "Is something going on?" he asked. "I am filled with such an intense sense of

warning and caution. I have never felt such dependence on the Lord. Is something happening on your
end?"

In astonishment, he read the response from headquarters: "O God, what turmoil fills my heart. I went
into my quietness to meditate and I realized what a
slippery path they walk, those who plot against our
great God.

"You will send them sliding over the edge of the
cliff and down to their destruction, to an instant end
to all their plotting, then an eternity of terror! They
will awaken to the truth as one awakens from a
drunken binge.

"O Lord, when I saw this vision, what turmoil
filled my heart! I saw myself so stupid and ignorant.
But, even so, You love me! You hold onto my right
hand and do not let me sink into my despair.

"You guide me with Your wisdom and counsel and
receive me into the very glories of heaven! Whom
have I in heaven but You? I desire no one on Earth as
much as You! My health fails, my spirits droop, yet
You remain! You are the strength of my heart! You
reign forever!" (Ps. 73: 17-26).

"Amen!" typed Huck on his screen.

"Amen!" responded somebody in Amsterdam.

"What is going on?" typed Huck.

"Nothing that we know of," responded Amsterdam.
"Watch and pray. Know that He is God."

"Thanks," tapped Huck.

Then he heard the helicopters. He stepped outside. Loudly, almost blowing over his tent, the chop-
pers landed in the clearing beside Lake Nyamulalengai.

Three foreign soldiers wielding assault rifles
charged toward him.

"Where are we?" demanded a sergeant.

"What?" demanded Simon, coming up behind Huck.

"Where are we?" roared the soldier impatiently. "We lost our bearings. We have a chopper down somewhere near here, but we were out of contact with our base and our navigations were going crazy."

"You're just inside Tanzania," said Simon. "Sitting on the Uganda and Rwanda border. Where are you from?"

"Eritrea," growled the soldier. "Which way is Lake Victoria?"

Simon pointed west.

"Eritrea?" exclaimed Huck. "That's way up north of Ethiopia on the Red Sea. What are you doing down here? You're half-way to South Africa!"

The sergeant glared at him. "We have a chopper down. We are trying to home in on its emergency beacon. Have you heard anything?"

Simon shook his head.

"A chopper?" asked Huck, looking skeptical. "What was an Eritrean helicopter doing in Tanzania?"

"It wasn't an Eritrean chopper. We're part of a multi-national search effort. We were looking in southern Ethiopia, but the search has moved south."

His words were suddenly drowned out by a formation of jets screaming overhead. Simon gawked. They bore Egyptian markings.

"Good grief! Who was in that chopper?" exclaimed Simon. "The King of England?"

"I don't have that information," growled the sergeant. "But there's a big reward."

"A reward?" Simon's interest was stimulated.

"A million pounds," said the sergeant.

"Eritrean pounds?" asked Simon.

"British pounds sterling — in silver bullion."

Simon almost choked. That was more than a million dollars. "What are you looking for?" he gasped. "How can I help you?"

A lieutenant ran up from the chopper. He wore a

Somali national army uniform.

"Sir!" exclaimed the sergeant, spinning around. "We are in Tanzania."

"Do you know where we can get a native guide?" asked the lieutenant, shaking hands with Simon, then Huck.

"What's this about a million pounds?" gasped Simon.

"We're looking for a missing helicopter," said the lieutenant. "The reward is for the return of an electronic device that may have been stolen from the chopper wreckage. The occupants were headed in this direction and had described on the radio a great plain that ended in bluffs. Our information is rather sketchy."

Simon nodded, his eyes a slit. It sounded like everything he had ever heard about the hidden valley settled by Matthew's secretive bunch. Once Matthew had described his village briefly, telling him how he believed God had led his people there and describing the ancient burial caves up in the cliffs.

Simon had scoffed. Matthew was a mystical know-it-all. Something within Simon told him that he just might be a rich man by morning.

His eyes danced. With a million dollars, he could blow off this smelly lake with its disrespectful savages.

"I think I may know something about your device," smiled Simon. He ducked into his tent. He emerged with a flare gun. "Can you take me to the other side of the lake?"

The lieutenant nodded.

Simon, Huck, and the foreign soldiers clamored out onto the muddy shores on the far side of Lake

Nyamulalengai.

Simon held up the flare gun. He fired it into the sky.

The lieutenant turned and looked at him inquisitively.

"Now, we wait," said the Bible translator.

"What?" demanded the sergeant.

"There's a tribe of refugees from Uganda that has a village hidden nearby," said Simon. "They've gone back to their traditional ways — living off the land, poaching wild game, that sort of thing. I trade them various trinkets from time to time. They always want bright-colored baseball caps. They trade me skins, and onions that make the most delicious soup."

"Where is their village?" demanded the lieutenant.

Simon shook his head. "They are very paranoid. They survived Idi Amin and Milton Obote. I've sent up our signal. Now, build a fire and put some green leaves on it to send up smoke. They'll send somebody along presently."

The lieutenant returned to his chopper. "Navigation and radio are out again," he told the sergeant when he came back. "But I radioed our position."

He glared at Simon. "You have no idea where their village is?"

Simon shrugged and shook his head. "They'll be along. Be patient."

But patience was not one of the lieutenant's virtues. He ran back to the chopper and called in help.

Up in the burial cave, the LORRD computer monitored the activities all around it.

It began to plot.

It did not like this one called Huckleberry who was downlinking to Amsterdam. He would have to die.

So would Matthew and Patrick.

The great, insidious evil inside the computer

laughed in glee at the idea.

These goody-goodies would have to pay.

And everyone would see who was the most powerful.

❖ ❖ ❖

"Look!" yelled Molech, pointing.

Valentina saw the flare, too.

A squadron of helicopters lined the far horizon — headed straight for Lake Nyamulalengai — answering the newest, urgent pleas for help broadcast by the computer.

"They're looking for us," bellowed Molech, running toward the flare.

Panting behind him, Valentina howled protests.

❖ ❖ ❖

"Look!" exclaimed Daniel, pointing at the flare.

"A flare!" yelled Patrick. "Who is it?"

Matthew looked perplexed. "It is Simon," he answered. "A very disturbed Bible translator who brings us our antibiotics. He is not trustworthy. Mostly he supplies us with baseball caps."

One of the men of the scouting party called to Matthew and pointed. Molech and Valentina were trotting toward the flare with renewed energy.

"Come," motioned Matthew.

Silently, the men and boys followed. Soon a thin plume of smoke rose into the sky where Simon waited.

Molech and Valentina became even more excited when six more helicopters crossed the sky from the east and south, putting down at the source of the smoke.

❖ ❖ ❖

"Where are we?" demanded a Tanzanian colonel

trading salutes with the Eritrean lieutenant.

"Lake Nyamulalengai," volunteered Simon. "What's this that I hear about a million-pound reward?"

The colonel turned and looked him over. "Who are you?"

"I'm on the payroll of the Tanzanian education ministry," oozed Simon, extending his hand. "We're putting local languages into written alphabets."

"Linguists," muttered the colonel. "Jesus missionaries."

"Oh, no," assured Simon. "I am in very good standing with your people. We are bringing literacy to the savages."

The colonel snorted his disgust and turned away from Simon. "A private plane is coming in from Mombasa. Where is a good place to land around here?"

"Oh, we've used the road as a landing field a number of times," offered Simon. "It can land right here."

The colonel nodded in agreement.

❧   ❧   ❧

Down the breathtaking escarpments following the Gomaliki River north of Lake Nyamulalengai, three squadrons of Tanzanian jets screeched in search of Molech Gordini.

Seven times they roared down the narrow valley directly over the distinctive fields and pastures of the hidden valley, then along the wide river where Britanga men and boys fished, and right over the tall granaries and symmetrical family hut clusters of Britanga itself.

But they did not turn.

They did not circle.

They did not report that they had found anything.

They did not see the unmapped plateau and its unexploited herds of game — enough to feed the Britanga people for many decades.

The hidden valley remained hidden.

Up in the dark cave, the LORRD computer watched in disgusted silence.

It was as if a mighty wing was hiding God's people, and the enemy was rendered blind and powerless, as if every weapon formed against the Britanga people simply failed.

"The earth shakes at the sound of His voice," whispered Sarah on the seventh pass of the jets. "A mighty warrior is the Lord our God, fearless in battle. His armies outnumber our enemies. When they shout, the strongholds of Satan come crashing down."

Beside her, Zuni watched the jets. "They've seen us," she said.

Sarah shook her head.

"The Lord is our Saviour. Gracious is He. The Lord is full of compassion. His army is also His family. When they shout, the strongholds of Satan come crashing down. It is happening. All across the globe, God's people are shouting. The Lord has given us power and authority. They are praising His holy name."

Zuni looked up. The jets were gone. "How did you do that?" she whispered in awe.

"I did nothing," exclaimed Sarah. "Our God reigns. Jesus reigns. Open your heart, Zuni Graham, and welcome Him in and He shall reign in your heart, too. Dark days are upon God's people, but He is our mighty refuge. Open your heart and He will reign and you will be unafraid. His mighty Comforter, the Holy Spirit of God, will fill you with joy and peace and you will tremble no more."

Zuni stared at her, startled by the sudden sales

pitch. "I don't believe in that sort of thing," she struggled out.

Sarah smiled. She touched Zuni's hand. "Yes, you do," she said softly. "You are not a fool. Only a fool in his heart says there is no God. You can see all around you the testimony of the hand of the Lord. Those airplanes did not see us. Their eyes were blinded. If they had cameras, they malfunctioned. There will be no report of this refuge of God's people."

"You can't hide here forever!" exclaimed Zuni.

"How do you think your great America was founded?" asked Sarah. "Refugees that you call pilgrims suffered terrible hardship and came to your Massachusetts where they could worship without persecution. Your Quakers followed in Pennsylvania, then your Baptists in Rhode Island. When white men first came to Virginia, they knelt on Cape Henry and proclaimed that America would be dedicated to God. And the Lord has protected America for more than 200 years."

Zuni did not answer. Sarah was a constant surprise. Zuni had not expected an American history lesson from a black tribeswoman in the middle of the Great African Rift.

"Your great rivers and forests were first discovered by missionaries," said Sarah. "Your capital city is filled with praises to God. Did you know that the highest building there, your Washington Monument, has the words 'Praise God' carved at the very top in Latin, facing your Capitol Building? God has blessed America although it has been battered and seduced by the evil one.

"And so, God protects us here, too. Perhaps from Britanga will rise a new Africa someday. An Africa that does not hide its proud culture and its rich traditions, but knows the great joy of Jesus Christ instead of the murder and pain of false, futile religions devised over the centuries by the evil powers of darkness."

Zuni stared at her. She did not say anything.

"You have seen terrible hurt," said Sarah gently. "You have known great hardship and heartache. God has brought you here to recover."

"Why would He care about us?"

Sarah smiled. "He loves all His children."

Zuni smiled politely.

"Where is your husband?" asked Sarah.

"He has divorced me," said Zuni, surprised at the question.

"Did he leave you?"

"I left him." The noise of the village filled the great silence. "He was having an affair," said Zuni. "I found out and I threw him out. I told him I never wanted to see him again."

Sarah nodded sympathetically. "He must have been a very terrible man."

"No." Zuni's eyes were faraway and suddenly filled with tears. She searched for words. "I . . . I scared him. He enjoys a safe, conservative life. He takes no risks. I like risks."

Sarah studied Zuni's face. "Did he beat you?"

"No."

"I did not mean with fists. Was he cruel?"

"No . . . not really."

Sarah nodded, trying to understand. "He went to live with this other woman, this adulteress?"

"No, he swore it was a one-time thing, a mistake."

Sarah smiled. She reached out and touched Zuni's hand. "You knew that he was lying."

"No, he was telling the truth."

Sarah gripped Zuni's hand. "But you were so hurt that you did not wish to sleep with him ever again?"

Suddenly, Zuni was crying. "How could he do that to me? How could he do that? How could he betray me? I had given up everything for him. Instead, I did all the things he wanted me to do. Then, he went to 'her'."

Gently, "You must forgive him."

"Forgive him?" whispered Zuni.

"God has forgiven you. You cannot do any less."

Zuni shook her head. "Never."

Sarah patted her shoulder. She quietly prayed.

Zuni closed her eyes.

"Forgiveness is hard," said Sarah. "We all must forgive if we are to exist together. I have to forgive you. You have to forgive me. You have to forgive your husband and you must forgive yourself, just as Matthew had to forgive himself."

Zuni sighed. "I know that Patrick needs a father image. I believe in marriage, but . . ."

"It is not easy to be alone," agreed Sarah gently. "I know. I went through a terrible time trying to accept the massacre of my husband and my boys. The worst part truly was just being alone afterward. All alone. My boys were falling apart . . . I was falling apart . . . my life had completely fallen apart. I had no money, nothing. I had no one but strangers to turn to."

Zuni nodded.

"I cried out to the Lord," said the old woman. "I had to be strong. I could not be weak. I could not cry in front of my boys. I had to be strong for them. But I should have cried. I should have held them and let them comfort me. Yet, I was determined to fight back."

Zuni understood only too well.

"I was not really strong when I threw Noel out," she said. "I was mean and hard. It was not me — but what else could I do?"

"I had to accept the will of God," said Sarah. "I had to learn to trust Him with everything. I had to cry out to Jesus and ask Him to help me bear the hurt, the pain, the anger."

"I don't think that would work for me," said Zuni.

"I realized that He had been so good to me," continued Sarah. "So gentle in comforting me — in sending people to rescue me. You know, my husband was a good Christian. He was ready to meet God. So were little Mark and Luke. They were Christians. They had obeyed the Lord. They are with Jesus.

"But . . . John." Her voice cracked unexpectedly "I do not understand about John. I like to believe that he is still alive and that he has come back to the Lord — but . . ."

She was silent.

Zuni gripped her hand.

Beside the silent Matthew, Patrick gawked in disbelief. Molech and Valentina stumbled into the clearing on the shores of the lake.

Officers from eight African nations stood in amazement and respect as Molech roared an introduction of himself and demanded the use of a radio.

The Tanzanian colonel stepped forward, introduced himself, and handed Molech a cellular phone.

"Give us a helicopter," demanded Valentina. "I know where to go. I know where to go."

Instead, Molech was barking orders into the phone.

Patrick watched from the high grass. Back in communication with the outside world, Molech Gordini was once again the commanding, dangerous man that Patrick remembered.

Overhead, two large cargo planes lumbered into view, searching for Simon's camp on the other side of the lake — and the landing strip road.

"You," Molech said, staring at Simon and clutching a phone to his ear, "where are these caves?"

Simon sputtered something about the reward.

"Take us now," ordered Molech.

"I don't know where they are, exactly," said Simon.

Molech stared at him. With cold calm, he reached over and removed the colonel's revolver from his hip holster. Without even blinking, Molech leveled the gun at young Huck,. Then he fired.

Patrick gasped.

The young Bible translator fell, a small wound neat and centered in his forehead, right between his eyes.

"Now," said Molech. "You will take us to the caves."

In horror, Simon looked down at his dead co-worker. His fear was overpowering. He did not mourn the young troublemaker. He did not weep for the injustice of a young life snuffed out. Instead, he cowardly, cravenly, babbled promises of complete cooperation.

Moments later Molech, Valentina, and Simon were airborne. This time, Molech sat at the controls of the helicopter. He turned off the radio and stared at Simon.

"Follow the river," said the Bible translator, completely intimidated. He had no idea if there were caves or a hidden valley along the little stream.

But he did not want to die.

Huck's body was left in the dust as the last helicopter lifted off and returned to the other side of the lake. There, a tent city was being erected. Six cargo planes had landed and unloaded a command center worthy of an emperor. Simon's satellite dish was taken over as well as his computers.

With a single motion, a Gordini technician accidentally erased every bit of Bible translation that Simon had done in the months that he had toiled in the stench of the lake.

Gone forever was the detailed research Simon had done into the mechanics of the local dialect — its sounds, its inflections, and its subtle variations.

The alphabet he had thrown together for them was wiped out, too — gone. He had never bothered to back any of it up on disks or dump it into the network, using his satellite dish.

It was as if Simon Webster had never been there.

❖ ❖ ❖

"Yes," exclaimed Valentina as the chopper swept down over the great cliffs that rose over the widening river. "Yes!" she screamed, her voice high and otherworldly. "My LORRD awaits! There! You fool! There!"

Molech's eyes grew black and small with anger. He gently guided the chopper to where the madwoman pointed.

High up in the sandstone cliffs were hundreds of small caves, the ancient graveyard of a civilization long departed.

"Yes!" shrieked Valentina, pointing to one cave in particular. She yammered wildly.

Gently, Molech set the chopper down on the dusty riverbank. The frenzied Valentina babbled, her face glued to the tall bluffs, her eyes fixed on a particular cave. She was then out, scrambling over the sacred remains of a vanished people. Babbling, weeping, Valentina stumbled excitedly, her feet crushing ancient funeral statuettes, overturning earthenware burial objects arranged on the ground. The great mass of pagan relics — weathered and fragile from centuries out in the elements — shattered under her stumbling feet.

Valentina was up a narrow trail, carefully finding the old log ladders and footholes in the cliff. Solemnly,

Molech followed.

Inside the cavern, he shivered in discomfort, stepping carefully among the human bones that covered the floor and crowded the mouth of the cave. Trembling behind him, Simon tried not to disturb piles of human mummies packed into the cave like so many bolts of cloth.

Who were these dead? How had they reached this ancient graveyard in the cliffs? Were all the other caves also full? Dusty bits of cloth hung in the stillness, faded, but still bearing native patterns.

Valentina saw none of it.

She was tearing open three crates. Excitedly, she ripped the lids apart with her chubby fingers, howling in delight. Shaking, she lifted out the undamaged components of her LORRD.

Then, she almost dropped them.

Recoiling she mumbled in confusion to herself. She touched the machine daintily — as if it burned her fingers. She looked immensely confused. "What has happened here?" she whispered.

Atop the dusty, upturned crates, she fumed as she assembled her little mega-computer, talking to it as if it were a live thing, baffled that it did not seem to answer — assuring it as if it were a pet or a human being with very real feelings. Her face grew increasingly troubled. "You are diminished in power," she whispered. "It was those natives, wasn't it? They've meddled where they should never have come. Well, come back, come back, my friends. I am here now. Everything is back to normal."

Simon watched with revulsion. The machine was nothing like he had expected. It certainly did not seem to have any life of its own. Sure, with no visible power source, it hummed to life as Valentina connected cables and threw switches. But this was not the evil machine he had expected.

Bending over it, Valentina cried, "Why don't you answer?" her voice almost a chant. "What is wrong? Why don't you come back?" Squatting in a tangle of ancient human ribs and vertebrae, she carefully touched the keyboard.

"Doesn't it work?" demanded Molech.

"Well, yes," whispered Valentina, her left hand hovering warily over the console. She looked away, self-consciously. She tapped cautiously on the side of the monitor.

"When will it tell me the future?" demanded Molech.

Valentina looked up in disgust. *You are still a fool,* she thought. *Even as we speak, we are taking him to the threshold of a great and wondrous day. The entire world is at our fingertips. Our LORRD has been downloading for months from every computer worldwide, every communications network, every electronic device that transmits even the weakest signal. There are no secrets.*

"I want to know the hour of my death," demanded Molech.

"Fool!" shrieked Valentina. "I know how to input your stupid program. It can project the millions of variables, but such time wasted is an absurdity in itself. You will die when you will die."

She laughed under her breath as she tapped the keyboard.

Then, she looked up in horror and disbelief.

Molech had his pistol leveled at her face. "I already have all the riches of any man alive. There will be time for your little financial games and much, much more that I desire. But this moment, I require the knowledge of the hour of my death."

Valentina stared at his pistol. "You are a pitiful joke," she sneered. "You would not kill me. No one else can make this machine do what I designed it to do."

Molech cocked the pistol.

She spat venomous objections. Then in Russian, she uttered an ancient curse from the Siberian highlands. She leered her rebellion and began to laugh.

Molech fired the gun.

The bullet streaked past Valentina's ear, creasing it and burying itself into the sandstone wall of the back of the cave.

"Fool," spat Valentina. "Fool! Fool! All right. But it will take hours and perhaps days. Weeks!"

She tapped in the fortune-telling probability-projection program her spirit guides had shown her. She hissed her hatred of the fool who wanted to turn the most powerful computer in the world into a crystal ball.

"At my fingertips is a new world order," she muttered under her breath. "A new monetary arrangement forced upon every living human being who trades or earns money." She glanced up at the spellbound Simon.

Molech stared out the door of the cave. He did not see the thriving village or beautiful fields of Britanga.

"At my fingertips is a new fiscal order that I can drop into place overnight in a technological coup that will catch even the superpowers by surprise," hissed Valentina, watching Simon. She typed madly on the keyboard, pausing every few seconds and holding her fingertips in the air, as if she hated touching the keys.

"All nations of the world will bow down to me. We are God. The Arabs. We are God. The Yanks. We are God. The Japs. We are God. The Aussies. We are God. The Frogs. The Brits. The Chinks. The Krauts. WE ARE GOD. Everybody. I will give Mother Russia new life. We are GOD! A new world awaits!" Crazily, Valentina chuckled, suddenly infuriated again that Molech somehow no longer shared the urgency of her scheme. She squinted conspiratorially at Simon. "Kill him," she whispered. "Knock him from behind. Throw him off the cliff. Then you and I will rule Earth."

Simon licked his lips.

Ruling Earth sounded too mad to be taken very seriously.

"I understand there is a reward for this computer," he whispered. "One million pounds sterling."

Valentina was ignoring him. She typed madly on the keyboard, staring into the monitor. "Fool," she whispered. "Kill him. Hit him from behind." But she did not seem to be talking to Simon any longer. Under her breath, she was babbling with beings unseen.

Curious, Simon peered over her shoulder. What she was typing was not any computer language Simon had ever seen. It was a mass of numbers and symbols jumbled crazily in an unending stream. It did not even look like the baffling assembler codes that Simon had hated in college.

There were no neat rows.

No data lines.

Just a jumble.

"Idiots," muttered Valentina. "Everything has been ready and is just waiting. The world's financial structures are interfaced. Today, all humankind could bow to a new, peaceful ruler — but no, here I am squatting in a burial cave in darkest Africa, playing Gypsy fortune-teller."

She was typing so fast that sparks seemed to fly from her fingertips. A constant muttering flowed from her lips. "In a matter of moments, no monetary exchange could take place without my knowledge. But no, I have to play witch." She leered at Simon. "Kill him," she ordered, "throw him to the jackals."

Simon crossed his arms. He glanced away. He wasn't about to pick a fight with a man who commanded soldiers from ten countries. A man able to offer a million-pound reward and holding a cocked pistol.

❖　　❖　　❖

Patrick knelt over Huck's body. The Bible translator's eyes stared unseeing at the heavens. His face was calm, however. It was obvious he had not feared death.

"Hey," Patrick whispered. He shook the lifeless shoulders. "Hey, Man." The grey coldness of death was unmistakable. Matthew leaned against his spear and gazed across the lake. It was as if a new city had sprung up.

"I must go over there," he said softly.

"What?" demanded an older man beside him.

"The Lord would do a mighty thing today," said Matthew softly. "Empty, hurting souls from many nations are gathered across the lake, waiting for an answer. I can give them their answer."

Daniel stepped up beside his father. "I'll go with you."

The other men began to debate in their native language that Patrick could not understand. He looked up, baffled. *Why didn't they care about this dead body?*

Beside Patrick knelt young Andrew. He had sensed the fourteen-year-old American's grief. Gently, he touched his hands to the dead Huck's eyes and closed them. Nudging Patrick's sunburned ribs, the twelve year old lifted his hands to heaven. He smiled blissfully, praying.

Patrick understood — although he did not know the words. Andrew was thanking God for the life of this stranger. Both boys sensed that Huck had been a believer, for there had been no terror in his eyes, no scream on his dead lips.

Daniel touched Patrick's shoulder. "We're going over there," he said, his voice strangely resolute. "I believe we are going to die. Andrew will take you to your mother."

"What?" exclaimed Patrick, jumping up. "Why? What are you talking about?"

The men of the scouting party were gathered around Matthew, who was kneeling on the ground. They laid their hands on Matthew's shoulders and head and began praying aloud.

Their voices grew in volume and emotion. It was not a death chant — more a celebration of joy and wonder.

Matthew stood.

Daniel stood tall beside him.

"No," said Matthew. "You must stay and lead our people."

"What?" wept Daniel, understanding exactly what his father was saying.

"You cannot come where I am going."

Daniel threw himself on his father, his voice full of grief and pleading. Gently, Matthew held him close, as if the lanky teen were a little boy again.

"You are a man," said Matthew. Spear in hand, the chief of the Britanga people trotted off along the shoreline of the lake.

Daniel stood bravely, his eyes filled with tears. "He will live!" he proclaimed aloud in English, then in the tongue of his people.

The older men stared after Matthew.

Patrick stood. "Yeah, Matthew!" he announced. "He will live." He realized that his eyes were filled with tears. Unashamed, he felt them running down his cheeks. "He will live!" proclaimed Patrick again.

Beside him, Andrew stood and shouted agreement, although he could not have understood what Patrick had said.

Daniel turned. "The Lord Jesus Christ promised to us that whatever we agree together to be in His name, He would give us." Daniel stared after the disappearing figure of his father. "We agree! My father will live!" His young voice carried across the still water.

The boy saw the spear of his father rise into the sky in agreement.

Daniel fell to his knees, weeping in joy, unashamed of his tears.

"He will live!" yelled Patrick. "He will live! He will live!"

For the first time in Britanga history, a stranger stumbled into their hidden valley. Searching jets and helicopters had unsuccessfully scoured the area. But a lone embassy worker named Noel MacDougal walked into the valley, wearing a backpack and following the satellite coordinates that had been broadcast by the megacomputer in the burial caves.

Why had no one else managed? They had failed because their eyes had been blinded. Their minds had been clouded. Their instruments had been dumbfounded — all at the hand of Almighty God. They could not see what God chose for them not to see.

It was certainly within the Lord's desire for Noel MacDougal to be reunited with the two he so urgently sought.

So it was that Noel knew exactly who the white woman was beating laundry against the rocks of the river downstream from the village he had not yet seen.

Noel watched Zuni and wondered.

Had she changed? His body shook, realizing that his love for her had never left him. It had been buried in hurts of the past.

She seemed lighthearted. Could that be? She was supposedly missing — the object of a massive, international search. Yet, scrubbing laundry in the middle of a crowd of tribeswoman, she seemed relaxed and . . . happy.

There was a worried stir among the women when suddenly he was spotted.

Zuni stared in absolute disbelief.

As if in a trance, she stepped out to greet him.

Running to her, he said, "So, this is where you've been hiding," his voice gentle but cautious. Carefully, he touched Zuni's hand. She did not pull away.

"I've missed you so," he declared awkwardly, reciting a speech he had practiced in his mind for hours and hours. "Zuni, my life is so empty without you. There's no reason for anything unless I'm with you. I can't concentrate on my work. I can't find any purpose for living. Zuni, my greatest joy in life is knowing that you are happy. Please forgive me and come back to me."

The renegade missionary daughter looked down at his hand on hers, then up into his eyes. Noel could see the tears well up within her eyes as she whispered, "Oh, my love, kiss me."

Noel paused for just a moment in pure ecstasy. Then like a hungry lion, he engulfed her lips with his. Zuni thought for a moment she was going to faint from the dizziness that overtook her. "Zuni, I love you more than I will ever have words to express it to you."

"Yes, Noel. I can now sense and feel that love. Something has happened to me that now gives me the ability to know and receive your love," Zuni said tearfullly.

"I don't know what it is but I like it," responded Noel. He then took Zuni into his arms once again. For what seemed like an eternity they hung in each other's embrace, trying to understand why they had ever endured a moment apart. Then they kissed again, a long, soulful kiss from deep within as two hearts reunited. "Let's go someplace where we can be alone," Noel breathed into Zuni's ear.

"Yes, let's do that and now," Zuni responded. And quietly they walked into the bush.

Suddenly, the ladies of Britanga were applauding. But it was not Western-style hand-clapping. It was their joyous, rhythmic clapping that always filled the village, now joined with happy voices.

As soon as they were alone, Noel grabbed and hugged her tight. Zuni responded with an embarrassed, shy school-girl look. (It had been so long since she had seen him or felt his touch.) "Wait, Noel, wait. Before we go any further I have something that I must tell you." It was obvious to Noel that she was afraid as she haltingly spoke, "Noel, please forgive me for judging you so harshly. I love you and always have. Please, my love, forgive me."

Noel gently took Zuni into his arms and whispered, "Of course, I forgive you. I am the one who did you wrong. Will you forgive me?"

"Oh, yes, I forgive you," Zuni tearfully responded.

Noel sighed at the touch of her womanly figure as he caressed and kissed her. Zuni's mind exploded with showers of emotion. A moan of delight escaped her lips. *"Mi corazon, mi vida. Tu eres el sol que me calienta. Tanto que te extrañe."* (You are the sun that warms my life. I miss you so much.) After Noel kissed her again, Zuni moved closer and said, "Kiss me again, my precious love."

Noel couldn't believe his ears. *This can't be the same woman I was married to,* he thought. Zuni began trembling. She had been without him for so long.

"I'm scared," she sighed. She had always wanted to give herself completely to her estranged husband, but she had always held back. She had been so cruel, arrogant, and selfish, ever going in her own direction. Zuni had always felt, at least subconsciously, that

Noel was something less than a man, a wimp.

It was strange but now she realized that he was indeed a man deserving of her love and respect. *Could it be God who is giving me all of the new feelings?* she thought. In a playful and giddy mood from their rediscovered love, she told Noel about how she used to view him: "Honey, I know now that you are man." She giggled a bit and then continued, "But one thing, why do you only have three little hairs on your chest?" As they laughed, Zuni realized that as a Latin, her image of masculinity was a hairy-chested man. She knew now how wrong she'd been.

"Do you realize how much your body, your lips excite me?" Noel asked. "I've never told you that before, but from now on you will be hearing that very often. You are such a brave woman, a survivor. You really have been an excellent mother for Patrick. I trust you so much." Tears now welled up in his eyes and he groped for words. "I never want to lose you again. I've missed your black Spanish hair. I bought a gift for you, Darling." He handed her a white, snug-fitting dress. "Still a size 8, right?"

As Zuni removed her very masculine shirt and jeans Noel was once again amazed how feminine Zuni started looking. As she slipped on the sleek white dress even Zuni had to take a second look at herself, for this was the first time in years that she looked or felt like a real woman. As Zuni approached him she spoke in a soft, passionate voice, saying, "Oh Noel, I'm so happy that you still think I have a school-girl figure."

"We'll see how good your figure is tomorrow when we run five miles together like we used to. Will you be able to handle it after tonight?"

For almost a full minute she looked at him with a child-like gleam in her eyes and then shouted, "Let's go for it." And slowly, holding hands, they walked deeper into the bush.

❖   ❖   ❖

In the presence of the Almighty, Lucifer again made his accusations against the Britanga people and Matthew. "They do not follow You," he whined. "They follow HIM."

The Lord shook his head in disagreement.

"Let me take him," pleaded Satan.

"Why do you wish to kill this one?"

"I want You to see how they will all turn away from You," snarled Satan. "They are not Your disciples. They are his."

"I have heard this accusation before," said the Lord. "You said that those who put their eyes on the corrupt televangelists of not-so-long-ago would return to their sins when I let you bring their leaders down."

"Many did," whined Satan.

"Most did not."

"Your churches are filled with lazy, self-centered liars," said Satan. "Just look at . . ."

"Just look at the Chinese Christians," said God. "Look at their affliction and distress. Even in the midst of it, they knew they were rich. Look at how they have bravely faced persecution — dismissing their dread and fears. Even when I allowed you to throw so many of them into prison, they stood firm in the truth, knowing I had not deserted them. Look at how they were tested and proven worthy — loyal even unto pain of death."

"Some faltered," hissed Lucifer. "Some denounced You."

"Most did not. Nor did the Christian remnant of Iran — although they sit in a spiritual wasteland, old Persia, a stronghold where you, Satan, sit enthroned. Even still, they are clinging to and holding fast My name and did not deny Me even during the Ayatollah's worst reign of terror when many were martyred."

"Oh yes," whined Satan. "but look at them now. Look at that one there — he proclaims his Christianity from safe exile, yet he is not interested in returning at all. There's too much money to be made as a noble spokesman-in-exile. Oh, how he tells such lies in pursuit of money.

"He'll say anything if it makes him a buck. Look at his personal gluttony as he moves among the Christian big shots, eating their food, standing in their pulpits, and proclaiming his love for his persecuted brethren. What about that secret perversion of his? Among his staff, he loves to discuss in detail all the Americans' sexual problems. That's your best Christianity can produce? You must let me expose him for the fraud he is. He whispers that he is willing to die for You. He deserves to. Let me have him. I'll expose him for the fraud he is."

"No," said the Lord. "I will send my angels to him once again — and true Christian exiles to convict him of his gluttony and his love of money and his lies. He lies almost as well as you.

"I despise his sin," the Lord said. "But I love him as my very own son. You may take away all of his money one more time because of his continual lying.

"I desire that he should conquer. I wish him the best that I can give him. Joy immeasurable. A new name. Eternal life."

Lucifer glowered. "He deserves to die."

"No," said the Father. "He is a bright and shining light in the wilderness of Iran."

"A filthy and shameful flame festering in Your sight," hissed Satan. "Let me have him."

"He is My child. He says that he loves Me.

"Convenience," whispered Satan. "Let me give him what he deserves — public exposure, humiliation, and denunciation. Then let's see if he will continue to mouth his empty religiosity."

"No," said the Lord.

❖   ❖   ❖

In the darkness of the burial cave, Valentina sighed and sat back.

"Okay," she spat at Molech. "It's ready."

Gordini strode through the musty bones and peered over her shoulder. "Tell me," he sputtered, his voice hoarse and dry.

Valentina punched the keys.

What she saw took her breath away.

"No," she gasped.

"What?"

She tapped away on the keys. She shrieked. She tapped again.

"What?" demanded Molech. Simon peered over his shoulder.

"You will never die," whispered Valentina. "But your human life will end tomorrow. Everyone's will. It's all over. Everything is over. It all ends tomorrow."

"What?" exclaimed Simon in horror. "How can everything end?" He was filled with a terrible fear and dread. The very answer that man had sought for two thousand years now flashed on the computer screen before him.

"Nuclear war?" demanded Simon.

"No," rasped Valentina. "The return of Jesus Christ."

In the dark heavenlies, there was a horrible scream. What had been hidden for millennia from the commanders of the rebel archangel now flashed before them on the little computer before Valentina.

"Attack!" came the horrified scream.

"ATTACK!" shrieked the princes of darkness infesting the world.

In a panic that filled the Earth, a great and terrible oppression of evil swept over mankind — a desperate last-ditch assault to claim as many human victims as possible in the moments that remained.

In the same instant, the intercessors of the world were shaken awake. Millions fell to their knees in urgent and powerful prayer.

The howls of evil filled the darkness.

In the blackness of his earthly realm, the renegade archangel who had tempted Eve and tormented Job and who had mistakenly sent Jesus Christ to the Cross knew that he had been betrayed.

Humiliated, he stood in the presence of God and renewed his accusations against Matthew and the Britanga.

He did not even mention the obvious — that no human computer could accurately project the great and secret day known only to the Lord God Almighty. Jesus himself had admitted that He did not know the day or hour when the Creator, His wondrous Father, would bring human time to an end.

It was not known to the angels. It could not be calculated by even the most righteous searchers of Bible prophesy or the most powerful computer ever constructed.

The world would not end tomorrow.

The attack was called back.

But the intercessors did not retreat.

They were strong. They had experienced anew the joy and peace that comes from gathering around the throne of their loving Father. Across the globe, millions raised their voices and hands — defying religious traditions and doubts and fears of centuries.

Five million of them were kids.

Kids in the ghettos, barrios, subways, and streets, crying out "Holy, holy, holy. Around Your throne, we magnify Your name. Holy, holy, holy is the Lord! Lord God Almighty who was, who is and is to come! Holy, holy, holy is the Lord of all. Jesus Christ, we lift You high and give You the glory! Jesus Christ, we magnify, we honor You and lift up our highest praise."

Against this horrible counterattack, the evil forces retreated from ancient strongholds, reeling at the sound of such praise and honor of the One they hated and feared so.

"Father God, we honor You and give You the highest praise!" declared a tall black preacher on a street corner of East Los Angeles. "Jesus Christ, we acknowledge You, King of kings, Prince of Peace, Lord of lords. God the Holy Spirit, we thank You for the great comfort, joy, and power that You give us!"

"The Earth shall be filled with the knowledge of the glory of the Lord, just like the waters cover the sea!" shouted Miguel in his hospital room.

"Hallelujah!" bellowed an Iowa farmer atop his tractor. "Hallelujah! Hallelujah!"

"You are Lord, Jesus Christ," wept a little boy in Poland.

"We praise You!" cried a hotel maid in Australia.

❖   ❖   ❖

"No," whispered Valentina, hitting the side of her darkly glowing LORRD. "No, what's wrong here?"

She slammed the computer with the side of her hand. She looked up at the distraught Molech.

"The program has crashed," she said. "You didn't give me a chance to debug it. You're in such a crazy rush to know secrets no man is supposed to know. Let me do what we came here to do."

Across the globe, voices were raised in a new chorus of prayer. In spiritual realms, the Earth seemed to shake.

The glowing computer screen went blank. "No," screamed Valentina.

His face a death mask, Molech ran to the mouth of

the cave and looked out at the dusty ruins. "Everything ends tomorrow?" he whispered. "Everything? Everything?" He spun. In his fist he clutched his pistol like a club. "You witch," he raged. He screamed and ran toward Valentina with death in his eyes. He knocked over the computer, yanking out the cabling as it fell off its crate.

Valentina shrieked as her monitor screen went dark. Fingernails and teeth bared, she tore into him, her screams filling the cavern.

There were four quick shots.

Simon hid his face, afraid to watch.

When he looked up, Molech was awkwardly throwing Valentina's body off him. He struggled to his feet. "Witch," he spat, aiming the pistol at her again. He fired three more times, point-blank into her skull.

She did not move again.

Crazily, Molech stared at Simon. He then spun and was gone.

Disbelieving what he had just seen and heard, the Bible translator ran to the mouth of the cave and watched Molech scramble into the helicopter.

The chopper lifted off.

Simon was then alone amid the death of centuries. He squatted in the dusty bones and stared at Valentina's unmoving body. Beside her, the computer flashed and purred.

It was undamaged, but its mad master was dead.

Simon sighed.

He strolled over and tapped on its keyboard, then recoiled. There was something eery about the machine.

It seemed to be laughing.

He stood back, spun on his heel, and fled the cave.

An enormous male lion lounged against an acacia

tree and watched the scouting party running along the edge of the plain toward the cliffs of Britanga.

Heat waves danced over the ground.

At Simon Webster's camp, Matthew strode up unafraid and made conversation with the first guards he encountered. They laughed at the sight of him — a primitive tribesman in athletic shorts, carrying a tall spear.

He laughed with them and began to preach.

His gentle sermon was humble and easy to understand: Jesus Christ loved them.

They did not hear anything — except perhaps the evil taunts of a hidden computer. "Kill him," hummed the LORRD. "Kill him. Kill him."

Their ears irritated by something they did not understand, they ridiculed the tall preacher, laughing at the extreme darkness of his skin, the primitiveness of his bare feet and his proud spear. And they turned ugly.

Angry as the unheard hum grew.

Toward the east, thunder clouds gathered over Lake Nyamulalengai and the tent city that had been Simon and Huck's camp.

Running toward the hidden valley, Daniel halted. "We must go back," he announced. "Something great and terrible wants to kill my father."

There was no dissent. Matthew had said nobody could go with him — not that they could not follow later.

Excitedly, the men and boys turned. They charged back through the grass. Out of breath, they ran along the edge of the lake.

They arrived just as Molech Gordini's helicopter fluttered into view, landing in the middle of the camp.

Matthew was standing handcuffed by a Ugandan helicopter — under guard, but talking with a group of soldiers. Loudly they laughed, then slapped him across the face.

"Kill him," taunted the distant, vengeful computer. "Kill him."

They cheered drunkenly — leering their disrespect for his simplicity, his gentle goodness, his jovial laugh even when the joke was at his expense.

Gordini virtually fell out of his chopper in his urgency to get out. In absolute terror, he ran toward a commander who was stepping forward. "The world is ending!" Molech shouted. "I have seen it. It ends tomorrow."

Officers from six African nations glanced at each other in disbelief. Before them ranted one of the most powerful men on earth. Their governments had ordered them to give him every assistance he needed.

"I have seen it," screamed Molech. "Everything ends. EVERYTHING! Everything!"

A Ugandan colonel motioned to Matthew's guard. "Sir," he announced, "here is a savage who admits he helped hide your computer in a cave up in the cliffs nearby, but he will not tell us where. He is a Christian infidel. A dupe of missionaries. A crazy man."

"You!" shrieked Molech, aiming his gun at Matthew. "You! What do you know about all this? What does your God say? THE WORLD IS ENDING TOMORROW!"

Matthew looked perplexed. He gazed up at the sky, then down the barrel of Molech's pistol.

"I do not know what to tell you," he said. "But I do not believe that the Lord my Father, the God of Abraham, Isaac, and Jacob, will allow any man to know the day of His coming. The world will only know when Jesus comes in power and glory."

"Fool!" shrieked Molech. He pulled the trigger. But the gun did not fire. Molech shrieked his anguish. He grabbed an assault rifle from one of the soldiers. And he opened fire.

Bullets raked Matthew's chest and neck, throwing him backward against a truck. In complete surprise, the ebony giant stared at Molech.

"Jesus Christ loves you," he proclaimed from the dirt, his voice weak, but unafraid. "You will have nothing to fear from His return if you will bow down before Him and allow yourself to be filled with His Holy Spirit." Blood ran from his mouth.

"Yes," hissed the unseen computer. "Now the other one."

Matthew looked puzzled, then glanced over at the high grass and saw his sixteen-year-old son Daniel.

"Today," proclaimed Matthew, "I live. Forever." Then he was gone.

The camp was silent, except for the sound of the wind and thunder high in the clouds above them.

"Now the other one," hummed the computer. "Kill him, too."

In the high grass, Patrick stared in disbelief at the still figure.

"No!" screamed the white boy, admitting to himself for the first time how much he loved the black giant. Jumping up, the boy ran to him. "MATTHEW!" Patrick charged into the camp. "Don't go, Matthew! Hold on! We'll get you to a doctor . . ."

"KILL HIM!" shrieked the computer.

Shots rang out.

Startled, the boy was spun around backward. He gawked, as if not understanding his sudden, intense pain.

He looked down at his bloody chest.

He struggled to his knees, but was slammed forward as laughing soldiers poured more bursts into him. He slowly moved.

Sunburned, his narrow shoulders blistered from the sun, his skinny body clad only in the filthy remains of his hacked-off khaki pants, Patrick did not cry out.

A soldier strolled over and stuck his rifle barrel into the back of the boy's head.

There was an incredible peace on his fourteen-year-old face. A peace that would not have been there days before.

The peace that surpasses understanding.

In the sky, a great vulture circled.

Patrick Graham MacDougal, the white city boy who had wanted to be a black man running free forever in the rich, unmapped highlands beside his wise, loving giant, reached out and touched Matthew's handcuffed wrist.

"MATTHEW," he mouthed. He looked up at Daniel. On the adolescent American's lips was another silent, urgent message: "My mom."

Daniel stared, then nodded. Tears flowed down his dark cheeks.

Clutching Matthew's big hand, Patrick sighed and relaxed.

There was one last, unnecessary gunshot, but the boy was already dead.

❖　❖　❖

"No," wept Johanna Graham on her face before the throne of her great and beloved Creator.

Twenty-four thrones surrounded the great throne of God and on them sat the twenty-four elders arrayed in white with crowns of gold on their heads. Out of the great throne came flashes of lightning and rumblings and peals of thunder. And in front of the great throne blazed seven great torches.

In front of the throne was what appeared to be a glassy sea — as if made of crystal. All around the throne were great and terrifying beings whose voices thundered together: "Holy, holy, holy is the Lord God

Almighty who was and who is and who is to come."

Gabriel, the messenger of heaven, stood in silence. Battle-weary Michael, commander of the heavenly fighting forces, knelt with head bowed.

The Master of the Universe was in pain, His mighty love extended to an old friend who wept aloud in her rebellion. The scrawny old warrior on her knees pleaded her case.

The Almighty Father was unchanged.

I will have no other gods before me, He spoke into her tender heart, His own heart breaking.

In her darkened bedroom, Patrick's grandmother fumbled with her Bible and worn prayer journal. "Father," prayed Johanna Graham, tears rolling down her wrinkled cheeks, "I surrender. I give them up. I repent of my idolatry. You alone are my God."

Filled with continued dread, Johanna shook. "You have told me to rest in Your goodness. So, I give that boy up to You, Lord. He is Yours. I love him so, Father ..." She paused. "But You are God."

In the dark night, the Almighty Creator of all things was pleased and His hand moved.

❖ ❖ ❖

In the Great African Rift, at the headwaters of the mighty Nile, that life-giving father of waters, the hot afternoon was shattered by a lion's thunderous roar.

It was not the soft moaning sound of a mother lion calling her cubs from their hiding place in the rocks.

It was not the warning roar of a lioness telling a strange lion from another part of the grassy sea to retreat from this playground of her cubs.

No, it was the mighty roar of a great male declaring his domain.

Into the tent city strode the great lion and soldiers jumped up and took aim, but none fired.

The lion seemed in search of something or someone. Unafraid, it strode into the human domain like a giant house cat.

It found what it was looking for in the tent of the commander. There, the supposedly non-drinking Muslim Molech Gordini was guzzling Russian vodka and desperately screaming into a cellular phone.

The lion stared him in the eye, roared once more, then was gone.

It did not disappear. It just slipped out like the great hunter that it was.

Shaken, the soldiers of the camp whispered to themselves. This was a sign, a terrible sign.

They had been warned.

"Do not go," whispered the silent hum of a computer up in the dark cliffs. "There is much to do here."

The hyenas then came and the soldiers no longer seemed to hear. Laughing, tearing down tents, snarling, unafraid, the stocky animals stalked through the camp — staring eye-to-eye with the soldiers, mocking and laughing.

The commanders huddled. Yes, they had all sensed the hum.

This place was bewitched and it was time to go.

Without a word, the highly superstitious Ugandans were the first to go. They loaded into their helicopters and jeeps and retreated back into their blighted homeland.

The Sudanese, Malawians, Somalis, Kenyans, Rwandans, and Burundians slipped away after them. Soon all that remained were some very rattled Tanzanians, who began firing wildly at the hyenas, killing four or five.

Unaware of it all, Molech ranted into the phone, convincing even the highest government officials that he was completely mad.

The Tanzanians, too, got permission to go. Their

big cargo planes roared into the evening sky. Their helicopters rattled off toward the horizon. Their trucks roared away.

Molech was left with a tent, an old truck, and the two bodies that nobody had touched.

Insane with fury, Gordini climbed into the truck and ran over the corpses over and over, smashing their faces into the dust as he howled aloud to heaven and drove into the lake.

As the sulfurous waters of Lake Nyamulalengai engulfed him, he changed his mind and tried to get out of the truck, but he was too weak.

As the hyenas watched, pacing the shoreline, only circles rippled the water where he had gone down.

The hyenas did not touch Patrick or Matthew.

"I do not understand," whispered Daniel, tears running down his young cheeks. The sixteen year old knelt beside his father's mutilated body.

Gently, the boy arranged his father's legs and arms so that he had an air of dignity. Then, weeping, he touched his father's unseeing eyes and closed the lids. Carefully, he stroked his father's nose.

"We agreed that you would live," wept the boy. "God, why did You not hear my prayer? What happened to Your promise?"

Beside him, his mother and grandmother waited with burial herbs and a shroud. In silent grief, old Sarah looked over the body of her eldest son — the last survivor of her family.

"Lord," she prayed silently. "You have been so gentle in comforting me. But this . . ." She swallowed and her pain felt like a knife blade in her throat. She fell forward and clutched her son's lifeless body in her arms. "Why could You have not taken me so that I would not have to see this?" she wept. "This is too much."

She began to rock, storms of pain and hurt raging through her heart. She held Matthew and she wept.

Noel knelt over Patrick, shaken, unable to speak as he looked at the abuse his son had suffered under the tires of the mad Gordini.

How could anyone have done this to a little boy?

He was such a good kid.

Such a unique boy.

Great wails filled the night. As was the tradition of the Britanga tribe, the village elders cried out under the moon, reciting the great exploits of their fallen leader. For the first time in remembered history, the young men of the tribe joined the circle, proclaiming Patrick's bravery — how he had taught them to swim, how he had skillfully fled the crocodile when he went to get water for the scouting party.

How he had burst into the enemy camp, unafraid, in defense of the fallen Matthew. Yes, everyone knew that Matthew and Patrick now lived forever, but it did not ease their pain.

Matthew, the one who had led them so well for two decades was gone. What would they do without him? How could his son lead them with wisdom and justice? Could a mere youth be fair in judging disputes? What did young Daniel know of the great ways of the Lord God?

Indeed, Daniel was overcome with grief. The women waited for him to give permission to prepare the body.

Little Andrew gently put Patrick's boots on his lifeless feet, then crying unashamed, the twelve year old helped Zuni slip Patrick's shirt over the dead boy's shoulders. Carefully, Andrew placed Patrick's new baseball cap on his head and stood back. Noel stared at him, trying to understand how a little black native had loved his white son.

Andrew lifted his hands to heaven and cried out his anguish.

Zuni stroked her boy's hair. He was all she had. She had loved him so. He was such a good boy. Patrick was always funny, clever, loyal, and full of idealism. So ready to defend her.

She thought back to the acacia thorn hedge he had built around the crashed Martin.

Now that she and Noel were back together, it was not fair. NO! Tears rolled down her cheeks. It was not fair. Patrick had so wanted to see his parents back together. "Jesus, Jesus, what are You doing to me? Patrick has always been such a fine son. He does not deserve this!" she screamed.

Kneeling beside her, Noel stroked the boy's smooth face. Zuni whispered, remembered carrying him in her womb. The night of his conception, she had known that this child would be special.

Tears rolling down her cheeks, she remembered his first words, his first steps, his first sentence. The first finger-painting he had proudly dragged home from kindergarten to give her.

Gently, Noel held her, but she was inconsolable.

She had been Patrick's whole life when he was small and he had become hers when Noel had deserted them.

She needed Patrick so. Her life would have been so empty without him. He had filled up her life and had brought her such joy. He had taught her love as only the mother of a son knows.

Yes, she loved him — with the deep, wonderful, and forgiving love that only a mother can give freely and without complaint.

His adolescence had amazed her. He did not become the gangly misfit rebel that she had been. No, he seemed to know he had a purpose.

A meaning for being on Earth — a destiny.

Zuni touched his so-adult chin, then his manly young nose. *How could this be his destiny?*

She turned to Noel. "What has this accomplished?" she demanded. She leaned forward, holding her son's cold body tightly, her ear pressed to his chest, as if she were hoping that perhaps she would hear the stirring of a heartbeat, the rasp of a breath . . .

"He was such a good boy," she wept, her voice hoarse. "Growing so tall and his voice was deepening with such youthful masculinity."

Enviously, Zuni had watched him grin at young girls — and had watched them melt under his smile, giggle at his jokes, happily accompany him anywhere — even to the fuel dump to look at rusty drums leaking World War II kerosene Zuni had salvaged from the sands of the Sahara.

Noel touched her shoulder. She jerked away.

Patrick had made her so proud.

If she could not get her own life together, at least she had succeeded in producing such an extraordinary young man and future leader — a stalwart who caught the eye of everyone. Even the vicious, self-serving Molech Gordini had taken an interest in Patrick, offering to put him through college.

Zuni clutched his skinny chest. What had this boy's senseless murder accomplished?

Had he threatened anyone?

Was he a danger to the armed soldiers?

No!

He had been just a heart-broken, loyal boy, crying out in protest at the unjust execution of the good, decent, loving giant who had won his fourteen-year-old heart. His hero.

"Tell me again the story of how you first met my son," asked Sarah kneeling beside Zuni. Matthew's body was wrapped for burial. It was time to prepare Patrick's.

The people gathered around. As Noel sat silent, Zuni laughingly told how the spear-wielding Matthew had jogged up with Patrick, looking like some sort of Zulu warrior, but speaking perfect English as he knelt and prayed for her ankle.

Daniel translated.

The Britanga people laughed.

Someone else told a story about how as a boy, Matthew had hated stacking harvested millet spikes. They had to be stacked in wide circles to dry or else they would rot. So, he had tried everything under the sun to get out of stacking them — even mopping his father's supermarket.

Then Zuni told how Matthew had prayed for her broken ankle.

His eyes dancing, Daniel knelt beside Zuni. "And you were healed?" he whispered.

"Oh, yes," said Zuni. "I think that was when I first believed that Jesus Christ was my Saviour." She looked around self-consciously as Daniel translated. Lydia smiled and took Zuni's arm. Noel thought to himself as he longingly looked at Zuni, *I have got to know God like that.*

Suddenly young Daniel proclaimed with a shouting voice, "I believe that my father will live again!"

The people of the village murmured their agreement — yes, in the final resurrection, Matthew would again live. They would see him again and it would be glorious.

"No," said Daniel, his voice strong. "My God raised Lazarus from the dead."

There was silence as his words sank in.

"Dear Jesus of Nazareth, You care," he declared, looking up toward heaven. "You really care." Daniel's voice choked. He tried to continue, but had to look down, tears stinging his eyes and rolling down his cheeks. His speech resumed, just above a whisper.

"You are touched by our suffering.

"You wept when Your friend, Lazarus, died. I believe You are weeping now over what they did to my father."

The boy paused, his honest voice filled with deep conviction. "The Bible says that when You came to Lazarus' tomb, You were suddenly moved to tears. You WEPT. Why? You knew Lazarus was in heaven. He was fine. But You wept! My . . . my dad used to say that was shortest verse in the Bible — 'Jesus wept.' — and that it carries the most meaning. He told me this one little Bible verse reveals how much You care for me.

"God, You knew Lazarus was safe and so happy in heaven. He was better off! He had begun his eternal reward. But You could not ignore the sorrow of his sisters, Mary and Martha! They were so devoted. So many times they had taken care of You and ministered to You and sat at Your feet.

"For them You wept!

"Now . . ." Daniel choked again. "Now, are You crying again for us?"

Daniel sank to his knees. "Do You care?" he wept awkwardly. "Of course You do."

The sixteen year old paused, unable to go on.

The people stared in silence.

Then, little Andrew jumped up.

"I, too, believe that Jesus cares!" he declared. The adults stared at him, not really understanding. "Do you believe?" Andrew asked, his voice quivering with the emotion of a twelve-year-old boy. "Do you believe?"

Nobody said anything. Andrew was just a child.

He stared at them. A new flood of tears suddenly began flowing down Daniel's face.

"Who believes?" demanded Andrew.

Suddenly, all the little kids of the village were

crowding around the unmoving Matthew and Patrick. With Andrew and Daniel, they laid their hands on the head and shoulders and chest of their slain leader and the fourteen-year-old American.

The youngsters began praying aloud and did not giggle or recoil from touching dead bodies.

"In the name of Jesus Christ," proclaimed Andrew in his high boy's voice. "Rise and walk."

The little kids around him loudly agreed.

Their high voices were full of simple faith and deep conviction.

Their hearts heavy from the grief of their parents, the children of Britanga commanded the dead to rise and walk in the name of Jesus.

It was the stuff of legend. It was the sort of thing that is explained away too easily by those who know better.

Matthew and Patrick had not been dead, some would whisper later; they were just stunned by the bullets or they had been knocked unconscious.

No, others would testify. They had seen the multiple bullet wounds and had wept over the crushed skulls and the faces defiled by tire treads.

The adults stood in shamed silence as Andrew and the children prayed in boldness and power. The grown-ups did not have to speak aloud their brutal facts: no resurrection would occur today; no life remained in these mutilated bodies.

But the children did not limit their God.

Of such is the Kingdom of heaven.

Suddenly the ground begin to tremble. At first, it was ever so slight. Then, as the declarations of the innocents besieged the heavens, the quake was impossible to ignore. It became very obvious that the hand of God was moving with a mighty force.

Fervently, with great faith, young Andrew continued praying aloud, blessing the Lord, and claiming the victory. As he did, with a burst of glory, the skies parted and the clouds were rolled back. Golden rays of the sun burst forth.

A voice rumbled out of the thunder. The voice was a mighty voice so holy that they fell on their faces in terror, shame, and wonderment. **"Matthew! Patrick!"** the mighty thundering voice declared. **"Arise and be healed!"**

Matthew's body trembled. Sarah and Lydia stared in awesome wonder. It was not from the quaking of the ground, but it was the very breath of God that was returning Matthew's spirit to his earthly body.

The bullet holes closed.

The tire marks disappeared.

The grave clothes shattered as Matthew stirred — like fine crystal being broken. His eyelids fluttered, then his eyes opened.

"The glory of the Lord is shining through his eyes!" Lydia exclaimed. "My husband has been restored to me. He is Alive! Praise the name of Jesus. My Matthew is ALIVE!"

Matthew stood to his feet but he did not speak. He raised his arms to heaven in silent praise.

As Noel and Zuni clutched hands, they dared to hope against all hope. As they sat there in an attitude of prayer, Patrick's miracle took place. Bullet wounds closed. Tire marks vanished. The boy stirred and sat up, singing a heavenly song that nobody had ever heard.

His father grabbed him, yelling as if he were in a dream: "Patrick, Patrick, please forgive me for all the hurt I have brought into your life. My son, my son, can you ever forgive me?" He cried, clutching the fourteen year old to his chest, then unapologetically kissing him on the temples and forehead.

"Dad," protested the boy. "When did you get here?"

At that moment the whole world seemed to stand still.

Even the birds hushed their singing.

A mighty wind surged around the boy and his father and his mother, but not a leaf moved. The Spirit of God was there in might and power. Patrick was all over his mom, then his dad, unashamed of his public affection. The boy hugged his father in a way that the man had not experienced since Patrick was a very little boy.

With tears running down his cheeks, the American state department staffer held his son and hugged his wife. "Zuni, he's okay," choked the man, looking around at the debris of the former tent city. "He's all right. He's been restored to us. Thank Jesus, our boy is alive!" Noel seemed awestruck and became very quiet. He bowed his head and began praying aloud: "This day, God, I have seen Your mighty power. I have known about You, that You sent Your Son, Jesus Christ, to die for me, but I have never acknowledged Him as my Saviour. Jesus, please come into my heart, forgive my sins, and be my Saviour. Amen."

Zuni was crying uncontrollably as Noel was praying. Joyously, filled with incredulous reverence, she hugged her husband and her son and wept for joy.

"Wow, it looks like somebody tried to fight the battle of Armageddon here," wisecracked Noel.

"Arma . . . WHAT?" asked Patrick.

"Armageddon," said his father. "The last great battle between the nations of the Earth. You know, the Mount of Olives will split in half. Gog and Magog will invade Israel from the north. All the nations of the Earth will turn their backs on the Jews — you know, Armageddon. It looks like somebody tried to fight it out right here."

"Yeah?" laughed Patrick. "Well, Molech would have liked to have made it happen. But it wasn't time yet. You can't make God come out and fight unless He's ready."

"Noel," whispered Zuni, holding her ex-husband tightly.

"Hey," breathed the man, hugging her and their boy. He nuzzled her hair.

From behind them Matthew announced, "Come."

Patrick hugged his father. "What?" he asked, turning.

"Patrick, it is time to do what you and I should have done long ago," proclaimed Matthew. "It's time to deal with that evil computer of yours."

"What?" asked Noel, one arm on his son's shoulder.

But the boy was anxious to go. "Come on," he whispered to his dad. "We've got the world's only Lasing Optical Repandant Refluent Drive computer hidden up in one of the ancient caves over the river."

Perplexed and concerned, Noel stared up at the cliffs in silence.

Could Matthew be so simple as to destroy the LORRD computer? It was just a machine. Machines can't be evil — can they?

Holding his dad's hand unselfconsciously, Patrick did not speak on the long walk around the lake, then the rocky trek to the cave. Did Matthew know what he was doing? The big black man paused three or four times, each time asking the Lord for a clear direction — for firm instructions on how to deal with the computer.

As the men of the village approached the burial cave, Noel shivered. Suddenly, he was very cold. Fear filled him. He thought he saw something horrible move up in the shadows. Or was it just his imagination?

Then Noel felt the humming. Ultrasonic — just below hearing level, it was irritating, grating on his nerves. The high, unheard whine was ugly and demoralizing — taunting.

An argument broke out between the men. Matthew's voice grew loud above the hubbub. "I come against you in the name of Jesus," he proclaimed, his hand raised toward the cave. "Stop it. I bind you. You will not divide us. In the name of Jesus, I command you to cease and desist this moment."

It did, but an occult darkness seemed to billow in from all around. The earth began to tremble. Rocks tumbled down the cliffs.

"I come against you in the name of Jesus," declared Matthew. "Stop that."

The earthquake quit. Beside Patrick, Noel gawked in wonder and wished he had brought his camera. But his son was filled with a deep sense of dread and fear. It overwhelmed Noel, too — unexpectedly, a realization that they were up against something far too evil and much too powerful for their puny abilities. After all, they were not even Britanga. They did not belong here — for they could not understand the ancient superstitions of a primitive people.

"What's the problem, white guy?" suddenly snorted Daniel, his eyes also filled with doubts and fears. "Don't you think the African can understand your magnificent technologies? Aren't we smart enough?"

"In the name of Jesus, stop it," commanded Matthew, pointing his spear at the cave. The air began to vibrate. "You will not divide us." He climbed the notched poles and peered into the darkness. The others pressed behind him, filling the opening of the cave.

The vibration grew — almost laughing, mocking — so strong that Patrick could feel the walls of the cave beginning to tremble. Suddenly, the darkness grew — and with it a strange and wretched coldness. A thick cloud passed over the face of the sun. A putrid smell of death and consummate sacrilege permeated the place.

Musty old bones of the ancient dead rattled in their dusty crevices. Whispers and quiet movement in the back of the cave turned shadows into ghastly, loathesome threats. Dread swelled in the hearts of all those who remained — dark, horrible apprehension of the unknown, the demonic undead, the stuff of children's nightmares. Fright gripped the minds of the small group. Great evil loomed all around them — and all were consumed with a deep foreboding that they were vulnerable, feeble, and unprotected.

Out of the misty shadows, the disheveled, bloody corpse of Valentina Vasilieva reeled upward, blocking their path. With screams of terror, many of the men and boys of the village fled. "Tokoloshe!" they shrieked in real horror, believing that they had, indeed, seen a ghoul from African folklore — a zombie from the living dead.

She was a horrible sight to behold — bullet holes gaping, her lifeless flesh quivering, gray with death, yet moving before them, her eyes turned back in her head.

"Who are you?" demanded Matthew, not budging an inch.

"Go," shrieked something evil and terrible within the unbreathing corpse. "GO!"

"NO! In the name of Jesus of Nazareth," proclaimed Andrew, stepping up unafraid beside Matthew, "we take this place from you, tokoloshe! You have no power here. You are the one who must go." Quietly Daniel blurted a translation for Patrick and Noel.

The corpse turned a dead eye onto Andrew. "I know your secrets, Andrew Britanga," it threatened in his native tongue. "I know the times when you have stolen sweets and lied about it. These people think you are a perfect little Christian. I know different. I know when you have gone swimming and told your mother you were at school. I know the time you hid in the shadows and watched the old women bathe. I know . . ."

"Get out," said Matthew.

"YOU!" hissed the cadaver. "I know the lusts of your heart, Mayor Matthew Britanga. I know your secret sins. Shall I recite them?"

"Get out," declared Daniel.

"And you, boy" hissed the thing, "does your sissy father know that you —"

"Out," proclaimed Patrick, surprised at his own voice. "In the name of Jesus! Out!"

Reeling as if in a burlesque show's melodrama, it whined, "O Patrick, I am your friend. I am going to show you the secrets of the universe! You and I are going to travel to mystical worlds in parallel dimensions. I am going to take you beyond the human veil."

"I have been there and I know the Creator of the universe," said the boy. "I don't need you. He says you are a liar."

"Oh yes, you need me. He is a tyrant," whispered the thing. "Is it right for all creation to praise Him? What kind of ego expects everybody to bow down to Him? He doesn't want you to be as smart as Him, Patrick. I can make you as smart as God. You can be a god, too. Yes! You know just how important this machine is. I am the only one who knows how it works. I built it, Patrick Graham MacDougal. I am the great Russian computer expert Valentina Sergevicha Vasilieva."

"You are a liar," said Matthew. "You are not any human. The woman who created this computer is dead. You are evil and you must leave."

"Leave?" The thing mocked his words in a singsong. "Leave? I am so much more powerful than you, Matthew Britanga. You cannot resist me. I am Lucifer. I think I shall kill you now."

"You must obey me!" scoffed Matthew, his voice soft. "I come with all the authority of the blood of Jesus Christ and I command you to leave this place."

Stepping up beside him Daniel accused, "Evil liar, you are not Valentina and you are not Lucifer. We break your evil power in the name of Jesus. We break your dominion. You are a rebel angel, a demon that infests the air, searching for foolish humans to torment. We command you to leave! Go!"

The earth shook.

"I break all the tentacles that bind," shouted Andrew as rocks began to fall out of the ceiling. "I throw you out through the blood of Jesus."

Frightened, several more men retreated outside. As they scrambled down the ladders, they could hear the thing laugh and say, "I am Lucifer. I do not have to mind any of you. I hold the power of death. Now you will die."

"We do not fear death," chided Matthew. "Go."

"There are many, many of us. We will return!" A great chill swept the place. The ground shook again and the mouth of the cave collapsed, plunging into darkness the few who remained. Matthew groped for Patrick, Andrew and Daniel.

Noel pushed forward. "I know your kind," proclaimed Patrick's father. "You feed on fear. Well, we are not afraid."

"Adulterer!" hissed the thing. "Patrick Graham MacDougal, do you know what this fornicator did that so hurt your mother? Do you know that he lusted after —"

"Silence," proclaimed Matthew. "Go. Leave this place now. In Jesus' name, GO! In the name of Jesus — *by the blood of Jesus!*"

The corpse let out a horrible scream and lurched directly at Patrick. Noel and Matthew both clutched the boy — Matthew holding the thing by its shoulders. Noel grabbed an arm.

"Who can cast out demons?" shouted young Andrew. "Mark 16:17 says it can be done by 'them that believe.' Do we believe?"

"Yes!" chorused the men and boys. Loudly, they began proclaiming their faith. "I believe," shouted Patrick. "In the name of Jesus, I believe. You gotta go! Go! Go!"

There was a horrible scream, perhaps high in the heavenlies, perhaps deep inside some adimensional darkness — but a very real howl that resounded in the domains of evil. "In the name of Jesus Christ, our Lord and Saviour," Matthew was saying, his voice booming with power and authority, "I bind you, O power of darkness. I send you hence. You are not welcome here. By the power of Jesus Christ, I command you to leave this precious valley. You cannot come here. I claim this mighty computer for Jesus Christ. Satan, you cannot have this machine. I command your evil demons to depart from it and from us."

Valentina's body went limp. The machine visibly rocked.

It shook. The cold and mist dissipated.

As the sweaty, emboldened group continued, marveling and praising Almighty God, the crates trembled, then lay still.

Outside, there was the sound of the others pulling away the debris blocking the mouth of the cave.

"Today, I dedicate this machine to the glory of God," declared Matthew. "In the name of the Lord Jesus Christ, I proclaim that this computer is Yours, O Lord. Let it be used only for good. Father, send Your mighty warrior angels to our aid. Send them to stand watch over this incredible device and to drive back any forces of evil which would return and subvert that which we claim for Your glory and honor!"

In the gloom of Earth's high airy places, defeated

rebel angels bowed before a furious, raging spirit lord. Their gasped report evoked even more hideous shrieks as the terror and chaos spread. Angrily, the rebel commander turned and sank his talons into another insidious officer kneeling beside him.

"Destroy and mute these meddlers!" he howled. "Follow me and we will throw out these interfering God-worshipers. Sorrow and sickness and suicide will be theirs!"

In a mad rush, a legion of mutineers joined his mob. Screaming for blood, they charged into the peaceful valley.

But what they saw sent them howling in retreat.

An angelic army of the Most High stood majestic guard around the high plateau. The captain of the host was Jesus Christ himself.

"You cannot come here," proclaimed a low-ranking warrior angel — not Michael or Gabriel or any of the others feared and respected in the demonic ranks. "By the power of the Father's Beloved Son, Jesus Christ, you may not come here — you or any other principality which exalts itself against the knowledge of Jesus Christ."

The promises of God given thousands of years before to Joshua and Jehosophat and Jacob and Joseph and John and Andrew and Peter and Paul resounded in the ears of the cowering, weeping demonic forces. They fled in every direction.

"Ours is the victory!" declared Matthew.

One of the old elders of the village suddenly prayed aloud: "Wake up, my brothers," he rasped, "the battle is ours but our deeds are far from perfect in the sight of our God. We must continue to go back to what we heard and believed to be right at the first. We must hold to it firmly and keep our eyes on Jesus Christ alone."

"Unless we do," said another of the men, "the evil

will come back suddenly upon us, unexpected as a thief, and will punish us."

"Let us claim Revelation 3:8 through 12," said another man. And together, the black natives — some clutching spears, some in long white shirts, others wearing only tennis or soccer shorts — raised their hands to heaven.

"I know well that you aren't strong," quoted Matthew aloud from the Scripture. "But you have tried to obey and have not denied My name. Therefore I have opened a door to you that no one can shut." Tears began to flow down the big man's cheeks.

"Know this to be true," quoted another native who wore a Los Angeles Lakers' visor, "I will humble those who have claimed to be Christian but who have followed Satan. They will be held up before all men as liars and thieves. They will fall at your feet and acknowledge that you are the ones that I love."

"Yes," murmured one of the elders. He trembled with emotion. As he began quoting the verse, the other men joined in with him: "Because you have patiently obeyed Me despite the persecution, I will protect you from the time of great tribulation which will come upon the world to test everyone alive!"

Their voices grew in intensity: "My children, I am coming SOON! Hold onto what you know to be true. Be strong in the Lord! Know that he who is not seduced by the devices of the devil will be honored as a pillar in the temple of My God! He will be secure and will go out no more. I will write My Name on him and he will be a citizen in the city of my God!"

At their feet, the world's most advanced computer hummed silently. Lights flickered.

It was just a machine.

A mighty machine.

Dedicated to Jesus Christ.

❖   ❖   ❖

Patrick ran up with Daniel. Now the fourteen-year-old white boy was waving a native spear — an adult-size spear that the village elders had awarded him.

Patrick had been made a full-fledged Britanga. Daniel had even given him permission to talk to the girls who giggled and watched him from their circles.

Patrick was particularly smitten with an ebony princess who couldn't have been more than eleven years old. Zuni and Noel didn't know what to say.

"I don't want to ever leave here," Patrick told his father. "Dad, these people have it all figured out. I'm not going back to our screwed up world."

Noel understood. So did Zuni.

They wept that evening as Patrick and Zuni and Noel were baptized in the river while the village sang beautiful, joyous choruses and the kids danced. Patrick announced that he wanted a new name — another Britanga tradition. No longer was he Patrick Graham MacDougal. Now, he wanted a Christian name.

He declared himself Timothy Britanga Graham MacDougal.

Noel nodded his consent.

"Can we still call you Patrick?" Zuni asked.

"Sure!" the boy exclaimed. "But the girls are already calling me Timmy."

Zuni sighed.

Johanna Graham wept.

A new fullness gently buoyed her tired spirit.

She had obeyed and released the boy she loved so much to the Lord.

It had not been easy.

She had resisted.

Then, she had obeyed.

And she had weathered the long night, knowing that he was in terrible danger — but repeating to herself God's promise that all things work together for good for those who love the Lord.

Now, she was filled with an exciting release in her spirit. A delight. A knowledge that all was well . . . again.

❖   ❖   ❖

"What was it like?" asked Noel.

"What?" asked Patrick, kneeling in front of a cook fire and slipping in a log. He did not comment, but was very pleased to see that his parents were holding hands.

"You know, being dead," said Zuni. "You've not talked about it yet like Matthew does."

The boy shrugged. "Well, I have some really neat memories, like being in a really peaceful dream."

His father nodded. "Did you see a white light down a long corridor? Did God beckon to you from across a wide, cold river?"

"Naw, nothing like that."

"Well?"

"Well," sighed the boy, self-consciously glancing around. "Okay, this is really weird, Dad. I have this really vivid memory of being in this enormous place kind of like a stadium or maybe a big concert hall. Everybody was singing and praising God and I was, too, and I LIKED IT. It was incredible — nothing like Grandma's boring church. And we weren't in white robes or playing harps or anything like that. I didn't have wings.

"And it wasn't like we were being forced to bow down to a great, glowing throne or anything like that. I was with a Friend. A really good Friend. He really,

really loved me and I was delighted to be there with Him — and I was singing all sorts of praise and worship songs. I liked it — A LOT. It was like I was thanking Him for being so good to me and He was right there as if I were the only person there — except I was with all these other people and great, important beings, too. It's impossible to explain, Mom. But it was really profound."

Zuni studied her son. "Okay," she said with a sigh.

"Hey, Kid, you are really something else," said Noel.

The boy grinned. "So are you two."

There was a new gentleness and peace to the boy. Was it because of his death experience? Because his father had been restored to him and he didn't have to try to fit himself into other people's families anymore? Because he now knew a true faith that genuinely satisfied his innermost longing? Or because the two people that he loved most — and who his deepest instincts demanded should love one another — not unabashedly whispered and smooched in the shadows outside the firelight?

It was all of these things and more.

Patrick finally belonged.

He was accepted unquestioningly in a rigid society governed by strict rules. He was respected. He, alone, could get the little computer in the burial caves to respond.

Under Noel and Matthew's watchful eyes, the youngster from Nairobi's Royal British Academy tapped on the keyboard, trying this, then that, then this, then that — each time becoming more and more excited.

On the half hour, the village elders gathered to lay hands on the now-benign machine, to continually reclaim it for Jesus Christ and to banish any lingering powers of darkness.

"Yeah!" Patrick would exclaim — sometimes in mid-prayer. "This is so simple!" But nobody else could make heads or tails of the seeming garble on his screen.

Finally Noel pulled up a crate beside his son.

"Show me what you're doing," he said.

"Dad, this is so neat," exclaimed Patrick. "Look." He tapped on the keyboard and the monitor filled with data.

"That's the AAA newswire of the Associated Press," exclaimed Noel. "How did you do that?"

"Simple," shrugged Patrick. "Watch." He plunked away at the keys. "Know what that is?"

"No," said Noel.

"Two Russian generals on the phone discussing the situation on the Chinese border."

"But it's in English."

"Dad, this computer can do anything."

"You mean it can take a Russian phone conversation in progress and give you a print-out in English?"

"Hey, Dad, a few minutes ago, I was playing around with the Tokyo Stock Exchange. I could shut it down if I felt like it. What is the Federal Reserve System?

"This computer seems to want to take it over. What is it? I was poking around in the Singapore Stock Exchange and the Brussels Commodity Markets, then I tried something with the Japanese market and I think I accidentally bought several million shares of stock in the Toyota Motor Company. I undid it, though.

"Want to see what the French are up to with their Arianne rocket program in South America? Hey, how would you like to see what the president of the United States is doing?" Patrick excitedly tapped away on the keyboard.

On screen, an unshaven chief executive grumpily

nursed a cup of coffee as he glanced through his overnight briefing sheets.

"I tapped into the White House security cameras," said Patrick. "Dad, this computer can tie into anything that sends out a broadcast signal, no matter what strength, and it's got no limitations on memory. Dad, this thing is bango — major serious." The boy grinned — suddenly inspired.

He tapped excitedly.

He sat back, pleased with himself.

"What did you do?" asked his father.

"On every computer monitor worldwide in the language currently on screen, I just announced 'JESUS LOVES YOU AND SO DO I, TIMOTHY.'"

"You didn't," exclaimed his father.

"Yeah," grinned the boy. "I did."

Johanna stood in great awe, her mouth filled with wonder. Astonished, she turned and sang out a song of joy and thanksgiving and faith.

"Oh, Father," she wept in incredible joy. "You alone are God! You are all that is. You are the One to whom I can turn. You never fail. You never falter."

Somehow the powers of evil again had underestimated a scrawny, little old lady. They had not understood her silent obedience on her knees before the throne of God.

Now Johanna Graham wept with joy. Her mighty praises rose heavenward. The prayer warrior humbly thanked the Lord for giving her such faithful intercessors worldwide.

Across the globe, Christians here and there paused as the old woman, quiet and unobserved, danced before her Lord — just like David had. She sang — just as the Psalmist had done so many times.

She was just an old woman.
Weak.
Tired.
Human.
And vulnerable.
But faithful.

❖   ❖   ❖

On the shores of putrid Lake Nyamulalengai, Simon Webster sat at his new laptop computer. With short stabs he poked at the keyboard and peered at the manuscript before him.

In the distance, the Virunga eruptions still raged. Spectacular fountains of fire were reaching 3,500 feet into the African sky — attracting more tourists and sightseers.

The stench of the lake still did not seem to bother Simon. His camp looked like a garbage dump. He still hated his job. He had even less rapport with the natives — especially after he had pooh-poohed their enthusiastic stories about resurrections from the dead. His was a powerless religion of form and no substance — but he wanted nothing to do with anything else.

Matthew had spoken to him very sharply about being so willing to lead Molech and Valentina to the hidden valley — just for a reward. Simon never had collected, despite numerous letters to Gordini's companies in Nairobi, London, Baghdad, New York, and Brussels.

He got one letter from a London attorney claiming the Gordini companies were bankrupt because of the SuperRich scandal.

As Simon tapped away on his keyboard, he wished the Tanzanian education ministry had not confiscated his telephone line. He rather wished he could be in contact with somebody in a civilized part of the world.

And he wished he had a drink.

He nudged open the ice chest beside his chair, then cringed, noticing a plume of dust out on the road. A familiar jeep with diplomatic tags roared into view.

Simon grumbled to himself. Noel MacDougal climbed out.

Simon pecked at his keyboard. Noel was opening the passenger door. An old lady stepped out, glancing around in wonder.

"Pew!" said Johanna Graham. "What is that stench?"

A blond, bronzed native in gym shorts and bright baseball cap jogged into the camp, his African spear held high.

Behind him ran two other boys, one a giant and as black as a Nubian. The other was just as dark, but a boy.

In absolute astonishment, Johanna surveyed the trio.

"Grandma," yelled Patrick.

Johanna hugged him. This was not what she had expected.

"Grandma," blurted Patrick. "Do you think people can be raised from the dead?"

"What?" exclaimed the old woman.

"Do you think people can be raised from the dead?

"Well," grinned his grandmother. "I suppose, but it would probably take ten million people praying for you."

Patrick grinned. "Yeah," he chuckled. "Or else you, Grandma."

Johanna smiled.

Under the cliffs of a hidden valley that night, a

blond African strolled with his grandmother in the moonlight. He took her to a renovated granary where a compact mega-computer silently blinked in the darkness. He waved his spear in delight as the two of them caught his mom and dad kissing down by the river.

On a street corner in East Los Angeles, tattooed kids in Leones colors passed out Christian tracts to stunned drug dealers behind a closed quick stop store.

On an Iowa farm and in a Canadian TV studio, intercessors looked up in sudden, inexplicable exhilaration. In a CNN news studio, and on a Virginia Beach talk show set, they felt incredible joy.

In Poland, a boy named Ladislav stirred in his sleep and whispered praises to the Most High. In Australia, an Aborigine hotel maid named Helen sang softly.

Their prayers had knit a beautiful blanket that had smothered every strategy of the enemy. Truly a united force, their intercessions had risen before the Throne of God, permeating His presence and influencing the events of this world.

When God opened the curtain, what a display of glory as billions and billions of angels stood amazed at the prayers of the saints ascending like an aroma to God! They were lined up and ready to rumble, just waiting for a command from the captain of the Lord's Army. Even Michael, that warrior whose one word could destroy a nation, bowed his head in quiet submission, waiting. The Creator was in conference with one of His children. The world had been shown that as God mobilized His "little" people, they became "giants" as intercessors. This was a spiritual war far mightier than anything man had ever imagined. This was the common denominator uniting all of these dissimilar individuals from around the world — intercession. Their tender hearts had followed the teachings of the apostle Paul when he said that "requests, prayers, intercessions and thanksgivings be made for everyone" (1 Tim. 2:1).

Light had reigned over darkness.

And they shared in the victory.

Each had a harp and were holding golden bowls full of incense, which are the prayers of the saints. The smoke of the incense, together with the needs of believers, went up before God (Rev. 5:8; 8:4).